W9-BME-861

My Heroes Have
Always Been Cowboys

My Heroes Have Always Been Cowboys

GEORGINA GENTRY

TERESA BODWELL

LORRAINE HEATH

KENSINGTON BOOKS
http://www.kensongtonboks.com

KENSINGTON BOOKS are published by

Kensington Publishing Corp.
850 Third Avenue
New York, NY 10022

Copyright © 2006 by Kensington Publishing Corp.
"The Great Cowboy Race" copyright © 2006 by Lynne Murphy
"Moonlight Whispers" copyright © 2006 by Teresa Bodwell
"The Reluctant Hero" copyright © 2006 by Jan Nowasky

All rights reserved. No part of this book may be reproduced in any form or by any means without the prior written consent of the Publisher, excepting brief quotes used in reviews.

All Kensington titles, imprints and distributed lines are available at special quantity discounts for bulk purchases for sales promotion, premiums, fund-raising, educational or institutional use.

Special book excerpts or customized printings can also be created to fit specific needs. For details, write or phone the office of the Kensington Special Sales Manager: Kensington Publishing Corp., 850 Third Avenue, New York, NY 10022. Attn. Special Sales Department. Phone: 1-800-221-2647.

Kensington and the K logo Reg. U.S. Pat. & TM Off.

ISBN 0-7582-1301-8

First Kensington Trade Paperback Printing: March 2006
10 9 8 7 6 5 4 3 2 1

Printed in the United States of America

CONTENTS

THE GREAT COWBOY RACE

by Georgina Gentry
1

MOONLIGHT WHISPERS

by Teresa Bodwell
85

THE RELUCTANT HERO

by Lorraine Heath
183

THE GREAT COWBOY RACE

Georgina Gentry

One

Early morning, June 13, 1893

If she hadn't been so desperate, Henrietta Jennings would never have run away.

The train pulled into the station with the conductor yelling, "Chadron! Chadron, Nebraska, this stop! Everyone off for Chadron!"

Henrietta grabbed her small valise and went down the aisle. She knew the father she'd never met owned a huge ranch outside town. In retrospect, why had she been stupid enough to think he'd take her in and rescue her from the society marriage her overbearing mother was determined would take place in July?

Henrietta got off the train and stared at the big crowds in the frontier town's streets. To the ticket agent, she asked, "What's going on?"

The old man pushed back his eyeshade and grinned with store-bought teeth. "Big cowboy race begins this afternoon, miss, from Chadron all the way to Chicago."

"Chicago? Why, that must be a thousand miles."

"Yep, but for fifteen hundred dollars, a new Montgomery

Wards saddle, and a fancy pistol as a prize, I'd almost get in the race myself."

She was intrigued, but she had personal problems to think about. "How—how do I get to the Rocking J. ranch?"

He pointed. "Due north about five miles, can't miss it. Old Henry Jennings must have fifty thousand acres."

She couldn't contain her curiosity. "You know him?"

The man nodded and seemed to notice her blue silk dress and expensive luggage. "You got business with Henry?"

She'd better not tell the man she was Henry's daughter as she wasn't sure whom she could trust. "Uh, just curious. What does he look like?"

The little man's false teeth clicked. "Tall, lean, tough as a longhorn steak. Blue eyes like ice and light-colored hair. He ain't a man to be messed with."

She must look like her father, but he sounded formidable. "He—he hospitable to visitors?"

She could see the curiosity in the man's eyes. "Oh, he ain't at the ranch. I put his private car on the line two days ago. He's gone to a big cattlemen's convention in Omaha. Won't be back for a week."

Uh oh. Now what was she going to do? If she waited around here for a whole week, her mother and Henrietta's fiancé might figure out where she'd gone and come after her. She was underage and short on money. Only desperation had caused her to take her fine gray Arabian, Lady Jane, and flee west to the father who had never even bothered to answer her letters in all these years.

She walked to the stock car to watch the unloading of her beloved mare. As the train pulled out, she stood indecisively with her one piece of luggage and horse, trying to decide what to do. Survival was not a subject that was taught at Miss Priddy's Female Academy in Boston.

However, she knew Lady Jane needed some grain and a good rest, so Henrietta led her horse to the livery stable. Now she leaned against the stall door and brushed wisps of yellow hair out of her eyes and considered what action to take. She might find out which Omaha hotel her father was staying in and wire him, but she was uncertain of his response. He might just alert her mother of Henrietta's whereabouts. No doubt the Pinkertons were already searching high and low, since her social-climbing mother, Matilda, was insisting Henrietta marry that rich, prominent Bostonian, Throckmorton P. Gutterstaff III. For all she knew, the detectives might be on their way to northwestern Nebraska at this very minute. Besides, she doubted she had enough money for a week's room and board while waiting to see if her father would help her.

Henrietta took her luggage and pushed her way through the crowds to the Blaine Hotel where she got the last available room. In the lobby, there was talk of nothing else but the Great Cowboy Race with men standing around betting on their favorites. An idea began to form. Henrietta was an expert rider, and Arabians were known for their endurance. Was there even the slightest possibility that she could pass herself off as a boy and enter the race?

What an absolutely crazy idea, she scolded herself. Yet she didn't have any better ones at the moment. For a girl, she was tall and lean and had a husky voice. By entering the race as a boy, her mother's detectives would be baffled in their search, and Henrietta would be safely away from here. Then, too, if she won, fifteen hundred dollars was a lot of money and would take her even farther out of her mother's reach. In her desperation, anything was worth the chance.

Henrietta went to the general store and bought herself a Stetson, some western clothes, and a pair of boots. She returned to her room, put the outfit on, and studied herself critically in the mirror. With her blond hair up under her hat and the oversized clothes, she might be able to pass herself off as a boy. It was worth the gamble.

She lay down and slept for most of the day. Late in the afternoon, she left the hotel and went to get her horse. Once she reached the stable, she looked at her reflection in a horse trough and had second thoughts about her hair. If her hat came off, the masquerade was over. There was only one thing to do, and no sacrifice was too much to escape marrying that stuffy toad. Henrietta took a pair of horse shears and hacked off her long locks.

Then she put on her hat and led Lady Jane down to enter the race.

As she approached the table to sign in, she noted the big cowboy already there. He stood well over six feet tall, with the broadest shoulders she'd ever seen. A shock of black hair hung across his dark forehead as he pushed his Stetson back. Was he part Indian? She'd never met a real live savage before.

Comanche Jones laid down his hard-earned money on the table and signed in. "Twenty-five dollars?"

The grizzled old man nodded. "Worth it, too. Big prize, fifteen hundred dollars, a saddle, and a fancy Colt pistol presented by Buffalo Bill hisself at the end of the race in Chicago."

"My horse is good enough to win," Comanche drawled as he laboriously signed his name.

"Everyone thinks his horse is the best," the other man said. "You sound like a Texan."

"I'm proud to say I am." Comanche nodded and stepped away from the table to roll a cigarette. There were hundreds of people including newspaper reporters on the dusty streets. The race was supposed to start in less than an hour. He looked around at the competition critically and didn't see many horses as good as his own bay stallion, Hombre. Now, that fancy gray Arabian that young boy was leading looked pretty good. Comanche watched the boy tie his horse to the hitching rail, come to the table, lay down his money, and sign in. Then the boy glanced over to where Comanche leaned against a post.

The boy was tall and lean with delicate features that lacked a tan and eyes as blue as a Texas sky. *City slicker,*

Comanche thought with disgust. Worse yet, the fine gray mare carried an English saddle. "We don't see many city folk out West," he said with a grin.

The boy only frowned at him.

Snob, Comanche thought with a frown and tossed away his cigarette.

Men were shouting up and down the street for the contestants to mount up. Comanche patted Hombre's nose and led him over to the starting line in front of the Blaine Hotel. The snooty boy had swung up on the gray Arabian and now rode to the line. It looked like there would be ten riders. Up on the balcony of the hotel, several dignitaries came out and waved for silence. The gathered crowd quieted.

"All right, folks, this is a big day for our fair city of Chadron!" the fat little man shouted. "As mayor, I welcome you to the Great Cowboy Race. A thousand miles clear to Chicago where Buffalo Bill hisself will be waitin' by the Thousand Mile Marker tree to award the prizes."

The crowd cheered.

"Now, you know you're allowed two horses if you want, and you got to treat them good because the Humane Society will be inspectin'. Also, there'll be newsmen along the route and at the check-in stops. Good luck to all of you! The fire chief will shoot off the pistol that starts the race!"

More cheering. Comanche swung into his worn old saddle. All the riders were mounting up now, and people were clearing out of the street. Silence fell over the crowd except for the snorting horses. The mayor up on the balcony shouted, "Is everyone ready?"

The riders cheered and waved their hats. With a great show of ceremony, the fire chief fired a pistol in the air, and the riders took off. Some of them galloped away to the cheers of the crowd; some of them trotted. Comanche put Hombre into a slow walk. With a thousand miles ahead of him, he didn't see any point in working his horse into a lather on a hot June afternoon.

The boy riding the gray Arabian also urged his horse into a slow walk, and soon only the two of them were left behind, the other eight galloping into an early lead. The boy looked neither right nor left, just stared grimly ahead as he rode. Comanche glanced over at the other rider and grinned. "Looks like we're the only two with sense enough to think of our horses."

His competitor barely nodded to him and smiled, then kept riding. The boy had light, sun-streaked hair curling under his hat and eyes the color of Texas bluebonnets, Comanche thought, compared to his own dark features, courtesy of his part-Indian mother.

They rode the first twenty miles in silence, the other riders strung out ahead of them, riding faster. At the first marker, there were two barrels of water set up for horses and men. Comanche reined in and dismounted, then let Hombre bury his muzzle deep in the water while he got himself a dipperful from the other barrel. "Hot day, ain't it?" he asked sociably as the boy on the gray Arabian pulled up and dismounted.

"Yes." The boy nodded and let his horse drink, then took the dipper Comanche offered.

"We don't see many fine-blooded horses like yours in the West," Comanche said.

No answer. The boy continued to drink his water.

"I'm Comanche Jones from Texas. Who might you be?"

The boy kept his hat pulled low. "Uh, Henry J.—J. Smith."

"You know, Henry, we might could help each other if we teamed up; reckon some of the others will do that."

"Don't need any help," the boy growled, put the dipper back in the barrel, and remounted.

"Well, damn your hide, you won't get it then. Anyways, you sound like a damned Yankee dude." To Comanche, that was the biggest insult he could think of, but the other only frowned and rode away.

Comanche shrugged and mounted up. Okay, he wouldn't

cut the dude any slack; he'd beat him just like he would the other riders. Comanche had come to Nebraska bringing a herd of fine horses from the Durango Triple D ranch to the Rocking J. empire. The other cowboys had gotten on the train and gone back to Texas, but Comanche had hung around to look over the country. Northwestern Nebraska was might nigh as pretty as Texas, but of course a poor cowboy couldn't afford to buy any land here, especially with that Henry Jennings owning most of the county. Then Comanche had heard about the Great Cowboy Race. Fifteen hundred dollars was a lot of money, pert near two years' wages for an ordinary cowpoke. It would buy that ranch he longed for.

It was sundown when the riders rode into the town of Long Pine, where crowds waited to cheer the incoming riders as they checked in. "Welcome!" the town officials greeted the riders. "We got a picnic dinner planned for you, beans and corn bread and beer."

That sounded good to Comanche, and he dismounted with a grin. "You got a livery stable for the horses?"

A little man with a goatee nodded. "And a good hotel for you to stay in."

The free food would be welcome, and maybe he and some of the others could pool their money and rent one room. He looked up at the sky. It might rain a real toad-choker later tonight. The dude, Henry J. Smith, reined in and dismounted, checked in, then looked about uncertainly. Comanche had decided he wasn't going to do anything to help the snooty boy.

All the weary riders led their horses to the livery stable, rubbed their mounts down, fed them, and walked back to the bandstand in the center of town. It was a hot night, but the townspeople had set up lanterns, and the local volunteer firemen's little band played "Bicycle Built For Two" over and over. Maybe it was the only song they knew.

The riders got in line to fill up on the free grub. The city slicker boy took a plate uncertainly. He looked as lost as a goose in a gourd patch or a church deacon in a whore house. Comanche watched the boy as he, himself, chowed down on the beans. "Eat up, kid. Never pass up free food."

The boy was holding the corn bread as if he didn't know what to do with it.

"It's corn bread." Comanche shook his head at the city boy's ignorance. "It's good crumbled in a glass of buttermilk, but not quite as good as a tortilla for soaking up your pinto beans. Here, have a mug of beer."

The boy accepted the big mug of beer and looked as helpless as a lost calf.

Comanche sighed. "Kid, I don't think you'll make it to the end of this race."

"Got to. Need the money."

Comanche snorted. "No worse than the rest of us, and some of these hombres will do anything to win."

Henry continued to just pick at the food.

"Well, if you ain't gonna drink that beer, pass it this way," Comanche ordered. "Shame to waste good beer." He took it out of the boy's delicate hand and downed it.

Henrietta had never felt so out of place as she did now in the midst of these Westerners. She kept her head low and ate some of the strange food. She watched the big, rugged cowboy. What was his name? Oh, yes, Comanche Jones. He might be in his mid-twenties, and he drawled when he talked. She couldn't decide if his skin was dark because he had Indian blood or simply tanned from being outdoors. He wore a Stetson and a denim shirt open at the neck. His sleeves were rolled up in the June heat, and when he moved, his hard muscles rippled. This was the man to beat; she was certain.

The riders were all walking away from the bandstand. She looked toward Comanche.

"I reckon they're goin' to the saloon"—he nodded—"to celebrate."

"Celebrate what?"

He shrugged. "It don't make no never mind. Cowboys

don't need much reason to drink. There's probably women there, too." He started walking away.

Oh, my. "W—wait for me." She didn't know what else to do, so she followed after them, although she was having a difficult time keeping up with Comanche's long strides.

"Kid, can't you walk any faster? I ain't got all night." Looking at the pretty boy, Comanche felt an emotion that made him as uneasy as a rattlesnake on a hot griddle. The kid was sticking to him like an orphaned calf. Comanche was feeling protective toward the young city slicker and maybe something a little more. That made Comanche as nervous as a long-tailed cat in a room full of rocking chairs.

They went into the saloon. The place was full and noisy, the locals looking for any excuse to celebrate and the participants in the cowboy race being as good an excuse as any. Comanche pushed through the crowds and bellied up to the bar. The dude hesitated by the swinging doors. "Come here, kid, and I'll buy you a drink."

The boy came forward and leaned on the bar like the other men were doing, but he looked as ill at ease as a baby chick in a coyote's mouth.

The other riders were already there, shaking hands all around, accepting free drinks and introducing themselves to each other. "I'm Comanche Jones," Comanche said, "and this here is Henry J. Smith. I reckon you've all howdied but you ain't shook."

"How do you do?" Henry stuck out his hand very hesitantly.

The others looked at the kid and hooted. "Ain't this the dude who's riding that silly English saddle?"

The kid looked uneasy. "I—I got a good horse," he said.

The old gunfighter named Doc Middleton laughed. "You might as well drop out, boy. You ain't got a chance against real western cowboys."

"Oh, don't hooray the kid," Comanche said. "He's game enough to try."

A big bartender in a dirty apron wiped the bar in front of the pair. "What'll it be, gents?"

The dude said, "Sherry, please."

All conversation stopped as the others stared in surprise.

"Sherry?" said the barkeep, and his lip curled in scorn. "What in the hell is that?"

Comanche sighed. The kid was going to be a problem. The other men were looking at the dude with ill-disguised scorn. "Henry, you can have whiskey or beer."

"Or maybe sarsaparilla!" Doc Middleton hooted, and the other cowboys roared with laughter.

The bartender slammed down two foaming mugs of beer.

One of the cowboys winked at Comanche. "Some of us is going upstairs. You two want to join us?"

Comanche shook his head. "Like to, but don't have the dinero. Maybe Henry, here—"

"I don't either." The boy looked relieved and made a face as he tasted his beer.

"Talkin' about women," one of the riders said, "when I get to Chicago, I want to go to that big World's Fair they got there."

Comanche shrugged. "What's that got to do with women?"

Several of the men laughed. "Ain't you heard? That hoochy-coochy dancer, Little Egypt, has everyone talkin'."

"Disgusting," Henry muttered.

The others turned and looked at the dude.

"Speak for yourself, kid," Comanche laughed. He was more and more uneasy about the boy. Henry Smith had eyes as blue as a Texas sky. Hell, he'd never paid attention to a man's eyes before. Maybe he'd been too long without a woman, but he damned sure didn't have extra money for a whore tonight. "Maybe I can get lucky in a card game." He turned away from the bar and ambled across the saloon, several of the whores smiling at him. When he stopped, he realized Henry was as close on his heels as his own shadow.

He turned. "Look, kid, you don't have to bird-dog me.

Go find yourself a lady. If you charm her enough, she might give you a free one."

"A free what?"

Oh, Lord, what had he done to be saddled with Henry? "Never mind. We'll just get ourselves a table in the corner away from the noise until the other hombres decide they've had enough beer."

The kid slid into a chair, but kept his eyes lowered. "You a real Texas cowboy?"

"Yep," he said between drinks of beer, "came up to bring some fancy horses to that big Rocking J ranch."

"You ever met the owner?"

Comanche shook his head and wiped his mouth on his sleeve. "Nope. I was told the old codger is gone to a cattlemen's convention. My boss, Ace Durango, handed the horses over to his foreman. They say old Henry is as tough as a boot heel; carved himself an empire out of the Nebraska plains, fightin' Injuns and anyone else who tried to take it."

"Hmm," the boy said.

"Now, what I want to know is what a dude is doin' so far from home and in this race? I'd say lookin' at your fine horse and saddle, you don't need the money."

"I—I think the Pinkertons is looking for me," the boy blurted.

"That so?" Comanche threw back his head and laughed. "What'd you do? Steal a stick of peppermint out of a candy store?"

"No. You—you won't tell anyone, will you?"

Comanche was mystified. "Well, in Texas, it ain't polite to pry into a man's background, although you don't look the type to rob a bank or nothin'"

He would have sworn the boy had tears in his eyes.

"I've got to win this race," Henry said.

The kid sounded desperate, and Comanche's heart went out to him. "Still, you got to beat me and these others to win."

"I plan to do that," Henry snapped.

Comanche was annoyed at the boy's shortness. "I don't know why you need money so bad, kid, but you got a long, long ride ahead of you, and honest, you don't seem tough enough. Me, I don't care about the pistol, but I'd like to own my own ranch, and I never will unless maybe I win this race. That prize would make the down payment."

About that time, a pretty girl in a skimpy red dress got up on the stage and began to dance and kick up her heels to the rollicking song "*Ta ra ra boom de-ay.*" The appreciative cowboys left the bar and came over to sit down at their table, which was closer to the stage.

"Gold dern it," old Joe swore, licking his lips, "Little Egypt don't have nothin' on Nebraska gals."

Henrietta kept her head low and tried not to cough at all the cigar smoke. It annoyed her the way all the men, including the Texan, were ogling that saloon girl as she flipped up her skirts to the music.

"Want a chaw, boy?" Doc Middleton asked.

A chew of what? She was afraid to ask and betray her ignorance. "Sure," she said.

At that point, he pulled out a knife, cut a hunk off a plug of something, and handed it to her. She hesitated. All the men were looking at her. "Been looking forward all night to a good chaw," she said with more confidence than she felt and popped it in her mouth. It was strong, bitter tobacco. She wasn't certain what she was supposed to do now. She looked around. Men were spitting at the brass spittoon on the floor. She had to do something; the wad was choking her. She tried to spit and instead dribbled it down her chin. Comanche Jones was looking at her strangely. She swallowed a couple of times, tried to spit again, and again dribbled it down her chin.

Comanche pushed his hat back. "You okay, Henry?"

She nodded, but she was beginning to feel queasy.

"You sure, kid? You look a little green."

At that point, she broke and ran for the front door. She

barely made it and grabbed on to the hitching rail, throwing up. She felt so sick, she just wanted to die. For a long moment, she almost wished she was back in Boston making wedding plans with Throckmorton. No, she wasn't that sick. Henrietta heard someone come up behind her.

"Kid, you okay?" asked Comanche.

"I—I think something I ate disagreed with me."

"Uh huh." He took her arm, led her over to the pump, and began to pump water. "Here, rinse your mouth out and wash your face."

She felt too shaky to do anything but obey him. Oh, my, it was tougher behaving like a man than she'd expected.

"Boy, why didn't you tell them you don't use tobacco?"

"I was afraid they'd laugh at me again." She swallowed hard to keep from sobbing.

"Well, gettin' laughed at ain't the worst thing in the world as long as you're all right with yourself."

"I—I got to prove something." She wiped her face on her sleeve.

"Maybe what you're gonna go through on this trip ain't worth it," Comanche suggested.

"I'll stick it out."

"Well, at least you got grit. In Texas, we set a heap of store on grit."

She shook her head. "I don't know what that is."

"Well, little Yankee dude, grit is when it's tough and you keep right on goin' and don't quit. Most folks ain't got grit; most Texans do."

Thunder rumbled in the distance.

Comanche said, "Looks like we got a gully washer comin'. Reckon we'll all share a room to save money."

The thought horrified her. "I—I thought maybe I'd just camp out on the prairie."

The thunder rumbled again, and across the horizon, jagged lightning cut through the black sky. "You'll get wetter than a drowned rat," Comanche said.

Somewhere in the distance, something howled. It echoed and reechoed across the prairie.

"What—what was that?" Henrietta said.

"Coyote." Comanche yawned.

A few drops of rain fell around them. Just then, the cowboys staggered out of the saloon, singing off-key: *". . . There is a tavern in the town, in the town, and there my true love sets him down—"*

"Oh, hush up," Comanche said, "you hombres sound like coyotes in a trap."

The cowboys leaned against each other, laughing.

"Where's the hotel?" One hiccoughed.

Comanche nodded toward the frame building across the street with the faded sign over the door. "Reckon all of us can fit in one room?"

"Yep," old Joe said. "Iffen there's two beds, we can sleep four to a bed, but someone gets the floor."

Maybe she'd better opt to camp out. "I—I don't think—" she began.

About that time, the coyote howled again, and the rain began in earnest. The big Texan grabbed her arm. "Come on, kid, let's make a run for it!"

All the cowboys staggered across the dirt street toward the hotel.

"I—I don't mean to cause you any trouble," she said to the big Texan.

He looked at her with a crooked grin and a twinkle in his eyes. "Kid, you've been causin' me trouble almost since the first time I saw you."

"I don't think anyone wants to be saddled with a dude."

"Now, ain't that the truth? But we won't leave you out in the rain. Come on."

"But—" She tried to protest, but Comanche was dragging her through the rain toward the hotel. She couldn't spend the night in a hotel room with nine men. *Oh, my, what am I going to do?*

Two

The old hotel smelled like cigar smoke and boiled cabbage. A sleepy little clerk clad in a nightshirt came out of the back room when the cowboys banged on the desk. "All right! All right! I'm comin'."

"We want rooms," John Berry shouted.

The clerk held up his hands for quiet. "I ain't got but one room left, but it's got two beds."

"That'll do," old Joe Gillespie said, weaving a little on his feet. "Pony up, boys."

Each man began digging through his pockets. Henrietta looked uncertainly toward the door. There seemed to be a second Noah's flood in progress. "I—I think maybe I'll sleep in the lobby."

The little clerk scratched himself. "Against the rules, cowboy. We ain't givin' free sleepin' here."

Comanche put his arm around her shoulders. "Now, little dude, be sociable. Cough up your dime and share with us. Or are you too good?"

The other cowboys turned and glared at her, although most seemed to be having problems focusing.

Doc Middleton pulled at his mustache. "Maybe we ought to toss the uppity dude out into the street."

The others grinned and nodded. Evidently tossing anyone out into the mud would be a lot of fun.

"Now, wait just a damned minute," Comanche growled. "Henry here's a little strange, I'll grant you that, but maybe it's because he's a Yankee and he can't help that. He'll be happy to share and share alike, won't you, boy?"

What else could she say? "Of course." She dug into her pocket for her dime, which was difficult with the big Texan leaning on her shoulder. He smelled of wind and sun and beer.

The clerk frowned as he handed her the key. "Now, don't you boys be slippin' any women upstairs. It's against the rules."

Comanche shrugged while the others hooted and hollered. "We can't afford no women, can we, Henry?"

She shook her head and followed him toward the stairs with the others trooping along behind, singing about a good cowpony called Old Paint.

"Hush," she muttered, "you'll get us all thrown out in the rain."

She had the key, which was a good thing since besides Comanche she was the only one sober enough to find the door lock. She opened the door and led everyone in. The one called John was attempting to light a lamp, and she had a sudden feeling he'd burn the place down. She grabbed the match out of his hand and lit the lamp. Its dim glow revealed a shabby little room with two broken-down beds. With a sigh, she went to the window and looked out. Sleeping out on the prairie, even with rain pouring and coyotes howling, looked better and better to her.

Old Joe growled, "Which unlucky sonofabitches gets the floor, or do we fight over it?"

"No!" Henrietta whirled away from the windows. "No noise. I'll sleep on the floor."

Comanche leaned against the bedpost. "Now, ain't that nice of the Yankee dude?"

Little Davy said, "I'll sleep on the floor, too." He took a quilt off the end of the bed and tossed her one.

Comanche turned loose of the bedpost and started taking off his shirt. All the men struggled to undress, except Jack, who collapsed on the bed and began to snore.

Henrietta was in a panic. She'd never seen a naked man before, and she didn't want to start tonight.' Most of them were down to their long handles now.

Comanche said, "Henry, you gonna sleep in your clothes?"

"I—I'm cold."

"Cold? It's June, for Gawd's sake. We're all sweatin'."

They were, too. She could smell them. The reek was distinctly Dirty Cowboy. She didn't say anything else, just took her quilt and lay down in a corner while the boots hit the floor all around her, and from one of the other rooms, someone yelled about the noise.

"One of you bastards blow out the damned lamp," Old Joe yelled.

"Why don't I just shoot it out and save the trouble of gettin' out of bed?" Comanche said.

"Never mind!" Henrietta jumped to her feet and blew it out herself. She didn't want the room to catch fire.

Some of the cowboys lay in bed, and one started a belching contest. For some reason, all the men seemed to think this was hilarious. Worse yet, they had all filled up on beans at the picnic, and now they were having another type of contest. Whew! She held her breath as she got up and stumbled across the pile of boots to open a window.

"Now, there's a handy idea!" Old Joe said and got up, went to the window, and began to pee out onto the street. "Wasn't sure where the chamber pot was."

Immediately he was joined by two more cowboys, all seeing how far out the window they could direct a stream while the others roared with laughter.

"Now, Joe," Doc warned, "anybody passin' by underneath is gonna wonder why the rain is so warm."

All the cowboys laughed some more.

She huddled down under her quilt and watched Comanche's silhouette as he stripped down to nothing but his long johns. He had wide shoulders, rippling muscles, and the tiniest behind.

Henrietta Jennings, she scolded herself, *no lady would stare at a half-naked man in his underwear and think about the size of his rear. What are you thinking?* She closed her eyes and tried to concentrate on something besides those big shoulders and that lean bottom. It was difficult. She sneaked another peek as the men all piled into the beds while the springs groaned in protest.

Soon they were snoring, except Henrietta, who could barely breathe. Whew!

The floor seemed to be made of stone. She tried to take small breaths and fluff her thin quilt so that the floor would be softer. No luck. Outside, the rain poured down. This was the most miserable night she had ever spent. Worse yet, if Throckmorton ever found out she'd spent a night in a hotel room with nine cowboys, her mother wouldn't be the only one who would need smelling salts. Her body felt as though she'd been run over by a stampede, but she was so weary, gradually, she dropped off to sleep.

She didn't know how long she'd been asleep when a small noise awakened her. Henrietta lay very still and kept her eyes closed. The rain had let up, but the snoring and the other impolite noises the sleeping cowboys emitted made it difficult to hear anything. She turned her head to one side and opened an eye. The moon had come out, and in the dim light, she seemed to be eye to eye with a monster that reared up on its hind legs and stared back at her. It took a split second for the image to register in her weary brain while the furry beast wiggled its whiskers and nibbled a crumb of bread.

Henrietta came up off the quilt, shrieking. All she knew

was that she had to get off the floor before the beast ran up her pants leg. The cowboys came awake as she hopped up into the middle of one bed and landed on Comanche. Under the added weight, the bed groaned, swayed, and then came crashing to the floor while men cursed in startled surprise and Henrietta continued to shriek.

Comanche shouted, "What the hell—?"

She could only scream and point at the furry monster.

The others lay in the tumble on the floor, everyone shouting and cursing.

"A mouse!" Comanche yelled. "The dude's afraid of a mouse!"

The cowboys hooted with laughter as the tiny gray creature scampered away to a hole in the baseboard.

Someone lit the lamp, and the disheveled, sleepy cowboys stared at her.

"It—it seemed bigger." She gulped.

All the cowboys were grumbling as they untangled themselves from the sheets. Comanche stumbled around the room, cursed as he stubbed his toe, and hopped about.

John Berry peered sleepily at his watch. "It's almost five."

"Well, hell," Comanche grumbled, "it's rise and shine time anyway." He reached for his pants.

Five A.M.? They were joking, weren't they? Henrietta sat on the mattress and watched them all grabbing for their clothes. She fell back across the bed as the men filed out of the room.

"Hey, kid"—Comanche paused in the doorway—"you not ridin' today?"

"In a minute," she muttered and closed her eyes. Right now, she was so tired, she didn't care if hell froze over or who won the race. That was the last thing she remembered as she drifted off to sleep.

When she awakened, it was the middle of the morning,

and the other riders had been gone for hours. Oh, my. Now she was way behind, and she'd have to ride hard to catch up.

It was a long, hot day, and she never saw another rider. They all must be way ahead of her. That was okay, too, because Lady Jane was a good horse, and the race didn't always go to the swiftest. What was it the Texan had said about grit? Well, she might not be a Texan, but she thought she had that quality. She wasn't going to give up without a fight, even if she did have to deal with a bunch of stinky cowboys for the next few days.

Henrietta caught up with Comanche at almost dusk that evening. He didn't seem very glad to see her.

"Howdy, dude, you get plenty of sleep back there?"

She merely nodded. "Where we going to camp?"

He frowned. "I was hopin' you'd stay in town with the other hombres. There's bigger things than mice out here on the prairie."

She felt her face burn. "Sorry about that."

They rode out to a likely campsite, unsaddled and hobbled their horses, then turned them out to graze. When she looked up, Comanche was staring at her. He looked troubled.

She bit her lip. "If I'm too much trouble, I guess I could ride by myself tomorrow."

"I'd be much obliged," he said as he got his blanket and curled up by the fire.

Was that cowboy lingo for agreement? She was afraid to ask. Somewhere a coyote howled, and she jumped. This was a long, scary journey with rough men and in a hostile environment. She wasn't sure she was up to traveling a thousand miles across the prairie alone. On the other hand, she didn't think she had any choice. By now, her mother might have figured out that Henrietta had tried to reach her father and have the Pinkertons on the train headed for

Nebraska. She could only hope that when her mother discovered her errant daughter was in this race, Henrietta would have already won it, thus getting her father's admiration and acceptance, and if not that, at least she'd have the prize money for her escape.

Henrietta got her blanket and curled up by the fire. She had never slept on the ground in her whole sheltered life. She was shivering in the cool June night, but she wasn't sure if it was from the cold or the fear of that pesky coyote that sounded as if it might invade their camp. Henrietta edged closer to the sleeping cowboy. He probably had a gun and knew how to use it. That thought was comforting.

When Comanche woke up at dawn, the young dude was right up against him. For a moment, Comanche blinked, rather enjoying the boy's warmth, and then he recoiled in horror. His worst fears were realized. He jumped up as if he'd found a rattlesnake in his blankets. When he did, the boy came awake, too, looking up at him. "Boy, don't you say a word," Comanche growled. "I ain't ridin' with you no more; you're on your own."

"But what did I do?"

"Nothin'. Just don't ask." He was in a panic from his own reaction to the young man. Without even making a cup of coffee, he saddled up and rode out.

Crushed, Henrietta stared after him. Somehow, she'd really offended him, and now she'd have to find the trail and ride alone. Well, maybe it was better that way. There was less possibility that he'd find out she was a girl. She made herself a cup of coffee, combed her chopped-off hair with her fingers, and put on her Stetson. She could follow the trail by Comanche's horse tracks. Well, Mr. Comanche Jones could just go to hell. She'd finish this race, and she'd win it, too, without any help from that annoying Texan.

All day she rode while her bottom grew more tired. She began to wish that she, too, had one of those big comfortable stock saddles the cowboys were using. Lady Jane seemed to be holding up fine; after all, Arabians were bred for endurance in the deserts, so this June weather and the rough terrain were nothing to the mare.

In the afternoon, she came across young Davy. He was dismounted and looking sickly.

"Are you all right?" she asked.

He shook his head, and his freckled face was as pale as milk. "Think I'll have to drop out. I'm feeling poorly, and I just don't think I can make it the whole way. Wish the others luck for me."

"Can I do anything to help?" Her heart went out to him, but she felt inadequate. She wished Comanche were here; he'd know what to do.

He shook his head, and reluctantly Henrietta rode on. If a young, strong cowboy like Davy had to quit, what chance did she have of making it? There were probably ten days of riding ahead of her. Maybe she should give up and quit, wire her mother where she was. As tired and discouraged as she felt at that moment, becoming Mrs. Throckmorton P. Gutterstaff III didn't seem so terrible after all.

Comanche felt a little guilty when the dude never caught up with the other riders that day. Then he was angry with himself for feeling guilty. After all, he hadn't been elected nursemaid to that Yankee city boy. Losing him just put Comanche one step closer to winning, and most of the trip still lay ahead. Anything could happen, and it was almost night and time to check in at the next stop.

Doc Middleton was back on the trail before dawn the next morning. He smiled to himself, thinking of the cowboys still asleep back at the third check-in point behind him. Slipping a little horse medicine in everyone's beer but Comanche's last night had made them oversleep this morning. He'd do anything, anything, to win this race.

The men who had laid out the race had set up wooden signs pointing the way to the next check-in point. Doc leaned on his saddle horn and looked at the sign. *It would be a dirty trick to move that, now, wouldn't it? Leavin' the other contestants uncertain which way to go?*

He laughed as he dismounted, pulled up the sign, and tossed it into a nearby ravine. "All's fair in love, war, and a horse race," he declared and mounted up, then took off again at a gallop.

It was mid-morning when Comanche reined up in the clearing and looked around. His head ached like an Injun war drum, so he must have had a better time than he thought last night. It was past time to spot another sign pointing the trail, but there was none to be seen. He dismounted and studied the ground. There were hoof prints all right, but were they headed in the right direction? He knew there were several hombres in this race who weren't above dirty tricks. He tied his horse to a tree, rolled a cigarette, and walked about, checking out the hoof prints that he soon lost on hard scrabble rock a few hundred feet away. "Hell, as a Texan, how am I supposed to know if this trail leads to the next town?"

He heard hoofbeats coming and brightened. Maybe it would be one of the hombres who was a Nebraska native. Comanche was more than willing to be friendly and help a rider if he would return the favor.

The young dude on the fancy gray horse rode up. Comanche scowled. "Oh, it's you. I told you I didn't want you shadowin' me no more."

The boy kept his face ducked low under his hat. "It's a free country," he growled. "By the way, I ran across Davy yesterday. He's dropping out sick."

"Tough luck." Comanche sighed and tossed away his smoke. "You see any of the other riders?"

The dude grinned. "Passed some of them along the trail. They looked surprised to see me."

"Any cowboy that'd sleep past dawn can't be expected to compete and win."

"Just watch me."

Comanche couldn't believe the kid's bravado.

"What are we looking for?"

"*We* ain't doin' nothin'. Me, I reckon there oughta be a sign hereabouts, but I ain't findin' it. I don't reckon you—? Oh, hell, why am I askin'? You're from back East."

"Maybe I can help." The boy dismounted and began to walk in a circle.

"I don't need your help," Comanche snapped.

"Okay, then, maybe I'll help myself." The boy walked in an even wider circle, wandering around in the nearby gully.

"If there's a sign, it's probably over here in the brush," Comanche said and walked through the scrub just to one side of the trail.

The boy didn't say anything. After a moment, he mounted the gray Arabian and took off at a gallop.

"Hey!" Comanche shouted after him. "You know where you're goin'?"

The boy was grinning from ear to ear as he turned in his saddle, nodded, and kept on riding.

Damn the boy's hide, and to think Comanche had kept the men from tossing Henry out in the mud back in Long Pine. That was gratitude for you. If Comanche didn't get a clue soon, he'd be dealing with the other riders, who were probably only a few minutes behind him. He could stay here 'til hell froze over or take a chance that the kid knew something. The thought frosted him. "Damn it, anyhow." Comanche swung back in the saddle and took off. He didn't think the greenhorn knew any more than he did, but at the moment, what Comanche knew was nothing.

It took him an hour to catch up to the boy, who was dismounted and watering his horse from one of the two barrels along the trail.

The boy grinned. "What kept you so long?"

"Just how in the hell did you find the trail?" Comanche growled as he swung down, then led Hombre over for a cold drink.

"The sign had been pitched down in the gully." The boy leaned against a tree. "I saw it and took a chance."

"Why didn't you say so back there?" He nodded back down the trail.

" 'Cause you didn't want my help. Well, so long." The boy swung up on the big, gray horse.

"Maybe"—Comanche took off his hat and poured a dipperful of water over his head—"maybe we should throw in together after all. Two heads is always better than one."

"Unless one is full of booze."

"Don't get smart with me, dude. Can I help it if everybody in each town wants to buy the riders a drink?" Comanche grumbled and swung up on his horse. "Besides, a greenhorn like you could run into trouble. You got a pistol?"

The boy shook his head. "Do I need one?"

"Hell, yes. What you gonna do if you run up against an outlaw robbin' the stage or something?"

"I may be a greenhorn, but I don't think there's been any stagecoaches on these roads for fifteen or twenty years."

What a smart alec. "Well, maybe a snake, then."

The greenhorn's eyes widened. "Snakes?"

"Yep." Comanche grinned. He'd definitely ruined the kid's afternoon. That made for a good day. "From what I heard at the last town, the next check-in point is in Iowa. If we don't have any trouble, we might get there by dark."

They started out at a trot and rode in silence for several hours.

Finally the boy said, "Where are the other riders?"

Comanche shrugged. "Don't know. Some must be ahead of us and some behind us. When I find out who yanked up the sign, I'll make him holler calf rope."

"What?" the boy asked.

"Calf rope?" Comanche shrugged. "In Texas, it's the same as crying uncle; it means to surrender, something Texans never do."

"Texans," the boy sneered.

"Yankee city slickers," he snorted back.

They rode for another hour and then came to a small river. The boy reined in and looked at the water. "I—I can't swim."

Comanche grinned. "Well, then, looks like the race ends right here for you, kid." He dismounted and began to pull off his boots.

"What are you doing?"

"What does it look like I'm doin'? I ain't one to get my only set of clothes wet." He began to unbutton his shirt.

"You—you going to go into that water naked?"

"Sure." He peeled off his shirt and pants, then began to unbutton his long handles.

"It isn't decent." The boy sounded panicked.

"There ain't nobody here but us, boy, and I ain't about to wear wet clothes the rest of the day."

Henrietta watched in stunned silence as the cowboy unbuttoned his long handles. She wanted to cry out in protest, yet dared not. Now he stripped his underwear off, bundled his clothes in a piece of oilcloth, and tied them around his saddle horn. As she watched in shock, he dug a strip of rawhide out of his saddlebags, tied his boots together, and hung them around his neck.

All she could do was stare at this brawny, bare-bottomed man. She had never seen a naked man before, and this one was all man from his wide shoulders to his narrow hips. Because of the Indian blood, his skin was dark under his clothing, but not as dark as his suntanned, rugged face. The male part of him looked like a big sausage. She gazed at him in stunned silence.

"Look, kid," Comanche snapped, "it ain't polite for a man to stare at another man's whang, if you get my drift."

She felt her face burn and looked away.

The naked man remounted his horse and surveyed the water.

"What about me?" Henrietta said.

"Well, it's your call. You gonna get your clothes wet?"

What to do? If she told him her secret, he'd probably turn her in at the next check-in point, and maybe she'd be disqualified. On the other hand, if she stripped her clothes off, he'd know anyway. She hesitated, saying nothing.

"Well, I ain't waitin'," Comanche said and urged his horse into the river. She watched him dismount and swim next to the bay horse as they fought the current. He was a thing of beauty, his naked muscles reflecting the light.

When he made it to the other side, he called, "You comin', Henry? I ain't got all day."

She didn't know what to do, so she just shook her head.

"Suit yourself. I'll see you at the next check-in point . . . if you get there."

"You going to leave me here?"

"I ain't nursemaidin' a greenhorn anymore. That's one less competitor for me."

"Wait!" She took a deep breath and urged the gray Arabian into the water.

"Kid, you're loco, you ought to take your clothes off."

She didn't say anything, just kept urging her horse deeper.

"Henry, you're a damn fool."

The current was pulling at her now, filling her boots with water. She lost her grip on her saddle and went into the stream, thrashing wildly.

"Oh, hell!" Comanche swore, then dove into the river. He came up near her and grabbed her shoulder. He had her by the arm now, swimming with her and her horse to the shallows. Lady Jane staggered up on the riverbank and gave herself an indignant shake. Henrietta tried to stand but could not. Comanche swung her up in his powerful arms and carried her to shore. Only then did he seem to notice her wet shirt plastered against her generous curves. "Oh, Lordy, I don't know how I get into these fixes. What in God's name is a gal doin' in this race?"

She began to sob in sheer exhaustion and defeat. "I—I was desperate," she wailed.

He dumped her on the ground and grabbed for his pants. "You're either the dumbest or the damndest female I ever run across." He looked up at the sky, imploring. "Dear Lord, I don't know why I got her. Ain't there any other poor bastard in this race who deserves this hard luck worse?"

She shivered, wrapping her arms around herself. When she looked down, there was a small fish flopping around in one of her boots. She pulled off her boots and poured the water out, tossing the tiny fish back in the river. "Thank you for saving my life." She gulped. "You know, the Orientals think that if you save somebody's life, you're responsible for them."

"Oh, hell, no." He pulled his pants on and reached for his boots. "Missy, I don't know what you're doin' on this ride, but I've already done more than my share."

She shivered some more. "Where—where are you going?"

"Well, now, where does it look like I'm goin'? I'm headin' for the next check-in point, and you're on your own."

She tried to choke back the tears, but they filled her big blue eyes and trickled down her face.

"Oh, hell, don't start that," he snapped.

"Did anyone ever tell you you have a limited vocabulary?" She quivered in her soaked clothes.

"What? No, wait, I don't think I want to know." He sighed and paused. "You look like a drowned rat."

"I—I'll be okay." She let her teeth chatter a little.

He glanced up at the sun again. "I'm losin' time. Just why in hell is a gal doin' this?"

"Does it matter? You go on with your race."

"Winnin' is important to me," he muttered. "That prize

money would buy me a little ranch. I'm gut tired of bein' just a cowhand."

"I understand," she said and tried to wring some of the water out of her shirttail.

"Damn it all to hell," he growled. "I reckon I can't leave you like this. You probably don't even know how to build a campfire."

She sighed. "Worse yet, I don't have any matches."

"I don't know why I have to be the one to get stuck with you," he said as he began to gather firewood. "There's eight other hombres in this race you could have tagged after."

"Seven," she corrected. "I told you I passed young Davy on the trail. He said he got sick and was quitting."

"And I'm gettin' mighty sick myself. All right, I'll get you dried out, and then I'm ridin' on. Gal, you've slowed me enough."

She hunched closer to the fire he was building. "It hasn't been deliberate," she offered by way of apology. "I'm trying to win the race myself."

"Huh!" he snorted as he built a good fire and began digging in his saddlebags. "You look purty high-class to me. Why you need money?"

"Well, if I win, my father might forget I'm a girl when he wanted a male heir."

Comanche was having a hard time forgetting she was a girl with the way her wet shirt clung to her curves. "Well, poor little rich gal, that ain't as good as my reason."

"Well, how about this? Mother and my fiancé are looking for me. They've got the wedding planned, but he's a toad."

"Maybe he ain't so bad if you got to know him better—"

"His name is Throckmorton P. Gutterstaff III. Does that tell you something?"

Comanche winced. "So he's a toad. That prize money might take you out of his reach?"

She nodded and leaned into the warmth of the fire.

"If you'll get out of those wet clothes," he said, "I'll try to dry them out, whoever the hell you are."

"My real name is Henrietta." She hesitated.

"I won't look, okay? Here, you can wrap up in my dry shirt. Go over there in the brush and take off those wet things."

"Promise you won't peek?"

"Oh, missy, that dog won't hunt."

She stared at him. "I don't speak Texan," she reminded him coldly.

He took a deep breath and looked skyward as if asking for help. "What I mean, lady, is the only thing that looks good to me right now is that next check-in point where there's probably seven riders already ahead of me."

She took his shirt and went into the brush. Even though he tried not to look, he caught a glimpse of very fair skin and the length of her legs as she peeled off the wet pants. He took a deep breath and turned away, surprised that he was so aroused. It had been a long time since he had had a woman, and usually, it was one of the middle-aged whores at some cheap crib. It was a good thing he was a Texan. No Texan would take advantage of an innocent girl. However, he might think about it some and enjoy the images. There was no law against that.

She came tiptoeing out of the brush with wet clothes in hand. The shirt hung halfway to her pretty knees. "I wonder if there might be poison ivy in those woods."

He took the wet clothes. "That'll make for an itchy fanny if it's true."

"Don't be crude. Can you make some coffee?"

He sighed. "Look, Lady Prissy, or Henrietta, or whoever the hell you are, I am not your servant. I'm a poor stupid bastard who's tryin' to be gallant when any man with good sense would give you a quick tumble in the grass and then leave you to get on with winnin' this race."

Her face flamed, and about that time, she put her bare

foot on a sticker and hopped about, whimpering. The shirt went up so he got a better look at her thighs and bottom. "I should have picked a gentleman to ride with."

"I wish you had," he grumbled. "I might be ahead in this race now if I hadn't stopped to mess with you."

"May I remind you," she said with a tone sharp enough to cut a longhorn steak, "that I was the one who spotted the missing sign this morning? If it weren't for me, you'd still be wandering around back there."

"And I just saved your life, missy, so shut up and sit down here by the fire while I see what I can do about some food."

"I am not used to having anyone tell me to shut up." Her voice was icy, but she sat down on a log.

"And I'll bet no man ever turned you over his knee either, and I don't reckon Throckmorton P. Gutterstaff *the Third* is man enough to do it."

"And neither are you." She glared at him.

"Missy," he warned, "do not try a Texan's patience."

She thought about it a long moment, then decided he might not be bluffing. Why, the brute would probably enjoy it. "I—I'm sorry," she said. "I appreciate your saving me."

"And I'm much obliged to you for findin' the trail this mornin'," he said, "so I reckon we're even. Now, in the mornin', we'll ride on to the check-in point."

"We're gonna stay out here all night alone with no chaperones?" She looked around at the growing twilight.

He paused, sighing loudly. "Ain't you the gal that spent a night in a hotel room with nine men and one night on the trail with me?"

She felt the blood rush to her face. "Yes, but then you thought I was a boy. It's most unchivalrous of you to mention that."

He hung her clothes on a lariat stretched between two trees near the fire. "Believe me, I don't know what that big word means. As for your virtue bein' in any danger, I doubt you would shut up long enough to make it enjoyable."

"How dare you!" She bristled.

"See what I mean?" He finished hanging her clothes up, got some grub out of his saddlebags, and began slicing bacon. "You know anything about cookin'?"

"Nothing. Anyway, I can't bend over a campfire without exposing—"

"Well, I already seen most of what you got," he volunteered with a grin, "so if you want to bend over that campfire—"

"Don't be vulgar!" she snapped. "Whatever you cook is fine with me."

"Well, Miss High and Mighty, it better be. I'm beginnin' to feel sorry for old Throckie for wantin' you back. He don't realize that you runnin' off was his lucky day."

Henrietta snorted. "Throckmorton is rich Boston society, and Mother's gone through all the money Daddy's sent her, so she's eager to get me wed."

"My mama always said if you marry for money, you damn sure earn it." He continued to slice bacon.

"Are you married?"

"Now, missy, do I look like I can afford to be married? That horse and saddle are about all I got in this world. Not many women want a penniless cowboy."

She doubted that Comanche Jones would have any trouble attracting a woman. She watched him move around the fire. All he had on were his boots and tight denims. His bare muscles rippled as he worked, and when she saw the bulge in his tight pants, she remembered how it had looked and blushed at the thought. He was all man, all right, a big, brawny and uncivilized Texas brute. Yet she doubted Throckmorton, who certainly knew which fork to use, would have dived in that river and pulled her out. "Suppose we make a truce," she said. "We'll ride together until the last few miles, and then may the better rider win."

He looked up, a lock of his black hair falling across his rugged face. "Do I look like my mama raised a fool? I'm takin' you in to the next check-in and dumpin' you or maybe turnin' you over to the Pinkertons a'fore I get in trouble. I reckon you attract trouble like a dog does fleas, and I got plenty of problems of my own, thank you very much."

She let tears gather and trickle down her face.

"Now, you stop that," he warned. "I ain't gonna be swayed by alligator tears in them big, blue eyes. Here, I got some biscuits and bacon and some coffee made. Eat up, Miss Henrietta, but I ain't got no fancy napkins or silver like I reckon you're used to."

She took the tin plate and dived in, wolfing down the food in a most unladylike manner. It was good, hearty fare. Her shirt slipped so that it was showing a large expanse of her thighs, but she didn't care now because she had a new plan. Henrietta was desperate to stay in this race, even if it meant seducing this cowboy to buy his help and his silence. Frankly, she wasn't quite sure how one went about seducing a man, but she intended to find out.

Three

Back in Chadron, Henry Jennings' special train had just pulled into the station when the telegrapher came running to meet him. "Good evening, sir. How was Omaha?"

"Good." He nodded. "Got elected President of the Cattlemen's Association."

"I got a telegram for you, sir." The little man handed it over, his store-bought teeth clicking as he spoke.

"Hmm." Henry put on his glasses and studied it. It was from his ex-wife, so it couldn't be good news.

Henry: there is a big emergency. Stop. Henrietta has run away from home and may be trying to reach you. Stop. She has taken her gray Arabian horse. Stop. I'm sick with worry. Stop. What shall we do? Please advise. Matilda.

Henry took a deep breath and scowled. He loved this daughter he had never seen, and he was afraid for her if she tried to travel alone across the uncivilized West. To the telegrapher, he said, "You ain't seen anything of a young girl with a fancy gray horse, have you?"

The little man shook his head, then paused. "No, wait. There was a tall, light-haired young lady with big blue eyes asking for you while you was out of town, sir."

He smiled with relief. He'd never seen her, but Henrietta

must look like him because her mother was petite and dark. He'd married the big city beauty on impulse, but Matilda had never adjusted to ranch life and had fled back East after only six months. "You saw her? Where'd she go?"

The man shook his head. "Seemed disappointed you was out of town. Don't know where she went."

Now he was really concerned. He strode out on the platform into the twilight where his ranch foreman awaited his return. "Howdy, Buck. There been anything goin' on while I been gone?"

"Howdy, sir." Buck nodded. "Them blooded horses from Texas got delivered, and there's that big cowboy race all the way to Chicago."

Henry shook his head. "I meant—never mind."

"There was lots of good horses in that race," Buck said. "I had a good mind to enter myself. Why, there was even some young dude riding a fancy gray horse."

A warning went off in Henry's head. "A gray horse? An Arabian?"

"Well, yes, I reckon it was. Why?"

Henry thought a minute. He was a Texan himself, having come up to the high plains and fought Indians and rustlers to build his empire. He'd always regretted not having a son to pass his empire on to, which was why his daughter carried his first name. Did Henrietta have more grit than he had expected? Did she take more after her daddy than her citified mother? "Where'd you say that race ended?"

"Chicago, why?"

"Get the boys mounted and on this train. Load my best horse, too."

"But, sir, you just got home."

"You heard me!" he snapped, and Henry Jennings wasn't a man to brook argument. "See how close to that trail this train can follow."

Buck looked at him as though he thought he'd gone loco,

but he nodded and hurried off the platform. Henry turned to the telegrapher. "Jed, send a return wire to my ex-wife. Tell her to meet me at the end of this cowboy race in Chicago. I think we'll find our errant daughter there. Now, see how fast the engineer can reroute this train."

The little man paused, then nodded. "It don't follow the race route, except a few hundred miles. Then it angles off."

"We got horses, so we'll pick up the trail somewhere, maybe in Iowa or Illinois. Then we'll get back on for the last few miles into Chicago. Anything happens to my daughter, I'll skin some rascal alive. Now, get this train ready to roll!"

Comanche and Henrietta sat by the evening campfire.

"Thank you, that was good." Henrietta set her plate down and looked around for something to use as a napkin. The Texan was wiping his mouth on his bare arm. She tried not to wince. "I —I know I've been a lot of trouble to you—"

"That ain't the half of it," he snapped and gulped his coffee.

She leaned forward so that he could see the swell of her breasts in his oversized shirt. He didn't say anything, but he was staring so much that he spilled his coffee on his pants and jumped up swearing. "Missy, would you do me a favor and button that shirt?"

"Why?" She leaned even closer and pouted. Now he was staring at her lips. She licked them slowly.

"Stop that."

"What?" She blinked, moving her long lashes up and down like seductive fans.

"It's a good thing I'm a Texan, otherwise . . . ," he grumbled and threw the last of his coffee on the fire.

She didn't know quite what to do now. "Are you really going to turn me in tomorrow?"

He shook his head, obviously confused. "Hell, I don't know. Tell you what I'll do; after we check in tomorrow, you're on your own. That's the best I can do."

She really was sorry she had caused him so much trouble, especially since he needed the prize money as badly as she did. "I'm not sure I can finish this race on my own."

"Well, missy, that don't make me no never mind. There's other men in this race you can maybe talk into helpin' you."

"Oh, but I'm not sure I could—"

"Henrietta, you could talk a cow out of her calf, or a dog off a meat wagon, so I reckon you can talk some poor devil into helpin' you stay in the race. Now, let's get some shut-eye a'fore I do something a Texan would be ashamed of. Besides, we got to hit the ground runnin' at dawn."

Henrietta was relieved that she didn't have to go any farther with her seduction because, quite frankly, she wasn't experienced enough to know what to do next. At least he had promised not to turn her over to the authorities . . . if she could trust him.

The next morning, Comanche cooked up some bacon and biscuits, and then they rode toward the town.

Henrietta looked around at the landscape. "Where do you suppose we are?"

"I dunno." Comanche shook his head. "Reckon it must be Iowa; I see miles and miles of corn fields."

A large crowd had gathered to cheer the riders as they arrived.

Henrietta held her breath as she and Comanche rode up and dismounted. Three of the riders had arrived earlier and were standing around talking.

"Well, if it ain't the Texan and the prissy dude." Doc Middleton grinned. "Beginning to think you two was lost."

Comanche looked at her. "Well, we was for a while. It ain't like either of us know this part of the country."

"The dude looks tired," one of the others said. "You sure you ain't ready to quit? You ain't got a chance, you know."

She looked at Comanche, afraid to speak, afraid someone might finally recognize her voice as a woman's.

"It ain't over 'til it's over, and the dude ain't doin' so

bad," Comanche snapped, "although his horse ain't used to this kind of ridin'."

She smiled at Comanche, thanking him with her eyes for not telling on her.

Comanche glanced away. He was a goner when he looked into those eyes, bluer than a Texas bluebonnet. He reminded himself again that he'd have to be ruthless to win that money, and he was being slowed down by the girl. He ought to tell the check-in committee about her. It would serve the little gal right to be forced out of the race.

The gray-haired man at the sign-in table said, "You men can either rest and have some breakfast or ride on."

"Anyone already gone on?" asked one of the cowboys.

The official nodded. "One left less than an hour ago."

Doc Middleton said, "Me for some ham and eggs before I hit the saddle again."

"Me, too," said one of the others.

"I've already et." Comanche swung up into his saddle. "So I'll be movin' on."

The girl swung up onto her horse.

Damn, she was going to tag along with him. He'd hoped she'd pick on one of the others. "Dude, I thought we was goin' to part company when we hit this town."

She raised her eyebrows, shook her head, and smiled.

At this point, he was mighty tempted to expose her ruse, but he didn't. Comanche started out of town at a lope with the crowd cheering him on. The dude stayed right by his side.

When they got out on the trail, she said, "Thanks for not telling on me."

"You ain't welcome, missy," he snapped. "I thought we had an agreement that we'd split once we hit that next check-in?"

"I don't remember agreeing to any such thing."

"Henrietta, God's liable to knock you out of that ridiculous little saddle for lyin'." She had grit, he had to admit that. Even though she looked tired, she was staying up with him without complaining.

They rode for two more hours before Comanche drew in. "We ain't seen any signs along the way. I hope someone ahead of us don't want to win bad enough that they'd play dirty."

"They already have," she reminded him.

Comanche dismounted and checked the trail. He'd done a lot of tracking in his day, and after a few minutes, he picked up the faintest marks on the hard ground. "This way," he said. "I think the route is this way."

"I'll take your word for it," she said. "Honestly, Comanche, I wouldn't be able to stay in this race without you."

"Which makes me a damn fool," he grumbled as he remounted. "I ought to be tryin' to lose competitors."

They kept a steady pace, and along about sunset, they found a small creek to camp by. Up over the rise, he could see a distant town. "Reckon that's our next check-in point and none too soon. I think your horse has lost a shoe."

She dismounted and examined Lady Jane's hoof. "You're right. What can I do?"

"Well, best I can tell, Henrietta, you may be out of the race. They'll have a blacksmith in that town, but it'll take a couple of hours to replace it, and I ain't gonna wait."

She blinked rapidly and swallowed hard. "Okay. You've been good to help me this far."

Oh, Lord, he hoped she wasn't about to cry. He couldn't stand that. Comanche dismounted and hobbled his horse, then unsaddled and fed Hombre. "It ain't that I ain't a gentleman who'd like to help a lady; I just need to win so bad."

"Believe me, I understand." She began to unsaddle her horse.

"Here, let me do that," he snapped and came over, taking the saddle out of her hands. "A little slip of a thing like you got no business tryin' to lift a saddle. You sit down there on a rock, and I'll get a fire goin'. You look plumb tuckered out."

"I'm going to pull my share," she argued, but she plopped down on a rock anyhow.

He finished hobbling her horse and turned the gray loose. "You got grit. I'll say that for you. Texans like that in their women."

She started to tell him she wasn't his woman, but then she remembered that she was going to have to charm him into not leaving her behind, so she merely fluttered her eyelashes and sighed. "I'm doing the best I can, for a little slip of a thing."

He knelt and began to build a fire. "I'll get us some grub cookin', and then we'll bed down early. I hate to leave you behind in the morning, little gal, but it can't be helped."

"I know," she said, "and I understand. All of us have different reasons for needing to win."

He looked ill at ease. "Ain't you gonna cry or scream at me or anything?"

She let a tear slide down her cheek. "I—I guess I'm beat."

"Stop that," he ordered. "I can't stand it."

She managed to spill two more tears and buried her face in her hands. *Tonight,* she thought, *tonight, I'm going to do whatever it takes to stay in this race.*

It was dark when they finished eating and sat before the fire drinking coffee.

"It's been fun, Comanche. I hate to see it end." She moved a little closer so that she could lean against his leg as he sat on a rock before the fire.

"I have to admit you been a purty good sport," he said. "I didn't think you'd give up so easy." He knew he should ask her to move away, but somehow, the warmth of her against his leg felt good. Then the light from the fire shone on that tousled yellow hair, and before he was aware of his action, he reached out and stroked it. It was softer than a colt's mane. She turned her head and looked up at him with those eyes the color of a Texas sky. He felt very protective of this plucky female. "Maybe—maybe if the blacksmith can get right on it, you might could get back in the race."

Her lips opened, and all he could think of was how soft and moist they looked. "Without you, Comanche, I wouldn't have a chance of finishing, and I know it."

Her small hand reached to cover his big one. Her palm was as soft as feathers. He was paralyzed by her nearness. "Well, you might if the blacksmith could get right on it."

"No." She shook her head and then laid her face against his knee, looking up at him. "Tomorrow, I'll figure out what to do. Guess I might as well wire home and wait for the Pinkertons to come get me." She sighed. "If you'll help me up, Comanche, I reckon I'll get some sleep now."

"Sure thing." He stood and reached down, taking both her little hands in his big ones. As she stood, she stumbled and fell against him, grabbing on to him.

"Oh, I'm so clumsy." She was looking up at him, lips half opened. Her mouth looked soft and moist, and then she ran her little pink tongue across those lips.

He couldn't stop himself. He bent his head and kissed that mouth. Rather than pulling away in shock and slapping him, she put her arms around his neck and returned the kiss.

"Oh, missy," he whispered against her lips and pulled her tighter to his big frame.

"My name's Henrietta," she whispered, and then she kissed him again. She had never been kissed and here she was kissing a man with all the pent-up ardor she didn't know she possessed. Well-bred young ladies never, ever let a man kiss them until they were engaged and then maybe only a quick peck. This was more than a quick peck, it was hot and wild and delightful. My, she had really been missing something by not kissing men. Or maybe it was only because she was in the powerful arms of the big Texan.

She took a deep breath and ran the tip of her tongue across his lips which seemed to excite him even more. He tightened his grip so that she could scarcely breathe and sucked her tongue into his mouth while his hand stroked her bottom. The heat of his palm seemed to scorch her flesh.

Comanche felt like a hapless steer caught in a stampede heading toward a cliff. He might be able to get out if he wanted to bad enough, but the momentum was taking him forward to the canyon's edge. He pulled her so close, he could feel her nipples pressing into him through the denim shirt she wore.

Henrietta was shocked and surprised at her own reaction to the cowboy. She could feel his hot hands through her shirt and his arousal against her body. She had started out to seduce him into helping her, but now something in her stirred that she had not ever known existed. She felt very small and protected in his muscular embrace.

"Oh, Comanche, when you kiss me like that . . ." Her words trailed off as he kissed her deeper still. His tongue was hot in her mouth, pushing past her lips, and one of his hands went inside her shirt and covered her breast. In answer, she pressed up against his hand, wanting him to stroke and caress there. His hand felt hard and calloused, but his touch was gentle as he cupped her breast.

He swung her up in his arms, looking down at her in the firelight. His dark gaze smoldered with desire as she reached up and kissed his cheek, then laid her face against his broad shoulder.

"I want you," she whispered.

"Lord, missy, I don't need the kind of trouble you're gonna bring me. My good sense tells me to get on my horse and ride outta here," he muttered.

"But you don't want to, do you?"

At that, he groaned in surrender and knelt, laying her on the blanket, leaning over her. "Henrietta, don't do this to me. Tell me to stop while there's still time."

She knew that was what she was supposed to do, not give her virginity away to some penniless cowboy on a blanket out in the wilderness. Instead, she reached up and pulled him closer, desiring him in a way she had never felt before. Her body and her skin seemed to be aflame, wanting his touch, his kiss. "I don't want you to stop," she said and pulled him down on her.

With a groan, he tore at her shirt, freeing her breasts for his kisses as he tangled his fingers in her tousled blond hair.

She forgot that her goal had been to seduce him so he would help her stay in the race. Abruptly she wanted this union as much as he did, and in a frenzy, she ran her hands up and down his lean, hard body.

"Missy, I don't think you know what you've started here—"

She stopped his words with her mouth, reaching to unbuckle his belt, and pulled him to her. She wasn't quite sure how this was done, but she was confident he would know. His hands were experienced as he tightened his embrace and kissed her deeper still. Then his mouth went to her breasts. His rugged face was dark against the pale smoothness of her skin. His hands stroked her skin, up and down her thighs and she couldn't stop herself from trembling with anticipation. His black hair tumbled down his forehead and she reached up and tenderly stroked it away from his tanned face. Catching his face between her two, small hands, she kissed him gently, tenderly while he breathed deeper and tangled his calloused big hands in her pale hair.

"Oh, honey," he gasped, "I shouldn't be doin' this; tell me to stop. Tell me!"

She didn't want him to stop; she wanted it as much as he did. Henrietta gasped for air, her body hot as fever and it wasn't just the summer night as they came together in a wild, hard rush that was more exciting, more fulfilling than she had ever dreamed it could be. She was in the circle of his embrace and she felt safe there as she gave him her virginity.

He plunged deep into her, then shuddered and gave up his seed, covering her face with feverish kisses, panting hard. "Oh, little gal, I never had anything so good, no never. . . ."

They lay gasping in each other's arms.

"Neither have I," she said and hugged him to her. "Matter of fact, I never had any before at all."

That must have jolted him back to reality, for he rose up on his elbows and stared down into her eyes, blinking.

"Oh, missy," he gasped, "now I know I shouldn't have done that."

"I'm glad you did," she whispered and kissed his sun-tanned, handsome face, and pulled him down to her, curled up in the circle of his embrace. She smiled at the memory of the moment he had taken her so sompletely and laid her face against his brawny chest.

He stroked her hair once and she waited for him to say something romantic. Instead, after a moment, he began to snore. What? Surely he hadn't gone to sleep when she wanted to talk about this new experience, talk about her feelings.

Damn him, he was asleep, all right. Men, they weren't much better than hound dogs. After the rush, they didn't want to talk all night, they wanted to sleep. She was angry and disappointed at this betrayal.

Well, now she would do whatever it took to win this race. It served the cowboy right, and she didn't even feel ashamed at what she was about to do. Quietly, she slid out of his arms, checked to make sure her clothes were dry as they hung near the fire, and put them and her boots on. Still he snored the sleep of a satisfied, bone-tired man. She got her light saddle and bridle, then tiptoed over to Hombre. She would leave Comanche with Lady Jane, and he could get her horse shod. By the time he awakened, found a black-smith, and got a new shoe for the gray mare, Henrietta would be miles down the trail. Later she would figure out a way to reclaim her horse. Right now, she intended to win this race, no matter what.

Just as she was about ready to leave, she tripped over the metal coffeepot, and it fell on the rocks with a jangle.

Comanche came up off the blanket. "What the hell—?"

Desperate, Henrietta picked up the noisy coffeepot and threw it at him. He dodged and lunged toward her as she turned and ran into the darkness. Behind her, she heard him stumbling and cursing. Oh, there was no telling what he would do if he caught her. She dashed to his horse, mounted and took off up the trail at a dead gallop. Her heart pounded so hard, that was all she heard, but any moment, she expected to hear him galloping after her.

No, wait. She'd left him her horse and Lady Jane had lost a shoe. Comanche couldn't come in pursuit. Henrietta smiled to herself and kept riding.

Comanche had dodged the flying coffeepot and lunged for the girl, but his boot slipped on a loose rock. He tried to catch his balance, but it was too late. In the firelight, he saw the big rocks and tried to throw out his hands to catch himself, but he landed hard. Pain crashed through his head and then everything faded into blackness.

It was long after daylight when Comanche finally came to, tried to sit up, groaned. He had a splitting headache. It must be late and he wasn't sure what had happened. He stumbled to his feet, found his shirt the girl had worn last night, slipped it on. His head still pounded. With a tentative hand, he reached up and touched his temple, came away with a smear of dried blood.

"What the—?" He wiped his hand on his shirt. "Henrietta?" He hoped whoever had attacked him hadn't hurt the girl. He'd kill the villain who laid a hand on the helpless little thing. He looked around. There was no sign of her and Hombre was gone. Lady Jane grazed peacefully nearby.

He began to look for his boots. What was the coffeepot doing on his blanket? Then the memory of last night returned. It had been the best night he'd ever spent in a woman's arms, right up until . . .

Why, that little tart. She had seduced him, tried to hit him in the head with the coffeepot, and by the looks of it, had stolen his horse. Now he remembered slipping and falling on the jagged rocks.

He had trusted her and she'd done him in. If that wasn't just like a woman. Well, there was nothing to do but take the gray mare into town, check-in, get the horse shod, and ride on, trying to catch the crafty girl.

With his head aching like a two-week bender, he managed to stumble to the creek and wash his face to clear his mind. Then he gathered up the camp stuff and started walking toward town, leading Lady Jane. He should have known better than trust Henrietta, but when she'd looked up at him with those moist lips just begging to be kissed, and those soft blue eyes like Texas bluebonnets, he'd been done in like Santa Anna had by a woman at San Jacinto.

"Women," he snorted. "They all know how to take advantage of a man's weakness. Miss Priss, if I catch up with you, I'm gonna spank that purty fanny until you can't stand up." He smiled despite his aching head. It had been a pretty fanny, along with everything else about her, and it looked as though it had cost him the race and that big prize. With a sigh, he led Lady Jane into the next town.

First he went to the check-in in front of the hotel. "That young dude already checked in? Ridin' a bay stallion?"

The elderly judge nodded. "Hours ago, the first one to come through. You're a little late, young fella. The others already come through and gone. In fact, when I check you in, I'm leavin' town."

His head still ached. "I ran into a little trouble."

A trouble named Henrietta J. Smith, he thought grimly and hobbled over to the blacksmith shop. The blacksmith was gone on an errand, and there was nothing to do but await his return. Comanche tied the gray up and brought her some feed and a bucket of water. Then he lay down under a shade tree and dropped off to sleep, hoping to shake the headache.

He must have slept several hours when he heard a commotion, felt a crowd around him, and slowly opened his eyes. He was staring into the business end of a double-barreled shotgun being held by an angry-looking old codger with cold blue eyes glaring from under thin, light-colored hair. This cowman looked mad enough to take on a rattler and give it first bite.

"All right, you buzzard, where'd you get that horse?"

Comanche took a deep breath and sat up. "Someone took my horse and left me this one."

"You're a damned liar!" the older man shouted. "What'd you do with the girl?"

"Boss," said one of the cowboys with the old man, "he's got blood on him."

"It's my blood," Comanche said.

The old man swore. "Buck, I reckon he's killed her."

"Wait just a damned minute—" Comanche began.

"No, you wait, you bastard," the weathered cowboy called Buck said. "You don't know who you're talkin' to."

Comanche was getting as nervous as a whore in church on Sunday. Maybe that was why the one called Buck looked familiar, even though he couldn't figure out why. "I'm talkin' to a loco old galoot who won't listen to reason—"

"Let's string him up," one of the other cowboys said.

Comanche saw the sheriff running toward them, the star on his chest reflecting the light. He didn't know or care how this bunch knew Henrietta; he was only trying to stay alive. "Now, hold on just a damned minute. She tried to hit me in the head and stole my horse, left me with this lame one."

The old man waved the shotgun at him. "A likely story, a big hombre like you overpowered by a little gal?"

He started to say the girl had seduced him and got him to

lower his guard, but it didn't seem a gentlemanly thing to do, leastwise, not for a Texan.

One of the men shouted, "Who's for a necktie party?"

It seemed everyone except Comanche yelled approval. There must not have been much entertainment in these parts.

"Wait a minute," said the sheriff as he came up and waved for silence. "This man deserves a fair trial."

"You're right, Sheriff," snapped the old man. "We'll give him a fair trial, and then we'll string him up."

Comanche felt a growing sense of panic. "I tell you, she threw a coffeepot at me and stole my horse. If I'd killed her, would I be here tryin' to get her horse shod?"

The old man waved the shotgun again. "You didn't figure anyone would find out this fast."

The sheriff grabbed Comanche by the arm. "Let's throw him in jail until we can figure all this out."

"We'd rather string him up now." Several of the cowboys crowded closer. "Waitin' 'til tonight will interfere with our poker games."

"I ain't one to delay a good poker game," Comanche insisted, "but I ain't killed nobody. I tell you, the girl bedded me, then threw a coffeepot at me and took my horse."

The old man's eyes turned as cold as blue ice. "Bedded you? You callin' her a whore, you low-lived varmint? Now I'm really gonna lynch you."

"Easy!" said the sheriff. "Nobody's found a body yet. I'll toss him in the hoosegow and wire around to see if anybody's found her remains."

With Comanche still protesting, the crowd followed the pair over as the sheriff led Comanche to jail.

"That little tart," he grumbled as he collapsed on the bunk and listened to the growing crowd outside calling for his hanging. "She'll win the race, and I'll get lynched, still tryin' to explain."

What to do? There wasn't much he could do, and he wasn't at all sure the crowd of angry cowboys that old man led might not storm the jail before dark and lynch him. That little blonde had been mighty tasty, but she hadn't been worth getting killed for. Well, on second thought, it had been the best loving he'd ever had. He shook his head and closed his eyes. He hoped when she heard about it, she'd at least be sorry. He didn't know whether to hate her or admire her for her grit. "Damn, Henrietta, I never met a gal quite like you, and I hope I never meet another one. Of course, I don't reckon I'll get the chance. I expect to be dead a'fore midnight!"

Four

Still dressed like a boy, Henrietta rode the bay stallion into the next town. She was the first rider to check in which cheered her considerably. It was just past noon, and she'd been riding hard because there was no telling when Comanche would get the horseshoe replaced, and come after her like wild bees after a bear robbing a honey tree.

She decided she would feed and rest Hombre and do the same for herself rather than riding on immediately. If she was back on the trail this afternoon, she should stay ahead because Hombre was such a good horse. When the race ended, she'd reclaim her own beloved Arabian, but she wanted to give that Texan time to cool down. No doubt he'd be as mad as a rained-on rooster.

She got a late lunch at the local cafe: fried chicken, hot biscuits, corn on the cob dripping with fresh-churned butter, and some blackberry cobbler. As she finished and paid for her meal, she asked the waitress, "Anything happening in these parts?"

"Well"—the plump, gray-haired waitress leaned in closer— "Jack, the telegraph operator, just brought word that a few miles back down the road, they've jailed a killer, part of that Great Cowboy Race bunch."

"What?" That drew Henrietta's immediate attention.

The other nodded, evidently pleased to be the bearer of such interesting gossip. "Jack says the sheriff's holding this fellow after he came into town with blood smeared on him and leading a gray horse. They say he killed another rider and maybe he'll get lynched before morning. The town's pretty upset about the murder."

"Oh, no," Henrietta said, "I mean . . . the world's getting to be an evil place, isn't it?" She left the cafe and paused on the sidewalk, thinking. The man in question could only be Comanche Jones. At least now she didn't have to worry about that angry cowboy catching her. She hadn't seen any of the other riders, so it appeared she was in the lead. All she had to do was continue to ride hard and win.

Comanche. Was there any real possibility he'd get lynched? No, of course not; that was just small-town gossip. He was a tough, virile Texan who could look out for himself. Yet she felt as guilty as homemade sin about him cooling his heels in the hoosegow. Well, not really. She grinned, picturing that scene. Then she remembered last night's hot passion with a deep breath. That had been better than she'd ever thought it could be, but maybe he made love to all girls as if he cared about them. No way to know. Henrietta was in the clear.

And yet . . . She remembered last night and the taste of his kisses. If she went back to try to help him, it would throw her behind in the race. Besides, there was no telling what he would do to her if he ever laid eyes on her again. After all, she had thrown a coffeepot at him and stolen his horse. In Texas, that was probably a hanging offense.

Henrietta struggled with her conscience a few seconds and then sighed in defeat. Win or lose the race, she couldn't let them hang him. Maybe she could just send a wire to the sheriff, explaining things. No, she shook her head. She'd have to return to really convince the law Comanche hadn't killed her. It was a long ride back.

* * *

Comanche finished his jail supper and flopped down on his bunk. He lay there, staring up at the ceiling as night came on and deepened. If he wasn't in a helluva fix. From the tidbits he'd picked up from the deputy, that tough old geezer and his angry cowboys planned to break him out of jail and lynch him. Was it just for fun, or maybe they knew Henrietta? No, she'd said she was from back East. Maybe the old hombre just liked being the local vigilante.

Comanche sure hadn't bargained for this when he'd taken that little spitfire in his arms last night. If only she hadn't had curves so round and soft and eyes bluer than the Gulf of Mexico, he wouldn't have been such a fool . . . or maybe not. There had been something about her that had made him act like a loco pony on jimsonweed.

Finally he dozed off. A noise outside the barred window made him jerk awake. Was it the lynch party?

"Comanche?"

He jumped up, ran to the bars, and looked out into the bright, moonlit night. It was her all right, sitting on his bay horse, holding the reins of the gray mare. "You little rascal, you know what kind of fix you got me into?"

"Well, you shouldn't have gone to sleep on me. That was insulting."

"Listen, missy, they're gonna lynch me, you know that?"

"Who?"

"I don't know, a bunch of angry cowboys led by some light-haired old codger who looks like he could fight a cougar bare-handed."

She paused. "Oh, dear. Could it possibly be—?"

"Is that all you can say? Do you know him?"

"I—I don't think so. Anyway, I came back to help."

"Help? It was you who got me into this mess."

"I know and I'm sorry. Look, I got Lady Jane out of the livery. She's got her shoe fixed."

He sighed heavily. "Great. So I'll be sittin' on a horse with four good shoes when they run her out from under me and leave me danglin'.''

"I said I'd come back to help."

"Good. Then you just trot your little connivin' body around to the sheriff's office and tell him you ain't dead after all."

"I—I can't do that."

He grabbed the bars in frustration. "What do you mean, you can't do that? Did you not understand they're liable to stretch my neck before mornin'?"

"There's just too much to explain right now."

"Try!" he challenged.

"We don't have time. How about if I just tie the horses onto your jail bars and pull them out?"

"You loco gal, then they'll be after me for murder *and* for breakin' out of jail. They'll chase me all the way to Chicago."

She leaned on her saddle horn and grinned. "Well, you could always quit the race and go back to Texas; they wouldn't expect that."

"I've run across a lot of women in my time, but never one who would seduce a man just to win a race."

"It isn't just a race; there's a lot at stake here."

"Oh, Lord, tell me about it. I'm the one who's gonna get his neck stretched after that old geezer finishes a leisurely dinner, a game of poker, and a fine cigar." He touched his head against the bars. "What have I done to deserve this?"

"Oh, stop whining. Now get out of the way," she ordered. "I'm going to tie onto the bars."

He stepped back and watched her. "The noise is gonna bring half the town runnin'."

"Then you're going to have to move fast, cowboy." As he watched, she tied onto the bars, wrapped the lasso around her saddle horn, and urged Hombre forward. After a long moment, the bars groaned, but they didn't give.

"It's hopeless," he complained. "Do me a favor and just go explain to the sheriff I didn't kill you, at least, not yet."

"I told you I—I don't think I can do that. Now, shut up and—"

"Tie both horses to the bars," he said, "you hard-headed little rascal."

"You keep on, I just may leave you in there." But she tied both horses to the bars and urged them forward. He held his breath and watched as the bars groaned. Then they gave way, pulled out, and part of the wall tumbled down.

"Hey!" a voice called from the front of the building. "What's going on back there?"

Comanche winced. "Now you've done it! That's the deputy about to sound the alarm." He crawled through the bent bars. "Gimme my horse back!"

"No time. Take Lady Jane!" she shouted.

Behind him, he heard running boots and shouts. Any minute now, there would be a hue and cry raised with lots of bored cowboys joining the chase, no doubt led by that tough old codger with lynching on his mind. The gray Arabian danced about while he tried to swing up into the saddle.

"Hey, you, stop!" the deputy yelled, and a gun roared. That buckshot inspired Comanche to almost leap up into that unfamiliar saddle. The two of them galloped away into the night, with shots and shouting ringing out behind them.

They rode several miles through the darkness before they reined in under the shadow of some trees to rest the horses.

"Well, if we ain't in a mess now," Comanche complained. "That posse may chase us all the way to Chicago, especially that one old man. I don't know why he'd taken such a dislike to me, right after I told him I bedded you."

"You didn't!" In the moonlight, she looked horrified.

"It ain't that I'm not chivalrous, but I was tryin' to save my neck. I don't know why I was ever loco enough to get mixed up with you."

"Because you were wanting to get my drawers off."

"Little gal, you threw yourself at me, and it was good, all right," he admitted. "But it damned sure wasn't worth gettin' lynched for."

She drew herself up with indignation. "If I'd known you felt that way, I might have left you in that jail. I only came back because I heard what had happened, and I didn't think I could enjoy that prize if you got killed."

He pushed his hat back and glared at her. "I'm glad that the thought of me danglin' from a cottonwood would at least have dampened your fun while you was spendin' that money."

She sighed. "You didn't even thank me for saving you."

"Thank you? Ha! If that don't beat all. Gal, you was the reason I was in that mess."

"Details, details," she complained. "Well, now we're even, and we'll swap horses and be on our way. I warn you, this changes nothing. I intend to win that money, cowboy."

They changed horses and rode on. Only then did a thought occur to Comanche. "Hey," he said, "now you got a fresh horse."

She grinned. "Thank you for seeing that Lady Jane got a good rest. I don't expect to see you again until we reach Chicago. What is it Texans say? Oh, yes, *adios*. Watch my dust, you rascal." She galloped away up the trail.

He stared after her. If he ever caught up with her again, he might strangle her. After all, he'd already been charged with her murder. She was the most intriguing and annoying woman he'd ever met. Why, she was as sassy as some Texas gal.

About that time, he heard a train approaching, probably headed toward Chicago. He rode into the shadow of some trees and watched it passing in the moonlight. He was close enough to see the people inside the coaches as they visited and read their newspapers. Next came the boxcars. The door of one was open, and standing there looking out at the landscape was Doc Middleton, his horse beside him.

"Damn!" Comanche swore. "It ain't enough I got a feisty female to deal with and a lynch party; now I got big-time cheaters." A thought occurred to him that made him grin. "At least, with people cheatin', it might keep Missy from winnin' that prize."

Comanche sighed and dismounted, then began to walk up the trail leading his horse. It was probably a long way to the next check-in point, and he was wearing cowboy boots that weren't meant for walking. In fact, "walk" was a dirty, four-letter word to Texans. Still, he loved his horse, and he wasn't about to make the stallion carry any weight until he'd rested him some. "Comanche, you were a loco fool for a pair of big blue eyes and a handful of yellow curls. Reckon you got a lynch mob back there searchin' the countryside and the most ornery, stubborn gal you ever met ahead of you gonna beat you out of that prize money."

He snorted as he walked. Why, she was almost as smart as a man and a helluvalot purtier. Yet he was beginning to think the prize money wasn't enough for all the headaches he was dealing with. And it wasn't just headaches. The longer he walked, the more his feet hurt.

Finally he was forced to pull off in some woods near a little stream and rest awhile. He unsaddled his horse and staked Hombre out to graze, then pulled his boots off and groaned aloud. "Little gal," he promised through clenched teeth, "if I ever catch up to you again . . . " He couldn't think of anything terrible enough to do to her. Besides, when he thought about her, he saw those blue eyes and that mouth . . . oh, Lordy, that mouth.

He leaned back against a tree, closed his eyes, and remembered the scene on the blanket. He'd never had loving like he'd gotten the other night. He hated to admit it, even to himself, but he held a grudging admiration for the girl. In spite of being a back East greenhorn, she had grit, even when the going got rough, and after all, she had come back to rescue him.

Am I loco? He wouldn't have been in that mess in the first place and need rescuing if it hadn't been for her. Now here he was hundreds of miles from where this race had started, somewhere in Iowa and not even sure how many riders were ahead and behind him. One thing for certain, there was nothing to do with a sheriff and a posse behind him but to keep heading east.

He slept a little. During the night, he thought he heard at least one rider gallop past, but Comanche was too tired to care. At least it hadn't been a posse. Maybe they had given up the chase . . . or had simply wired ahead to the law and Comanche would be arrested if he dared complete the course and rode to the finish line in Chicago. He'd have to take that chance because a Texan was never a quitter. "Remember the Alamo!" he muttered to himself as he saddled up and rode out before dawn the next morning. He might not have a chance of winning, but he intended to finish this race. If nothing else, he wanted to catch up to that feisty gal so he could shake her 'til her teeth rattled.

Comanche rode steadily all day and the next. Hombre was a good horse, and Comanche knew he was gaining on the others when he passed one rider and then another. Some horses didn't have the stamina, and some riders just didn't know horses well enough to know when to rest their mounts and when to urge them forward. At the rate he was going, he was surely gaining ground on Henrietta Smith. When he got tired and his butt ached from the saddle, he pictured the surprise on her pretty face when he caught up to her. That thought kept him riding.

He checked in at the first town in Illinois late in the afternoon. "Anybody but me in so far?"

The old man at the table nodded. "Some fellow named Doc Middleton checked in to the hotel yesterday, but he never has left. I hear he's in the bar playin' poker."

So Doc was losing his ill-gotten lead at the card table.

"It's easy to get sidetracked, I reckon," Comanche said, "Anyone else?"

"Just one." The old man stuck a toothpick in his mouth. "Young fellow ridin' a fine gray horse. He's only a couple of hours ahead of you."

"Oh?" Comanche swung into his saddle.

"You ain't spendin' the night?"

"I reckon I'll join that young fellow out on the trail," Comanche said and nudged Hombre away from the check-in. He rode at a slow lope, smiling to himself. When he caught up to her, he was going to steal her boots, or turn her horse loose, or whatever it took to put her out of this race. She couldn't possibly need the money as badly as he did. He thought about having his own little ranch and sighed. Besides, he'd never be able to face other Texans if they found out he'd been beaten by a girl. Well, he wasn't ready to yell "calf rope" yet. She might think he was all gurgle and no guts—no, he was in this race to stay.

He came to a sign with an arrow pointing the way up the trail. Strange, it seemed to turn off to the right. He reined in and looked up at the sun, but it had set, and clouds had moved in so that he couldn't tell his direction from the stars. So he followed the sign's direction. An hour later, he came to another sign, and it was still pointing the same way, so he was reassured. Yet his Indian blood sensed there was something wrong. It began to rain, a cold, steady rain for June, and he'd lost his slicker in all that fuss escaping from the jail. He was hungry, wet, tired, and beginning to feel that he might be lost, yet he kept riding. Finally he saw a light up ahead at a small farmhouse and stopped to bang on the door.

A tousled, sleepy farmer in a striped nightshirt answered the door with an oil lamp in his hand.

"Howdy." Comanche ignored the rain dripping off the brim of his Stetson and down his neck. "I think I'm lost. I'm on a long-distance race and—"

"Mister, if you mean the Great Cowboy Race we heard

about, you're miles off course. Didn't you see any signs pointing the trail?"

"Yep, that's how I ended up on your doorstep."

The other man chuckled. "Stranger, someone must have moved your signs as a joke. Don't know who'd be rascal enough to do that."

"I think I know who the rascal is." In his mind, Comanche saw big blue eyes and yellow hair. "I reckon there must be some who's ornery enough to do anything to win."

"You're welcome to sleep in our barn 'til it quits rainin'."

Comanche sighed. "Good as that sounds, I got to catch up some miles. Just how far am I off course?"

The man gestured. "At least ten miles to the south. You can pick up a road there that leads into town. I hear that's the next check-in point."

"I'm much obliged." Comanche touched the brim of his hat and walked away to mount his horse again.

"You tell the race officials about someone moving them signs," the farmer yelled after him.

"Don't worry, I'll deal with that rascal myself," Comanche promised and reined his horse around. Why had he been so stupid? The gal was outsmarting him, and he didn't like that.

The rain stopped, and the stars came out so that he could figure out where he was. Finally he came to a sign that he didn't think had been messed with and followed it. Again Hombre set up a steady lope. "Hombre," Comanche promised him, "when we get to the next check-in, I'm gonna see you get more hay and grain than you ever saw before, and when I catch up to Miss Henrietta J. Smith and her fancy mare, I'll make her wish she'd left those signs alone."

He kept riding even though he was dozing in the saddle. It must have been near dawn when Hombre nickered. Comanche came out of a half sleep. "What is it, boy?"

About that time, there was an answering nicker. Comanche reined in, looking around. There was a small barn off in a peach orchard a few hundred feet away. Hombre's ears went up, and he started walking toward that barn. Comanche grinned. "Pretty mare over there, you think? We ain't got time to chase women, now, boy, but I reckon I ought to stop and get you some oats and hay."

He dismounted and led Hombre toward the barn. Just inside, he saw the bare outline of a horse. It was a gray horse. He tensed, listening. Then he heard faint snoring. He tied Hombre up and tiptoed over, looking into the stall. Henrietta lay curled up in the hay, sleeping soundly and snoring away. "Well, hello there."

Her eyes blinked open, and she sat upright. "How—how did you find me?"

"I followed your snoring."

"I do not snore." She jumped to her feet, picking hay off her jeans.

"You sassy little rascal, is that all you've got to say to me after—"

"Have you got any food?"

"Of all the nerve! Why, I believe you've got more guts than a slaughterhouse."

She wrinkled her nose. "Don't be crude."

"Oh, excuse me!" He pushed his hat back, seething at her apparent lack of contriteness. "Look, missy, you caused me to go miles out of my way and—"

"You ought to be more careful." She didn't seem at all apologetic as she combed her hair with her fingers.

"It was your fault!" he shouted at her.

"Why is it you blame everything that happens to you on me?" she asked and stepped around him.

"Because it always seems to involve you, and do you think I'd share what little food I got left with you?"

"You're selfish," she snapped, "and so ungrateful after I rescued you from jail and maybe my daddy."

"Your daddy?" He blinked, and then he knew why the blue-eyed old man had looked so familiar. "Your daddy was leadin' that lynch mob?"

"Well, from your description, maybe. The photo I've got of him is old, but now you see why I couldn't go tell the sheriff." She shrugged.

He groaned aloud. "No wonder he wants to lynch me. Your daddy is still on my trail because he thinks I murdered you." He sighed heavily. "At the moment, that don't seem like such a bad idea. All you had to do was tell him—"

"Tell him what? That you had your way with me out on a blanket? I think that would make him really mad."

He grabbed her arm. "You threw yourself at me, and bein' a man—"

"I know. Is that all men think about?"

All of a sudden, he realized he'd thought of nothing else but that since she lay in his embrace on that blanket. He couldn't stop himself as he pulled her to him and kissed her again.

His gesture caught her by surprise, and for a moment, she melted against him, dazzled by the male heat and passion of the man. When she pulled away, they were both gasping for air.

"Look," she said, "that's not going to cause me to back off and not finish this race."

"I wasn't thinkin' about the damned race." He looked a little foolish.

"I wish you wouldn't swear. You see any other riders?"

He shook his head and watched her wide-eyed as she began to saddle her horse. "Where are you goin'?"

"Now, what does it look like?" She surveyed him as if dealing with an idiot. "Lady Jane and I have had a nice rest, so we're ready to ride on. You're welcome to the barn."

"You've tricked me one too many times," he warned.

"On the contrary"—she winked—"I may have a few more tricks up my sleeve. I intend to win this race, cowboy."

As he watched openmouthed, she swung up on her horse and rode out of the barn.

"Hey!" he yelled in protest behind her, but she kept riding.

It was almost daybreak, Henrietta thought with satisfaction, and she was ready to continue. Was that her father chasing Comanche? Who else could it be? Well, she'd straighten out that misunderstanding once she crossed the finish line, just in case her father intended to stop her and return her to her mother. That Comanche Jones could just quit thinking about delaying her with those hot kisses, as tempting as they were. He might be willing to do anything to win this race, but she intended to outsmart every man in it and prove that she was more than just a pretty face. Barring that, at least she'd have enough money to escape from her mother and Throckmorton P. Gutterstaff III.

Five

The days had become a blur of exhaustion and Henrietta was riding until way past sunset as she traveled across Illinois. Comanche had finally caught up with her, and they traveled together in cold silence. Henrietta wasn't certain she could stand one more day of this, which was good because as she bedded down near Comanche when they checked in at the next stop and camped outside town, she realized that tomorrow's check-in was the Thousand Mile Tree on the outskirts of Chicago.

She awoke before dawn. Comanche still snored near the embers of their campfire. He was too good a competitor, and she knew she was going to have to resort to trickery to win. She couldn't let the fact that she was beginning to have feelings for this cowboy interfere with her plans. Too much depended on her winning this race.

Quietly, she saddled her horse and led her away from the camp. Henrietta wasn't certain just how far behind her the other riders were, but she knew if she didn't do something, Comanche, on his sturdy mustang, would pass her during the day and win. What to do?

She tied Lady Jane to a tree, tiptoed back into camp, and picked up the big cowboy's boots and took them with her.

She grinned as she imagined the scene when he awakened. Yes, he'd be madder than a rattlesnake on a hot griddle, but that was okay, too, as long as she stayed out of his reach. She noticed he had a big hole in the toe of one red sock. Poor thing, he didn't have anyone to mend his things or care for him. *Henrietta, are you out of your mind?* she scolded herself. *This man is out to beat you.* She tucked his boots in her saddlebag and mounted up, then took off at a lope.

As she passed the outskirts of the last town where she had checked in, she saw a funny sight. A strange little man on a bicycle came peddling out and tried to keep up with her as she loped along the road.

It must be a mirage, she thought with a shake of her head. She was so bone-tired and sleepy.

Then the little man shouted at her. "Cowboy, I'm a newspaper reporter. Can I have an interview?"

"May," she corrected and didn't slow her pace.

"Couldn't you stop?" he pleaded and pedaled even faster. "I can hardly take notes and—"

"Just tell your readers I intend to win this race!" she shouted back and kept riding.

He was losing ground. "What do you intend to do with the money?"

"I don't know; winning is the important thing right now," she yelled as she left him in her dust.

He called after her, "How many riders behind you?"

She only shook her head and shrugged because she really didn't know; she could only hope she was in the lead. One thing she did know was that there was one very angry Texan back there hopping about in the stickers with no boots and cursing every time he thought about her.

Noon came, and she paused to water her horse and eat a bite of cheese and crackers. She must be nearing Chicago because the number of wagons and buggies on the road was increasing. Up ahead, she saw a big sign that read "Great

Cowboy Race contestants, the finish line is only five miles ahead."

Five miles. And no one in sight behind her. Yes, she was going to win this race, and after that, who knew what would happen?

Henry Jennings got off the train on the outskirts of Chicago and yelled at his men. "Buck, look alive there and get those horses off! I intend to meet the riders at the finish line and stop my daughter's killer."

"Yes, boss."

A conductor ran up and handed Henry a telegram.

> *Dear Henry. Stop. Henrietta's finacé is with me and we'll intercept her at the finish line and take her back to Philadelphia. Stop. Thank you for your help. Stop. Matilda.*

Henry scowled as he crumpled the wire and watched his posse mounting up. He was in a foul mood and wondering why his daughter had run away in the first place. He also intended to deal harshly with that Texan who had abducted and seduced his daughter, then killed her. That was, if the cowboy was still in the race. "All right, men, let's go! I want to be waitin' at the finish line when he comes in!"

Comanche came awake with a start. He must have been bone tired because it was way past daylight. "Henrietta?"

No answer. He sat up and looked around. Maybe she was off in the brush answering nature's call. Good, he'd be saddled up and out of here, leaving her shrieking after him with her drawers down around her ankles. That thought made him smile. Yet he had to hand it to her. Even though he was going to beat her to the finish line, she had been a worthy opponent. Why, she was almost as game and gritty as any Texas gal.

He yawned, then reached for his boots. He rooted around under his blankets and came up empty. Now, what the hell—? Maybe some animal had carried them off. How stupid. No animal would be interested in taking his boots. He scowled, thinking. However, he knew a little bitch who might.

He crawled around on his knees looking for the missing boots and cursing. "Damn it, Henrietta, don't tell me you fooled me again. Of all the damn, dirty tricks!"

He stubbed his toe on a rock and hopped about, cursing louder. Then he stepped on a sticker and howled like a coyote. "Curses on that woman! I've had nothin' but trouble since the first time I laid eyes on her, and yet I keep lettin' her do it to me again. She should know it ain't fair to steal a man's boots."

The little rascal was determined to win, and he was loco enough to keep trusting those innocent blue eyes. Well, there was nothing to do but saddle up and ride on wearing red socks with holes in them. Comanche was out of sorts and hungry, and he really needed a cup of coffee; but that wasn't to be, because Henrietta had a head start and he wasn't about to let that feisty little bit of calico beat him to the finish line.

As he mounted up and started out on the road, a strange-looking little fellow pedaled up to him on a bicycle. "You in the race, mister? Can I interview you?"

"You see any other riders?"

The little man nodded. "Slim young fellow on a fancy gray horse."

Damn Henrietta anyhow. Comanche turned in his saddle and looked back down the road. On the rise far behind him, he could see the silhouettes of other riders coming fast. It was going to be a close race at the end, but he intended to win. "Mister, you get to the finish line and I'll give you an interview."

"Hey," said the reporter, "why are you not wearing any boots?"

He wasn't about to admit he'd been tricked by a slip of a Yankee girl who didn't weigh as much as his Colt pistol. "I'm doin' it for luck; it's a Texas custom." Then he urged Hombre on and left the reporter standing with his bicycle, still scratching his head.

Comanche took up the race in earnest. He was certain no horse could beat his mustang stallion in an endurance race, but there was no telling what kind of tricks Henrietta would pull at the end. Hell, here was one cowboy who wasn't buying in to her charm again. He was going to win this race, and the devil take the hindmost.

Matilda Jennings turned to Throckmorton as they stood in the shade of the tree. "Are you sure this is the finish line?"

Before he could answer, a tall stranger dressed western style wearing long silver hair, mustache, and goatee rode up on a fine white horse and dismounted. "Yes, ma'am, this here tree marks the end of that thousand-mile race. The reporters and the crowds will be gathering any minute now."

She frowned. "Who are you?"

"Buffalo Bill, ma'am." He took off his white hat and made a sweeping bow. "I'm here to present my share of the prize five hundred dollars."

Throckmorton looked utterly ridiculous in his striped vest and bowler hat. He pursed his thin lips. "I do hope Henrietta realizes what a fool she's made of herself. I intend to see that she learns better manners."

"Henrietta?" Buffalo Bill said.

"It's a long story and a scandal." Matilda shrugged, taking out a dainty hankie and wiping her eyes. "My daughter ought to be glad a fine scion of society is willing to forgive and forget, if she'll only become a dutiful bride."

The older man looked puzzled and started to say something, then seemed to decide that maybe he didn't want to know and lit a cigar instead.

As he had promised, a crowd was beginning to gather, including newspaper people with their pencils and little notebooks.

"Oh, dearie me," said Throckmorton, wringing his soft, pink hands together. "I just don't know what my dear mama will say about all this press. You know, society people have certain standards—"

"She'll do better," Matilda promised frantically, thinking of how badly she needed the Gutterstaff fortune to maintain her high lifestyle. She had to agree with her daughter that Throckmorton was a toad, but he was a *rich* toad. "She's just behaving like a silly little fool."

Throckmorton nodded in agreement, but Buffalo Bill frowned at her. "Silly? My dear lady, I think it takes a lot of bravery to ride a thousand miles across three states. Why, there'll probably never be another race like it."

"A woman?" a reporter asked. "There's a woman in this race?"

A murmur of excitement ran through the crowd as the reporters wrote furiously.

A man galloped up on a horse, shouting, "Telegraph says the lead racers are only a few miles out!"

The crowd cheered, and the newspaper reporters scribbled faster.

Back on the trail, Henrietta was so tired she could hardly keep her eyes open as she rode. Worse than that, she reached up and touched her face, realizing it was dirty. Her hair was windblown and dusty, but it didn't matter now because she was almost at the end of the race. She envisioned accepting the prize, loading her horse on a train, and disappearing into the West before her mother and the toad discovered where she had gone. Too bad she had never managed to talk to her father, but maybe he didn't want to know her anyhow. If he had, he would have answered at least a few of those letters she had written him over the years. Maybe he'd been disappointed she hadn't been a boy. Well, she'd proved she had the grit and gumption to be his heir, which satisfied her, but maybe her father wouldn't know or care.

She patted her horse's neck. "Only a couple more miles, Lady Jane. Then I'll get you some hay and grain, and we'll rest up some before we board a train for the West."

She heard hoofbeats behind her and turned in her saddle. In the distance, she saw Comanche coming at a fast gallop, and he was waving his fist at her and shouting. She decided she didn't want to stop to hear what he was yelling, but it had something to do with what he was going to do to a dirty varmint who stole a man's boots.

Oh, my. The boots. She reached back to get them out of her saddlebag and tossed them into the road behind her. His stopping to retrieve them would delay him. On the road behind him, she could see at least two other riders coming hard. Well they wouldn't catch her. She took off again at a gallop.

Comanche swore under his breath and urged Hombre to run faster. "I'll teach that sneaky little rascal to outwit me so she can win this race!"

When he caught her, he might shake her until those pretty white teeth rattled. That made him think about her lips and how soft they had been. "Damn it, Comanche, keep your mind on the race," he muttered to himself. She saw him, too. He was sure of it because those blue eyes widened and she threw his boots into the road and took off again in a cloud of dust.

Hombre was at a dead gallop, and Comanche wasn't about to rein in and retrieve his boots. That would be what she would expect. He would return for them later. He kept his horse moving. Behind him, he heard hoofbeats and turned in his saddle to see two riders only a few hundred yards back. Well, that pair would come in third and fourth, and the prize would go to number one, which of course, he intended to be Comanche Jones.

Up ahead, Henrietta had lost her hat, and the gray's tail was blowing out behind her like a flag. When he topped the next rise, he saw a crowd gathering in the distant valley under some trees. That had to be the finish line. He was gaining on the sassy girl. Oh, he could hardly wait to pass her and leave her eating his dust for a change. "Come on, Hombre, let's really go!"

His bay stallion seemed to understand and quickened his speed. They were gaining on the girl and her mare, Comanche thought with glee. He'd really enjoy galloping past her and on to the finish line. She glanced back, her face pale now as if she realized he might beat her yet. For a split second, he almost sympathized with the feisty girl, remembering how game she was and the joy he had found in her arms. Well, even if he won the race, she would turn up her nose at a poor cowboy with only a few acres to his name.

Her horse was tiring and lathered. He could see that as Henrietta urged the gray on. She was riding well, but Lady Jane had given almost all she had to give. "You know, Hombre," he muttered to his horse as they galloped toward the finish line, "you and that gray could turn out some mighty fine colts."

Am I loco? That snooty girl wouldn't allow her fancy mare to mingle with his stocky little mustang.

He was gaining on Henrietta. In a few more seconds, he would be almost close enough to touch her. Way ahead at the line of trees, he saw the crowd moving, beginning to cheer, realizing it was going to be a dead heat to the finish line.

And as the crowd roared its excitement, Lady Jane stumbled, and Henrietta cried out, grabbing for her saddle. The falling horse sent Henrietta flying over the mare's head where the girl hit the ground and lay still. The crowd grew suddenly quiet and white-faced. The mare staggered to her feet and stood lathered and blowing.

It was a trick, Comanche thought, a trick to keep him from winning the race. Oh, the little rascal had been full of tricks. He was a cinch to win now; all he had to do was keep moving, and he'd finish easily ahead of the two riders coming fast behind him.

As he approached the fallen girl, she raised up with difficulty on one elbow, her face a mask of pain. "I—I'm hurt, Comanche. I can't make it."

In spite of himself, he reined in. "How bad is it?"

"Forget me!" She gestured wildly. "There's two riders coming; go on and win that ranch you want so badly."

He hesitated a split second. The land he had always dreamed of was within his grasp. All he had to do was ride past the injured girl and claim the prize money. The injured girl. The ranch. Which meant most to him? It was no contest. He dismounted and hit the ground, running to her. "How bad is it?"

"Are you crazy?" she screamed, her face pale. "Get on that horse and go, Comanche! I want you to have that ranch."

Instead, he knelt by her and gathered her up in his arms, helping her to her feet. "I—I can't ride away and leave you hurt like this, missy. Damned if I know why, but I love you."

"Oh, Comanche!" She buried her face against his broad shoulder, shaking with sobs as he held her tightly. "I'm sorry. I'm so sorry for everything."

"I'm not." He held her close and brushed her wind-blown hair away from her dirty face. Tears made muddy trails down her cheeks. He took out his bandana and wiped them away. "As long as you're not hurt bad, it doesn't matter about the prize."

Even as he held her close and kissed her lips, two riders galloped past him, heading for the finish line.

She heard the cheers and turned and looked toward the

finish as John Berry galloped past the tree marker with old Joe Gillespie close behind. The crowds surrounded the two riders, congratulating them and shaking their hands. "Comanche, I'm so sorry I caused you to lose. I know how much that ranch meant to you."

"Well, hell, you needed the money, too."

She slipped her arms around his neck. "Not as badly as you did."

He looked down into her face. "If I'd gotten that ranch, Henrietta, it crossed my mind that . . . Well, I ain't got a pot or a window now, so—"

"Comanche, will you marry me?"

"What?" His rugged face looked startled. "Henrietta, I'm the one supposed to do the askin'."

She glared up at him. "Well, it didn't sound like you were ever going to get around to it."

He laughed. "You got grit, gal. Texans like that in a woman. Yes, I'll marry you." He swung her up in his arms and started walking toward the finish line. The crowd saw them coming and began to cheer. "Hey, look at the cowboy! He lost the race to help that girl."

She laid her face against his broad chest as he carried her. His grin spread ear to ear. "Well, I lost the race, but I got the gal!"

"Oh, no, you don't! You dirty drifter, put her down!"

They both turned, startled. "Mother!" Henrietta cried in dismay. "And Throckmorton!"

Throckmorton stepped up, looking a little ridiculous in his spats, cane, and derby hat. "You! You dirty peasant! How dare you lay hands on my fiancée!"

Stunned, Comanche slowly set her on a log. "This is him, Henrietta?"

She nodded, too upset to speak as her mother and her fiancé advanced on her.

Throckmorton grabbed her by the arm. "How dare you,

Henrietta? You've made a laughingstock out of me. It's a good thing I'm a forgiving person—"

"Let go of me, Throckmorton. I will not marry you!"

"But of course you will." He tried to pull her to her feet, but Comanche reached out and caught his arm. "Just a damned minute, Throckie, maybe you didn't hear the lady. She ain't goin' with you; she's goin' back to Texas with me."

"This is ridiculous!" Throckmorton jerked away from Comanche and tightened his grip on Henrietta. "You can't leave me for this—this cow person!"

"I warned you to get your hands off her, and I ain't askin' again!" Comanche hit him, a good, solid blow to the chin that sent him stumbling backward, away from Henrietta. "Now, get up and fight like a man!"

Instead, Throckmorton sat blubbering in the dirt. "I'm bleeding! Someone call a doctor! I'm bleeding to death."

"Oh, I just hit you in the nose, Throckie," Comanche grumbled. "You ain't hurt bad."

Henrietta straightened her shoulders. She was no longer the frightened little mouse who had fled west. "Throckmorton, maybe you didn't hear me the first time. Go back to Boston. I won't marry you."

"No!" Mother wailed, clasping her well-manicured hands together. "Henrietta, you don't understand! I've spent all the money your father has been sending you. I need the Gutterstaff fortune to survive."

Throckmorton turned deathly pale as he wiped the blood from his pasty face and turned toward her mother. "You mean—you mean there is no Jennings' fortune?"

"There sure as hell is!" growled an old man, pushing his way through the crowd, followed by a bunch of cowboys, "but a dude like you ain't gettin' any of it."

Comanche took a deep breath as he recognized the tough old codger with the light hair and blue eyes who had been planning a necktie party for him back at that check-in town. "Jennings? I thought your name was Smith. Sir, now you see she's alive—"

"Daddy?" Henrietta blinked.

The old man nodded. "Well, I'm glad to see you're alive. I been tryin' to catch up with you since a few days after the race began. I've had a bad opinion of you, Henrietta, since you never answered any of my letters or came to visit me."

"What?" Henrietta turned and looked at her mother. Matilda had a guilty look like a coyote caught with a chicken in her mouth. "Why, Daddy, I've written you many times, but when I didn't get any answer, Mother said you didn't want me at all."

They both turned and looked at her mother.

Matilda blanched. "Well, I just thought it was for the best that you two never met."

"Of all the rotten tricks," Henry Jennings growled, "Matilda, you've reached a new low. Damned if I send you another dime."

Mother began to wail. "I can't go to work. What will my fine friends think?"

Tears came to Henrietta's eyes. "Oh, Daddy, I assumed you wanted a boy and were disappointed you only got a girl."

Mr. Jennings grinned. "Well, it appears to me you got more grit than most boys. I'm right proud of you, daughter."

She limped into his arms and hugged him. "Daddy, now that we've found each other, we'll make a fresh start."

With Throckmorton busy tending his bloody nose, Mrs. Jennings wailing about money, and Henrietta and her father hugging each other and talking about the future, no one was paying any attention at all to Comanche. He sighed as he turned and started to walk away to get his horse. Well, he'd almost had the best part of his dream. She wouldn't want to marry a poor, penniless cowboy now with her daddy having all that money and land. Comanche couldn't blame her for that.

"Hey!" Henrietta called after him. "I thought we were getting married?"

Comanche paused and turned, thinking she had never been as beautiful as she was at this moment with her dirty face, tousled hair, and twisted ankle. "Well, I'm just a cowboy, missy. I can't expect you to live in some line shack and be poor. Your daddy can give you anything you want."

"Wait, Comanche!"

He shook his head and started to walk on.

"Comanche, I'm going with you."

Comanche stopped and turned to her. "No, I don't reckon it would work out." He shrugged. "Long as I got a biscuit, you'd get half." A Texan couldn't make a deeper commitment than that. "But I can't expect to compete with your dad's money. It wouldn't be fair—"

"Damn it!" Henrietta limped to his side. "Let me decide what's fair, or are you trying to back out of making an honest woman of me?"

Comanche flinched as the old man glared at him. "You ain't plannin' on walkin' out on my daughter, are you?"

The old man had to be a Texan. He looked as if he could bite an iron bar and spit out bullets.

"Look, sir"—Comanche gestured—"I'm poor—"

"Don't call me 'sir,' call me Henry," the cattle baron said. He turned to his daughter. "You love this poor cowpoke?"

Henrietta nodded. "He means more to me than your money, Daddy, so I'm going back to Texas with him—"

"Cowboy, you love my daughter?"

"In spite of everything," Comanche admitted. "I reckon that makes me a damned fool 'cause she's so ornery and contrary."

"Look, you two." Henry held up his hand for silence. "Now, I got a giant ranch, and I'm a lonely old man. I could use some company—"

"Now, Daddy," Henrietta interrupted, "I just told you I'm going to marry Comanche, and we'll—"

"Hush up, girl!" Daddy ordered and then winked at Comanche. "I reckon you got your work cut out for you to deal with this bossy britches, don't you, son?"

"What?" Comanche blinked.

Henry sighed and looked at them both. "What I'm sayin' is why don't you two get hitched and take over my ranch? Henrietta will inherit it someday anyway, and I'd like a houseful of grandchildren to play with. Son, you look like a man who could give me a bunch of grandkids."

Comanche grinned. "I'll do my best, sir, if it suits Henrietta."

She threw her arms around his neck and kissed him until they were both breathless as the crowd roared its approval. "It suits Henrietta just fine."

"Good!" Henry Jennings said. "What do you say to a big wedding at our ranch?"

"Yes!" they both said in unison.

Comanche hugged her to him. "I thought I was gonna lose you."

"Never!" she declared. "I'm sticking to you like a tick on a hound dog."

"You're startin' to talk like a Texan." Comanche grinned and kissed her again.

"Now that's all settled." The old man nodded. "Buck, get the boys to load up these horses and ship them back to the ranch. I'll show you two the sights of the World's Fair. Then we'll buy the fanciest wedding dress in Chicago, a pair of fine boots for my new son-in-law, and head back to Nebraska in my private railroad car."

"What about us?" Throckmorton wailed behind them.

Henry Jennings turned and glared at the pair. "You two are up a creek. I'll keep sending you money, Matilda, but I can't forgive you for deliberately keeping my daughter from me all these years."

"But—" Matilda said.

"Don't push me, Matilda," Henry warned. "You think it

over. You owe your daughter an apology for tryin' to marry her off for money."

The two turned and walked away.

Henrietta hugged first Comanche and then her dad. "I didn't win the race, but I won the cowboy, so I reckon I came out all right. Comanche, why are you limping?"

He looked down at his feet. One big toe stuck out of a hole in his red sock. "In case you forgot, missy, someone stole my boots. They're layin' back up the road. I reckon I'll go get them now."

Henrietta smiled innocently. "Now, who would do a rotten thing like that?"

Henry Jennings laughed. "Yes sir, boy, I reckon she's a handful all right. But being a Texan, I reckon you can handle her. Did you know I'm a Texan, too?"

"No, but I might have guessed," Comanche said.

Henry nodded. "Came up from Sweetwater forty years ago. Once a Texan, always a Texan."

Comanche took off his Stetson and held it over his heart. "Amen!"

Henrietta looked from one man to the other. "I guess we lost the Great Cowboy Race, but maybe we won something better."

Comanche grabbed her and kissed her like he'd been wanting to do, promising more with his lips when they were alone. "You got that right, missy. Now, let's go find them boots!"

TO MY READERS

Although my main characters are fiction, the Great Cowboy Race of June, 1893, is a bit of actual history that I stumbled upon while in Chadron, Nebraska, doing research with the Order of the Indian Wars group. The Blaine Hotel is still there, although its name has changed. The sleepy little town is much like it was over a hundred years ago, although automobiles have replaced the horses, and they've paved the roads. It wasn't difficult to stand out in that street on a hot summer's day, stare up at the balcony of the old hotel, and imagine the fire chief shooting off the pistol that began the race that intrigued the whole nation.

There were no rules against women entering, but none did. However, the rules stated that only western-type horses and saddles were to be used, and rider and saddle combined had to weigh at least one hundred fifty pounds. Eight riders began, but seven finished this thousand-mile race across three states; young Davy Douglas did drop out when he got sick. There were all sorts of accusations about cheating, and at least one rider admitted to catching a ride on a freight train. The winner of the race, John Berry, rode it in thirteen days and sixteen hours. He was presented Buffalo Bill's share of the prize and the saddle, but was disqualified for the biggest money because he had helped lay out the route, which some thought gave him an unfair advantage. Second place at the Thousand Mile Tree marker was old Joe Gillespie, who received the pistol and the major prize money, although all the finishers got a small sum. Doc Middleton came in sixth.

Further research for this story came from an article in the April, 1942, *Reader's Digest* and a special centennial edition of the *Crawford Clipper,* published in Crawford, Nebraska. If you would like to see an actual photo of two of the riders and their horses taken at the Thousand Mile Tree, log on to: www.thelongridersguild.com/chadron2.htm on the Internet.

If endurance races interest you, there is an Internet site for the Long Riders Guild: thelongridersguild.com.

Before anyone asks about the movie, *Hidalgo,* I'll tell you there is no proof that Frank Hopkins ever raced in the Sahara Desert or did any of the heroic adventures he claimed. For more details about this hoax, look up the Internet sites I have already listed.

For you non-Texans who might be mystified by the mention of Santa Anna at San Jacinto: the butcher of the Alamo was supposedly at that location, dallying with a pretty girl known by history as the Yellow Rose of Texas. I'm sure you've heard the song. The Mexican leader was so enthralled with her, he ignored Sam Houston's men sneaking up on his troops. The Texans took revenge for the defeat at the Alamo, the Mexican soldiers surrendered, and Texas shortly became a nation. It would not become a state for ten years.

Those of you who have been reading my books know all my stories hook together in one long Western saga. You have met Comanche Jones before as a minor character in *To Tame a Texan.* The latest of that saga, my twenty-fifth for Zebra Books, is in stores right now: *To Tease a Texan.*

If you would like an autographed bookmark, please send a stamped, self-addressed envelope to Georgina Gentry, P.O. Box 162, Edmond, OK 73083-0162, or check out my Web site at nettrends.com/georginagentry.

Long As I Got a Biscuit . . .
Georgina Gentry

MOONLIGHT WHISPERS

Teresa Bodwell

One

Washington Territory, 1862

Luke stomped into the saloon, ready to lasso and hog-tie his useless brother. A broom handle struck hard in the center of Luke's chest. He grabbed the little thing that was wielding the weapon, lifting her off her feet. When she let out a shrill yelp, Luke dropped her and stepped back.

"What the hell?" He scowled at the tiny woman clutching the wooden handle as if it might buck away from her.

Damn! He'd probably frightened the little filly.

"What is the meaning of this behavior, sir?" she snapped.

"Me?" Luke reckoned she was more angry than scared. "You're the one swingin' that broom like you aim to sweep me out with the dust!"

She lifted her chin, preparing to give Luke a good scolding, he suspected. The saloon owner stopped her with a hand to her shoulder. "Hold on, Isabelle. You want to drive all the customers away?"

She looked from the saloon owner to Luke, then back again—like a trapped animal trying to find a way to escape. "I'm sorry, Mr. Haverman." She dropped her gaze to the floor.

Standing next to the slight old man, she didn't look so small. Luke reckoned she was a good height for a female. He allowed his eyes to roam. About the right shape, too, so far as he could tell with that wide flowing skirt hiding most of her lower half. He wondered briefly what she wore under her dress that made her skirt puff out so. His gaze meandered back to her face, taking time to appreciate the curves along the way.

Danged if her face wasn't glowing bright pink from her lace collar clean to her ears. Even the wisps of hair that had escaped the tight ball she'd pinned to the top of her head seemed to blaze red.

"Don't matter, girl. Luke ain't much of a customer anyhow." Clyde Haverman seemed to be on the brink of laughter. "You go on back to the kitchen and get some dinner."

She bobbed her head, then floated away. Or so it seemed to Luke. The only evidence of any stepping was the swing of her hips causing the skirts of her impractical gown to swish back and forth.

Clyde cleared his throat. "Pretty little thing, ain't she?"

"Who?" Luke forced his eyes back to the old man.

"Isabelle," Clyde said as though he were speaking to an idiot. "Too bad we don't have enough work to keep her on here." He scratched at the white stubble on his chin and studied Luke for a moment. "What can I do for you? Whiskey? An early supper? Charlotte has fresh bread just out the oven."

"I'm lookin' for that worthless brother of mine."

"Matt?" Clyde showed the wide gaps between his few remaining teeth. "You're talkin' about my best customer. I'll thank you to show some respect."

Luke bit back a retort. Matt's love of gambling and drink might make him profitable to the saloon, but it sure as hell didn't make him useful as a rancher. "You seen him?"

"Ain't been in for days, I'm sorry to say. We could use the business."

Luke shoved his broad-brimmed hat back on his head and glared at the barkeep. "I ain't funnin'. I'm worried about the rascal."

"Ain't no jokin' matter as far as I'm concerned either. Last time he was in here was Monday—no—Tuesday. There were some miners, celebratin' a gold strike—"

"Matthew took up with 'em?" *As though I need to ask.*

"Well, you know Matt. He's always friendly. 'Sides, the miners was buyin'."

"Hell!" Luke ripped his hat off and had half a mind to crush it under his muddy boots. If he couldn't knock some sense into his little brother, at least he could damage something.

"Now, don't get yourself riled, boy." Clyde turned to wipe off a table. "You know old Matt always comes home."

"Any idea where that gold strike was?"

Clyde shook his head. "Hell, you know miners ain't much inclined to tell the whereabouts of their claim."

Assuming it was a real claim. Matt had been duped more than once. Not that he'd learned anything from the experience. His brother thought he'd find his fortune in gold. He might as well be hunting six-legged snakes. Matt didn't give a damn about Luke or the ranch. His brother would never make it back before the first snowfall, which meant that Luke was on his own to ready the ranch for winter. Again.

He turned and stared out at the gray sky beyond the window. The highest mountains already wore their white winter caps, but the valley was still more likely to see rain than snow. Little chance the dark clouds would drop much of anything today; the air didn't feel damp the way it should before a storm. Too bad. They could use the moisture.

Luke drew a long, slow breath as he surveyed the broad valley he called home. As far as he was concerned, the chance to tame a piece of this land and call it his own was a greater treasure than any gold. If only his brother would get some sense, he'd reach the same conclusion right quick and finally settle down. Matt was too restless—always looking for the excitement he imagined just beyond his reach.

Luke's eyes fixed on the bright autumn leaves still clinging to the cottonwoods along the river. Not much he could do about Matt's disappearance. Someone had to work the ranch, and as usual that person was going to be Luke.

When Matt did choose to come home, Luke would bite his tongue and welcome the scoundrel. He'd promised Pa he'd always look out for Matt. Luke wouldn't break that promise if he could help it, though Matt sometimes made it damned difficult for Luke.

"I'd best get home." He settled his hat back on his head. "You see Matt—tell him he's needed at the ranch." Little good that message would do.

"Say—you need some help at the ranch? How about you take Isabelle with you?"

"Isabelle?" Luke squinted at the old man. "She's a woman!"

"You noticed that, did you?" Clyde pounded a fist on Luke's shoulder. "Glad to see you can still recognize a female."

"I mean she couldn't do any real work. How would she replace Matt?"

Clyde scratched at his chin. "I see your point. She is a mite smaller than Matt. On the other hand, it don't seem like your brother's doin' a whole lot for that ranch of yours just now."

Luke recognized an argument he couldn't win.

And so did Clyde, judging from the old man's cocky grin. "Isabelle ain't a man, but she works hard. Think it over."

Like hell he would. "Nothin' to think about. I ain't got room for a female on my ranch."

Clyde shrugged. He tossed his cleaning rag over his shoulder and scraped his palms against each other as though wiping the subject away. "Thought I'd ask is all. Seems a shame." He glanced toward the kitchen door. "The little lady come all the way from Boston to meet up with her pa, and now she'll have to move on." Clyde shook his head. "We'll have to let her go come Sunday. A real pity."

Luke remembered the panicked look on the young girl's face when Clyde corrected her. She needed this job. "Ain't my concern." Luke took a step toward the door. "I've got a ranch to run."

"And no help runnin' it." Clyde threw the challenge out, but Luke wasn't about to argue the point. The old man turned to the window. "Looks like the weather's holdin' for now," Clyde said as he leaned next to the glass to peer up at the sky. "Sit down and have some of Charlotte's fine stew before you head out. It'll be warmer ridin' on a full stomach."

Luke contemplated the sky again. Those clouds were not going to do anything but block the sun and make his ride home miserable and cold. He might as well take advantage of the chance for a hot meal. At home he'd be eating beans, roasted potatoes, and smoked beef. Same as yesterday and the day before.

"Charlotte make one of her pies today?" Luke asked.

"Huckleberry."

Luke's favorite. "I believe I'll have some dinner before I head home."

Clyde favored Luke with a wide, jagged grin. "I'll let Charlotte know."

Luke hung his coat and hat on the rack near the door and made his way over the rough pine floor to a table near the window, far from the long bar that ran across the back wall. The small saloon and dry goods store the Havermans ran formed the heart of the Hell Gate trading post. The post, set as it was at the junction of five valleys, served as a convenient stop for miners, soldiers, trappers, and ranchers traveling in and out of Washington Territory.

Luke settled back into a sturdy ladder-back chair and inhaled the tempting aromas coming from the kitchen. A minute later a feminine hand set a steaming bowl in front of him and then placed silverware wrapped in a napkin and a basket full of bread on the table.

He looked up, expecting to see Clyde's daughter-in-law, but his eyes caught on a smooth young face—the color of cream with pink roses on her cheeks.

"Thank you, ma'am." It was pleasant to have the chance to view a pretty lady up close. Clyde's daughter-in-law, Charlotte, was the only young woman who lived at the Hell Gate trading post. Not that she was bad-looking—just not half so pretty as Isabelle. She was a sight. Of course, it had been weeks since he'd seen any female who didn't walk on four legs.

"You're welcome." Isabelle looked directly into Luke's eyes for an instant before turning to the bread basket.

Again Luke wondered what caused her response. She seemed to have too much spirit to be frightened. Maybe she just found him hard to look at. She was a city woman with fancy clothes, and he was a plain man. Unshaved and covered with dust from riding.

"Coffee?" Charlotte set a thick mug on the table in front of Luke and another across from him. She smiled at Luke. "I reckon you'd like some company. Isabelle was just about to have her dinner—how 'bout she joins you?"

Luke opened his mouth to protest, but Isabelle beat him to it.

"No!" She sucked in a breath. "I mean . . . I'm sure Mister . . . this gentleman doesn't want to have a stranger sharing his table. . . ."

"Nonsense, Isabelle." Charlotte guided the younger woman to the other chair. "Isabelle Millston, meet Lucas Warring. There, now you aren't strangers." She threw a smirk in Luke's direction. "Luke spends too much time alone." She turned to Isabelle. "I'm sure he'd love to hear all about your travels. He never seems to get away from his ranch, do you, Luke?"

"That's true enough." *I sure as hell don't want to spend any more time on the road.*

"There, you see? You'll be saving the man from his dull life." Charlotte placed a hand on Luke's shoulder. "Isabelle helped me make the pie."

"I—" Isabelle started.

"She's a wonder in the kitchen." Charlotte waved a hand, and Isabelle's mouth shut as though Charlotte could control it. "I've never seen anything like it. You just set and tell Luke your stories of Boston society."

Isabelle sat lightly at the edge of the chair opposite Luke, looking as though she were ready to spring away the first chance she had.

"There now," Charlotte said. "You make yourself comfortable and I'll bring your stew out."

"Oh, no." The words spilled out so light and soft they reminded Luke of the early spring melt trickling down the mountain. "It isn't right you should be waiting on me, Mrs. Haverman." Isabelle stood. "You should sit with the gentleman and—"

Charlotte placed a hand on Isabelle's shoulder and pressed her back into the chair. "I won't hear any argument, now. You deserve a rest. I'm nearly done with the baking, and you can do the washing up when you're finished eating." She glanced at Luke. "Now, don't either of you rush, mind. Have a nice chat."

Chat? Luke began to regret his decision to stay for the meal. Hell, he wasn't going to be chatting like a lady in a tea parlor. He leaned forward, thinking of an excuse to leave, and the smell of Charlotte's cooking filled his nostrils.

I'll eat, but damned if I'll chat.

TWO

As she watched Charlotte walk away, Isabelle concluded she had no choice but to entertain the gentleman. She glanced over at the rough cowman before picking up her white napkin and spreading it over her lap. "Gentleman" was perhaps not the most descriptive word.

Isabelle summoned a lifetime of hostess training, set her smile firmly in place, and looked directly at him. "Bread, Mr. Warring?"

He didn't seem to know what to do with the basket she held in front of him. Finally he took a slice.

"Thanks," he mumbled.

She watched him stare at the bread in his hand for a moment. Poor man must be a bit slow, she thought. Too bad, because he was pleasure to behold. He shoved a good bit of the bread into his mouth and ripped off a chunk with his teeth. He smiled as he chewed, apparently savoring the flavor. Isabelle could understand that—Charlotte was a fine cook. What she could do with the limited range of ingredients available to her amazed Isabelle.

She favored Luke with a smile and a nod, then set a slice on a small plate in front of her, placing the basket back on the table near Luke. He swallowed and shoved the rest of his bread into his mouth. She tried not to stare at the man, but her efforts to look down at the table were wasted. Her eyes kept straying back up to his ruggedly handsome face.

At this moment he had most of a slice of bread stuffed into one cheek, which did disrupt the elegant strength of his jaw. But that flaw did not take away from his other admirable features—a dignified nose and a firm chin that sported a small dimple. Isabelle stole another glance and considered Luke's face in more detail.

The perfect proportions of his features would not have attracted her attention if it had not been for his eyes. They were gray, which up until this moment she had thought a dull color. Luke's eyes were far too full of life to be boring. They reminded her of a shell she'd found on the shore as a child. The inside was gray, yet it sparkled like a fine jewel. If his rough manners and speech hadn't betrayed him, she'd have thought that shine signaled a keen intelligence.

Isabelle had seen her share of good-looking men. Her mother's parties always attracted Boston's finest gentlemen, many of whom seemed to take as much care with their fashion and coiffure as any lady. Luke Warring couldn't be more different. There was not a bit of the feminine in him. He carried himself with the complete confidence of a man who needed no pretenses. Even now as he relaxed in his chair, Isabelle sensed he was alert to the world around him—in command of the brute force that had lifted her off the ground as though she were no more than a feather.

"Would you care for some butter, Mr. Warring?"

He shook his head. "No, thanks, miss." He raised his cup, drank some coffee, and nearly choked. Once again Isabelle felt pity for the man. Gulping hot coffee as though it were water—he was bound to burn himself. She wondered if he was merely stupid, or perhaps he'd suffered some head injury. He set the cup back on the table. "You may as well call me Luke, everyone does."

"But, it wouldn't be proper. . . ." She looked down at the

hands on her lap. "I forget the standards of propriety are different here." She kept her eyes cast down, but couldn't stop the smile that sprang to her lips. *Foolish, foolish, girl.* She schooled her features into a proper, indifferent smile and forced her chin up until her eyes met his. "You shall call me Isabelle, then."

He nodded and continued shoveling down his meal as though he sat before the last food available on God's earth. Isabelle watched him for a moment. His hands, rough from work, his arms threatening to burst right out of the sleeves of his blue plaid shirt. Lord, she'd never seen a man his size who seemed so solid. The gentlemen she knew were either string-bean thin or broad and soft. It occurred to her that brawn had been built up from years of hard ranch work. No wonder he could toss her about with such ease. She wondered briefly what it would be like to touch those arms, that broad chest.

Isabelle Millstone, what would your father think of you? Allowing your mind to wander into fantasies of touching a man. A stranger at that!

Luke watched Isabelle as she tore a small corner from her slice of bread, spread a thin layer of butter on it, nibbled a bit, and set it back on the plate. At the rate she was going, it would take her hours to finish her meal. Lord help him if *the standards of propriety* required him to sit through the entire ordeal.

"Some nice hot stew for you, Isabelle." Charlotte placed a steaming bowl in front of the red-haired lady.

Luke examined her as he chewed. Yes, now that she was sitting in the good light near the window, he was certain her hair was red. Not a bright red, but dark—closer to chestnut than a sorrel. A most becoming color, not that he was any judge.

"Thank you, Charlotte." The lady beamed a smile bright enough to light the saloon. "I still don't feel right about you serving me, though."

"Nonsense." Charlotte shook her head. "The least I can do, seein's how you've been such a help to me these past few days. It's a damn shame we don't have enough work to hire you regular."

Isabelle's cheeks flamed, and she looked down into her bowl. Luke reached for another slice of bread and dunked it in his stew. He was not going to get caught up in Isabelle's troubles.

"Heard from Stephen?" he asked before ripping a bite from his bread. Maybe he could get Charlotte talking about her husband.

"Had a letter last week." Charlotte sighed. "I'll be glad when this damn war is over." She rested a hand on Luke's shoulder. "You enjoyin' that bread?"

"It's right fine."

"Wouldn't it be nice to have fresh bread at the ranch?" Charlotte winked at Luke, then marched back to the kitchen.

Luke stared after her. He reached his hand up to scratch at the back of his neck, thought of Isabelle watching him, and set his hand back on his lap. He smiled at his young dinner companion. First Clyde and now Charlotte seemed bent on convincing him to take Isabelle home. *She's their problem, dammit!* He had enough troubles.

He watched Isabelle move her spoon around in her stew. He'd wager she felt as awkward as he did as the silence extended between them.

"Boston home?" he asked her.

She paused, her spoon midway between her bowl and her lips. "I was born and raised there."

"What brings you to these parts?"

She ran her tongue slowly over her lower lip. "I've come west to join my father."

She dipped her spoon back into her bowl, filled it, tilted it to drop half the contents back into the bowl, then lifted it to her mouth. Luke stared at her blowing daintily on the spoon before placing it in her mouth.

Damn, but she had the nicest lips. Like the rest of her, they seemed soft. Delicate, but definitely not thin. He could imagine how they'd feel against his own lips—pliant and moist.

She watched him with a puzzled expression, and he realized he still held his spoon poised halfway to his mouth. He hastened to bring it the rest of the way, scraped it clean with his teeth, and dug into the bowl for another mouthful. This was exactly why he stayed away from women. They were distracting. A fella could spend hours in his day just watching this one eat a meal. What the hell would his life be like if he had a lady living in his house? He'd never get a lick of work done, that was certain.

And that didn't even take into consideration his biggest worry. He had his hands full looking out for his brother. Imagine keeping track of a fragile woman like this one. Likely she hadn't any idea how to survive on her own. At least he'd trained Matt to take care of himself—use his fists, a knife, and a gun. Isabelle was defenseless.

Luke smiled, remembering the ferocious way she'd held her broom handle. Maybe she could defend herself at that. She'd try, that was certain. But there were too many things in this rough country that could kill a woman when her man wasn't near. And a man couldn't keep watch every hour of every day.

"Where is your pa?" he asked.

"On his way here, I hope."

"Hope? You mean he didn't come with you?" Luke half rose out of his seat. "You're travelin' alone?"

"Certainly not!" She huffed out a breath as though he'd suggested she'd been walking on the moon. "I've traveled by train and steamship and most recently in a wagon with a very nice family." Before Luke could ask another question, Isabelle changed the subject. "Charlotte tells me you own a ranch near here."

He wanted to ask her why she'd come all this way with only a hope of finding her father. But it wasn't his business.

He nodded. "A few miles to the west. It belongs to my brother and me."

"The two of you work the land alone?"

Luke took a deep breath. "When Matt's around. Mostly I run the place. Hire extra hands sometimes."

"It must be terribly exciting—running a ranch."

"Yes, ma'am . . . Isabelle." It occurred to Luke that the name suited her. It was pretty and delicate, too. "If you were my daughter, I'd be here to meet you or send someone for you."

She scowled at him for a moment; then her face returned to that pleasant expression that seemed almost painted on. "Please, don't blame my father. It wasn't his idea." She stared into her bowl and then lifted her eyes back up. Green eyes, shining with unshed tears. "He wrote and told me he was coming here to settle. Papa left my mother and me in Boston some years ago to start a law practice on the frontier. He always writes to tell me where he is, where he's going. His last letter came just after Mama died."

Luke's gut twisted at the pain in her voice when she uttered those last few words. "I'm sorry about your mother."

"Thank you." Isabelle stirred her spoon around her bowl. "After she passed, I . . . I couldn't stay in Boston—so I packed my things and came here. I wrote Papa to tell him I was coming. I thought surely he'd be here before I arrived."

"Your pa the only family you have left?"

"There's an uncle in Boston." Isabelle wrinkled her nose as though reacting to an unpleasant smell.

Luke took another drink of his coffee, which had now cooled to a reasonable temperature. "What'll you do now?"

"I'll wait." Isabelle sat straighter in her chair. "The Havermans have been kind enough to give me a place to stay and a job. Temporary work. I'll find something else when I need to."

"Ain't too much work for a lady around these parts. Seems to me you'd be better off in Boston."

"You wouldn't say that if you knew my uncle." Isabelle shrugged. "Tell me more about your ranch. If I had to guess, I'd say your brother does the bookkeeping and you do the physical labor."

Luke snorted. Fortunately, at that moment his mouth wasn't full or something surely would have sprayed out over the table, and he reckoned that would upset Isabelle's delicate sensibilities.

"Hell, no. Beg pardon. I mean, no. Matthew does not take care of the books. That's my job." He filled his spoon with stew. "Tell the truth, it's all my job." He chewed on a piece of beef and swallowed. "Matt helps out with rounding up the cattle, branding and such. He's usually on hand for calvin', too."

"And during less exciting times, he leaves?"

Luke gave her a quick nod. He'd already told her more of his business than he'd intended. He spread some strawberry preserves on the last slice of bread in the basket and chewed slowly to savor the sweetened berry flavor mixing with the tang of yeasty bread.

"What is there to do on a cattle ranch?" Isabelle asked between her own miniature bites. "I assumed the cattle mostly graze and could be left alone."

"Mmm." Luke nodded as he chewed, then swallowed. "That is true as far as it goes. This land"—he waved at the valley beyond the window—"was planted by God with the richest grass you might ever hope to find. Makes the cattle fat and the beef full of flavor. But there's more to raisin' cattle than just puttin' them on fine grass. Plenty of trouble can come to a herd that isn't watched. Rustlers for one thing. Men who ain't willin' to work for a livin'. They help themselves to the grown stock after someone else spent time and money bringin' 'em here."

Isabelle sipped her coffee as Luke's story brought him to life. He might not be Daniel Webster, but the man could string words together and create complete sentences. He simply needed someone with the skill to ask the right questions. Mama had always taught her that men love to talk. The woman had only to find the topic that interested him and listen intently. The man would leave convinced that she was a brilliant conversationalist.

"And then there's the hazards of Mother Nature herself," Luke continued. "Winter could bring starvation to the whole herd. And don't let that river fool you—this is dry country— you can't be certain of water ever."

"It sounds like a real challenge." Isabelle had never met a man who seemed ready to make such an effort, except of course, her father.

"A challenge." His eyes held hers. "You chose the right word."

There it was again—that spark that betrayed a mind hiding beneath the gruff manner and slow speech. "And you enjoy the struggle?" Isabelle asked, intrigued.

"Never known an easy life. Might like to try it, if I had the chance." He favored her with a bright grin. "I reckon life on the ranch suits me. It's good to know I earned my rest after a day of hard work. And there's not a finer place to live than this valley."

"How can you be so certain? Have you seen much of the world?"

"Spent my childhood travelin'. Pa was always lookin' for the right place to settle." He lifted a full spoon, pausing to continue his story. "We lived all over. Kentucky, Missouri, California, Oregon Territory. When we found this place Pa said settlin' in this valley with the mountains shelterin' us would be just like livin' in the palm of God's hand."

"Your father must be a poet."

"Poet?" Luke shook his head. "Pa, God rest him, never learned to write a word except his own name."

"Nevertheless—he clearly had a gift with words." Isabelle looked out the window, sensing she'd tread into deep waters.

She decided to change the subject. "You and your brother mean to stay here?"

Luke nodded. "I reckon I've done enough travelin'. This is home."

"The palm of God's hand—and yet this place is named the gate of hell."

"True." Luke grinned. "When you feel the winter wind whippin' through that canyon to the east—you'll know why the name's fittin'."

He glanced down at the bowl he couldn't remember emptying.

"I thought maybe the Hell Gate referred to the entrance to Washington Territory."

Luke laughed. "I've traveled clear across this territory—all the way to the ocean. If this is hell, I can't begin to imagine heaven."

"Ready for that huckleberry pie?" Charlotte put a large slice in front of him and refilled his coffee cup. "Don't let me interrupt your conversation now."

He glanced up at Charlotte, but she scurried away before he could say a word. His eyes drifted back to Isabelle, who was spooning stew into her mouth. Conversation it was. Luke could not recollect the last time he'd put so many words together at one time.

"It is beautiful here," Isabelle said.

"Yes, ma'am." Luke pointed out the window. "Can you imagine a more wondrous sight than those mountains standing guard over the river?"

Isabelle's eyebrows shot up. "Wondrous?"

Luke turned toward the window, embarrassed. Maybe he'd used the word incorrectly. He'd read it, but never said it out loud before.

"Yes. I believe you're right, Mister . . . Luke."

He turned to see her leaning with her nose nearly touching the glass.

She glanced at him, then turned back to the window. "The land stretching out to those beautiful mountains. All the colors—so many shades of gray and blue. And scattered through it those bright fall leaves. Wondrous is indeed the perfect word for it." She sighed. "We have the fall colors in Boston—from so many trees—maple, oaks, chestnut. But it's different here."

Luke stood to get a better view. "Do you see where the gray has a bit of green to it?" He pointed at the mountains on the southern edge of the valley. "From here it looks like the mountain itself—solid rock. But go up into those hills and you'll find sturdy pine trees—excellent timber for building. And that orange and red on the mountains is from the larches that grow in amongst the pines."

She stood and leaned close to him, studying the view. He inhaled her sweet womanly scent. It was like walking through a garden in bloom. The light fragrance was nothing like the overpowering odor that had permeated every bit of the whorehouse Luke had visited once. He glanced down at her graceful hand perched on the windowsill. It was red and chapped from the work she'd been doing for the Havermans, but the fine lace on her cuff reminded Luke that this lady was not used to working for a living.

Again he felt anger churning in his belly at the thought of her pa allowing his daughter to be here alone in this dangerous country without a guardian. "Do you have a way to get a message to your father? Let him know you're here?"

"I did send a letter to the last address I had for him." Her smile held little confidence. "But I expect he'll be here before that message finds him."

He examined her clothing again. It was surely not designed for any sort of serious work, or even for travel. Those skirts would make it impossible to mount a horse and would be cumbersome even in a stagecoach as one woman would likely take up all the seats.

If she had talents, it wasn't as a cook or cleaning lady.

There was only one occupation she might enter in this territory. Luke had heard that the new gold finds were attracting every manner of sporting women. Not just ordinary whores, but fancy ladies who'd provide their services only to the wealthiest customers. Still, Isabelle could find honest work if she wanted it. Her family had money. Surely even if her father didn't come, she would not have to resort to selling herself.

"It don't seem right." Luke hadn't meant to express the thought aloud. "You bein' here on your own, I mean." *It ain't your business, Warring.*

Her smile vanished. "I'm a grown woman—nearly twenty-one years old." She pulled herself taller. "I think you may find I'm quite capable. . . . I have many talents."

Many talents, Isabelle? The talent to fool herself being chief among them. The truth was that her list of accomplishments was short and impractical. She could write poetry. She had a fine hand for needlepoint, and she could play the flute. *Flute!* Lord help her, even her musical talents were useless.

If she could play the piano and sing, Mr. Haverman said, he would consider keeping her on here. But who would hear a flute in a busy saloon? And damn her mother for failing to allow her to learn a single useful thing in the kitchen! It was no wonder Charlotte was anxious to keep her out of the way.

Feeling his eyes burning into her, she looked back up at Luke.

"You don't have any idea how you're goin' to make your livin', do you?"

"There's no need for you to concern yourself. If Papa isn't here within the week, I'll . . . I have things I can sell."

"Like what?"

Isabelle had spent a good deal of time thinking about this. "I have my clothes—the finest fashions. There is nothing like them available here."

"Men'll pay dear for what's scarce. But it has to be some-thin' they need. I can't think of anyone around these parts who'll be wantin' a fancy gown."

Isabelle scowled. "You needn't lecture me," she snapped. She regretted her show of temper instantly. The fact was, Luke was right. Her dresses might be worth a small fortune, but only if she could find a buyer. "My locket." She touched the small gold oval that hung from a chain around her neck. It was a gift from her father, and she hated to part with it, but if the alternative was selling herself, she'd make the sac-rifice. "And I have books."

"Books?"

"Yes—two volumes of Elizabeth Browning's poems. And some novels." And a copy of *A Lady's Guide to Home and Kitchen*, but that she needed if she intended to keep house for Papa.

"Maybe Clyde will trade for room and board?"

Isabelle nodded. No point in telling Luke that she'd al-ready asked the Havermans. They'd told her that her things couldn't sell here. Which really did leave her with only one marketable item. She glanced back at Luke. The shadow of a day's growth of beard darkened his jaw. Yet it was clear he owned a razor and knew how to use it. He kept his clothing relatively clean as well. If Luke were typical of men in this territory, it could be that making her living by the ancient profession would be tolerable.

She shuddered, thinking of the men who'd come through Hell Gate in the past few days, as well as all the men she'd met on the road. Ruffians who looked filthy and smelled worse. Papa must come for her. Surely he would.

Three

Luke sat a little straighter in the saddle as he caught sight of his log house, nestled among the foothills with a view of the river and mountains to the south. He'd built the place with his own hands, working alongside his father and brother. They'd unearthed the stones for the fireplace as they dug a root cellar and cleared land for their garden.

Pa had paid an old German stonemason to build the fireplace itself. Luke had worked with him and learned enough to build an outdoor oven where they cooked on hot summer days. Up the hill above the house and barn he could just see the headstone over Pa's grave. He nodded a greeting, knowing Pa was there looking over him as usual.

Luke had lost most of a day's work searching for his brother. At least his conscience was clear now. Matt had run off without leaving any word. Luke would be hard-pressed to chase after him, not even knowing which way his brother was headed. He cast a guilty look up to Pa's grave. "I did try," he muttered.

His trip to Haverman's had been worthwhile even if he didn't find his brother. He'd bought a sack of flour so he could make some biscuits. Not as tasty as Charlotte's bread, but they were good for sopping beans off his plate. And he'd enjoyed his meal at the saloon.

He scraped a gloved hand across his chin, picturing Isabelle sitting across from him. His dream was interrupted by the happy greeting of the ugliest varmint west of the Mississippi.

Luke dismounted and dropped to one knee to accept a nuzzle from Pennigan, his shaggy yellow dog. "Did you miss me, boy?" Luke scratched behind the mongrel's floppy ear, then ran his fingers through the thick, curly fur. "I don't suppose old Matt showed up while I was gone."

Luke led his long-legged gray gelding into the barn, hoping to see Matt's ride, but not at all surprised to find the stalls empty. After settling Cloud, he strode up to the house, ticking off the chores he hoped to complete before darkness fell. He looked up at the sky and took a deep breath. They might get a shower later tonight, but he had time to dig up the last of the potatoes and get them into the root cellar. It wouldn't be long before winter came and the ground would be frozen too hard for digging.

The thought of harsh winter weather brought Isabelle's face drifting into his mind again. If she waited much longer, she'd be stuck here. Surely Haverman wouldn't actually throw her out without anywhere to go. Luke slapped one of the pillars that braced the roof of the porch. It wasn't right to put the responsibility on the saloon owner to care for the girl, but someone needed to look out for her.

He found his spade and a basket and tramped out to the garden plot. Isabelle was not his responsibility. Clyde had Charlotte living with him. It would be far easier for him to deal with another woman. The last thing Luke needed was a fragile little lady to protect. Winter was hard enough on this ranch. Mighty isolated, too.

Not that Luke was lonesome. He was used to it. But a woman who had grown up in a big city like Boston couldn't manage with no one but an old cowman nearby. She couldn't be happy here. She should get to a town—Seattle maybe. Hell, she'd never make it over the mountains before snow blocked the passes. Maybe he could help her get up the Bitterroot Valley to the mission. The priests would be kind to her. She could help them teach the Indian children. And she'd be far away from Luke.

He rubbed a hand over the back of his neck, feeling the muscles knotted there. He could not take in a stray, especially a female. Pennigan whimpered and nudged at Luke's elbow just before the sky opened up and started dropping rain by the bucketful.

"So much for my weather predictions," Luke muttered as he gathered basket and spade and ran for the house. "Damn, that rain is cold," he said, throwing his hat over a peg and pulling off his coat. He shivered as he strode across the room and knelt to start a fire.

He could almost hear Charlotte Haverman asking, *"Wouldn't it be nice to have someone inside greeting you with a hot fire and a warm meal?"*

Pennigan slipped his head under Luke's elbow and rubbed against his ribs. "Don't worry, Pen. It might be nice to have some real food around here, but havin' a woman around . . ." Luke thought again about Isabelle's tempting lips. "No. You're companion enough for me. I don't aim to replace you."

"Luke is a perfectly nice man," Charlotte said as she placed the dried dishes back up on the shelf.

"So he is," Isabelle spoke carefully. The Havermans had been kind to her, and she didn't wish to offend them. Not that it was difficult to agree with Charlotte about Luke. He had been pleasant, outside of grabbing her when he first walked in the door. But in fairness, she had hit him with the broom. On the other hand, she felt certain Charlotte was scheming something.

"He lives alone, the poor man."

"I thought he had a brother." Isabelle's mind raced ahead. Surely Charlotte wasn't going to suggest Isabelle provide relief for the cowman's loneliness?

"Matt?" Charlotte laughed. "He comes around when he needs money, or when he's in trouble."

"Oh. That's too bad." Isabelle knew how important family was and how it hurt to know you couldn't depend on their loyalty. "Luke spoke as though they shared the ranch."

"I suppose they do if you look at what the deed says. Luke is the one who does all the work. If it weren't for him, there would be no ranch. He's a good man."

Isabelle nodded. "I think you're trying to tell me something."

"Clyde thinks it would be a good idea if you were to . . . stay with Luke for a while." Charlotte put the last dish up, but she didn't turn around. "Just 'til your pa comes for you, I mean."

"I . . ." Isabelle's mouth was suddenly too dry to speak. "Has Luke agreed to this?"

"No." Charlotte turned around and gave Isabelle a look of pity. "Not yet. But he will be here come Sunday."

"I don't understand."

"You can't stay the winter here. We told you as much when you first arrived."

"True, but surely winter's a long way off." Isabelle wiped her hands on her apron. "I know I haven't been much help to you, but I can learn."

"It isn't that. You've worked hard and done everything we've asked of you. Still—with the cold weather coming we won't have many customers. We just can't afford another mouth to feed." Charlotte made a weak attempt at a smile. "I'm sorry."

"What if . . . I brought in more business? I could . . ." *Say it, Isabelle. It is the only thing you have left to sell.* "What if I offered extra services to the customers."

"Extra?"

Isabelle drew herself up with as much dignity as she could muster. "More than one man has told me that I . . . I can be a tempting woman. I don't have any experience, it's true, but I—"

Charlotte put her hands over Isabelle's shoulders. "Honey, you don't know what you're saying, do you? A young girl like you—"

"I'm twenty."

"You've never been with a man. I won't tell you it can't be nice, 'cause that would be a lie. But it's only pleasant when the man cares for you. I've known women who've had to offer themselves for money. It isn't for a sweet thing like you. Trust me."

Isabelle sighed. "It's not as though I have a choice."

"You have Luke. He's your choice."

"And he wouldn't expect . . . ?"

"Luke'll give you room and board in exchange for your help with cookin' and cleanin'."

"But I can't cook—you know that!"

"Then I reckon you better start studyin' that book of yours. What's it called?"

"*A Lady's Guide to Home and Kitchen.*" She'd purchased the book with the intention of making herself useful to her father, not a stranger. Isabelle's stomach felt as if she'd swallowed lead.

"Between that book and what I can teach you in the next few days, you'll do fine. Luke is easy to please. Just good hearty vittles and plenty of 'em and he'll be content as a puppy on his mama's teat."

For some reason that image did nothing to ease Isabelle's mind or the heaviness in her belly.

Four

Come Sunday, Luke found himself riding Cloud slowly toward Haverman's Saloon. It was just curiosity. He had to know whether Isabelle's father had come for her. Of course he had. Hell, if Luke had a beautiful young daughter like Isabelle, he couldn't imagine leaving her alone ever. Especially not here so far from the civilization she was accustomed to. *No, sir. I'd be ridin' to find her and bring her home. And if I couldn't manage the trip, I'd find someone who could.*

Cloud walked patiently up to the hitching post in front of the saloon and waited for Luke to dismount. He saw Isabelle through the big picture window. *Damn!* There she was setting a plate in front of a hefty fellow Luke recognized as a maverick named Simon Vemonde. The man slapped his palm across her bottom, and Isabelle jumped. Luke could hear Simon's guttural laugh clean out in the street as that no-account pulled Isabelle down on his lap and tried to steal a kiss.

As Luke entered the saloon and strode across the room he reminded himself that he was not her protector. He should mind his own business, but damned if it didn't feel good to pull Simon clean out of his chair and hammer his chin with a ready fist.

"Argh!" The lout hit the floor and managed to pull himself to a sitting position. "What the—"

"I believe you're in need of some lessons on how to treat a lady!" Luke shouted. He reached down and pulled the man up by his leather jacket.

The big fellow had a good thirty pounds on Luke, but it didn't matter. Luke's anger made up for any disadvantage he might have in size. He dragged Simon outside for a proper thrashing.

"Enough!" Clyde yelled as Luke landed another punch in Simon's soft belly. "Luke, you get in here!"

Luke glared as Simon sank to his knees. "Keep your hands off her," Luke growled as he bent to pick his hat up off the road.

"She ain't yours, Warring!" Simon bellowed as Luke stepped into the saloon.

Luke bit his tongue. The only reponse he could make was to agree. She wasn't his, and he was glad. Still, that didn't make it right for Simon to help himself to her.

Clyde greeted him with his gap-toothed grin. "Pleasant way to act. And on a Sunday, too." Clyde shook his head. "Ain't like you, Luke."

"He had it comin'."

"I reckon he did," Clyde muttered. "Thanks for takin' it outside. I can't afford to keep replacin' the furniture every time that old boy comes in here."

Luke knocked the dust off his hat and set it back on his head.

"So, you come for her. I figured you would." Clyde nodded. "Had her pack her things so's she'd be ready."

"Come for who?"

Clyde didn't seem to be listening. "Isabelle! Luke's here to take you home."

"Now, you hold on a minute—" Luke stopped, aware that Isabelle stood a few feet away, staring wide-eyed at him. He turned to face Clyde.

"You gonna leave her to face the likes of him?" The old man nodded toward Simon, who stood glaring in the window.

Hell! Luke turned back to Isabelle. "I can't afford but room and board." He tried to give her a reassuring smile.

Apparently his smile didn't work because the young lady blanched so white he thought she might faint. Charlotte took the younger woman by the elbow and led her out to the kitchen.

Luke turned back to Clyde. "You know damn well I didn't come here intendin' to take her with me."

"No?" Clyde raised both eyebrows. "Strange you come the day I said we'd be throwin' her out."

Luke rubbed the back of his neck. "I thought her father would have come. But as she's still alone here and seein' how she's treated by your good customers, I reckon she'll be safer with me." *Lord help us both.* "Just until her pa comes. You be sure and send him straight out to my place as soon as he arrives."

"I'll send him out so fast he'll think this saloon was a dream."

Luke scowled at the old man. "It ain't no jokin' matter. I reckon she'll be safer on the ranch. But I probably won't get a lick of work done watchin' out for her."

"It'll do you good to have someone around to talk to." Clyde grinned. "And she's right nice to look at, too."

Luke watched Simon drop back into his chair and resume his meal. Isabelle was lovely and that was just the beginning of her trouble.

Isabelle wrung her hands. "You're certain he won't expect me to . . . ?" Just days ago she'd boldly suggested selling her services to any passing stranger. Now the prospect of being alone with Luke frightened her. Perhaps she didn't have as much of her mother in her as she had feared.

"Don't fret, honey." Charlotte pulled Isabelle's wool coat over her shoulders. "Luke is a real gentleman."

Isabelle's expression must have betrayed her thoughts because Charlotte laughed. An easy, comfortable laugh that Isabelle envied. If only she could be so certain of her place in the world.

"Takes more than fancy clothes to make a gentleman." Charlotte took a small parcel off the table and slipped it into Isabelle's bag.

"What's that?"

"You'll be wantin' a work dress. I reckon this one of mine will fit you well enough."

"Thank you." Isabelle threw her arms around the only friend she had. "I'm going to miss you."

"I'll miss you, too." Charlotte gave her a quick squeeze, then stepped back. "Now. Let's wipe those tears." She pulled her handkerchief out of her pocket and dabbed at Isabelle's cheek. "It won't do to have Luke see you sniffling like a little girl."

Unfortunately, at that moment Isabelle felt very much like a child. One who wanted her mama. And given the trouble Isabelle's mother had always caused her, that was a most unusual feeling. She sniffed and blinked back the threatening flood.

"He thinks I can cook."

"Well, then. I reckon you'll have to keep studying that book of yours."

Isabelle had great confidence in the teaching ability of books. But so far, she'd learned little of use from *A Lady's Guide*. Somehow it would have to be enough.

As Luke went around back to fetch Isabelle, his belly twisted, rebelling at the idea of bringing a lady into his ranch house. And thanks to his brother's disappearance he'd be stuck alone with her under his roof. When Matt got back Luke intended to wring his neck.

He stared at the kitchen door. Come to think of it, it was

just as well Matt wasn't home. Luke would have his hands full protecting the lady from his brother. Those womanly curves and pretty pink lips demanded male attention. Luke would have a hell of a time keeping his own hands off her. Matthew wouldn't even try. Luke would never get a lick of work done spending all day and all night keeping his brother away from Isabelle.

He stepped into the kitchen and caught sight of her walking toward him in a pale blue dress that hugged her figure so tightly it was hard for Luke to breathe. No wide skirts this time, instead the outfit tapered down her legs, leaving little to Luke's imagination. He slipped two fingers under his collar and tugged, but it didn't relieve his sudden need for air.

"I see you didn't bring a wagon," Charlotte said. Luke turned to her. Hell, he hadn't even realized she was in the room. "You can borrow one of our mules. Bring him back when you come with the wagon to fetch the rest of her things."

"The rest?" Luke asked.

Charlotte pointed to a teetering stack of luggage in one corner of the room. Two trunks and two smaller bags. *One woman had carried all of that from Boston?*

Luke shook his head. "She'll only be stayin' 'til her father comes for her."

"We'll keep her things here for a few days. If he don't come before winter—"

Luke glared at Charlotte, and she stopped. *Winter? Lord help us all, I can't keep the lady all winter.*

"I'm grateful to you, Mr. Warring." Isabelle's voice shook a bit, but still sounded as sweet as a meadowlark on a spring morning.

He wanted to tell her to keep her thanks, he'd changed his mind. This was a terrible idea. Instead he said, "I hope you'll be comfortable in my home. It's nothin' fancy."

"All I need is a roof over my head." Isabelle flashed a

timid smile that melted what remained of Luke's reluctance. "I packed what I need in this bag." Isabelle picked a substantial carpetbag up off the floor.

"That's fine." Luke took the bag from her.

"And here's something"—Charlotte handed Luke a large bag she'd packed with food—"so you won't have to take time to cook tonight."

"Charlotte." Isabelle turned to face her friend. "You and Mr. Haverman have done so much for me."

She threw her arms around the other woman, and Luke feared he might have to pry her loose, but she did back away after a moment.

"There now. You're gonna be fine, you'll see." Charlotte touched Isabelle's cheek. "Just remember your lessons."

Lessons?

Isabelle nodded and walked toward the back door. Luke hefted the bags and followed the ladies out.

"I've got Bluebell ready for you," Clyde said as he walked the mule toward them.

An amazing coincidence.

"Seems you had everything ready for me," Luke said as the two men worked together to lash the bags onto the mule's pack saddle.

"No need to thank me," Clyde said.

"Don't worry, I wasn't goin' to." Luke locked eyes with Clyde over the mule's back. "What if I hadn't come?"

"I told you. We'd have sent her packin'."

"You expect me to believe that?" Luke pulled the cinch tight. "I should leave now and call your bluff."

"Suit yourself. Seems a pity to have her sufferin' when you have Matt's room goin' empty."

"I'll find a way to repay you for this," Luke mumbled as he double-checked the packs held tight to the mule's back.

"As I said before—no thanks necessary." Clyde grinned.

Luke bit back the curse that came to mind. He turned to face Isabelle. Pushing his hat back on his head, he took in

the full view of her. *Lordy, she's pretty.* Just one more reason why this was a fool's mission he'd taken on.

Isabelle stepped so near he could smell her flower garden
scent. He looked at Clyde.

"As soon as her pa arrives—"

"I'll send him. I promise."

"Oh, dear!" Isabelle's face turned strawberry red as everyone turned to look at her. She threw Charlotte a pleading
look. "I didn't realize I'd be traveling by horseback."

"You never rode a horse?" Luke couldn't imagine such a
thing.

"Of course I've ridden, Mr. Warring."

"Then maybe you expected a golden carriage!" Luke
hadn't meant to shout. Now, seeing Isabelle on the verge of
tears, he wished the earth would just swallow him up, horse
and all.

"No need to fret." Charlotte took Isabelle's elbow and
tugged her away. "You gentlemen gossip a minute. We'll be
right back."

Luke stared at the two ladies walking away. This might
be a good moment to escape. *If I jumped on old Cloud and
galloped away . . .*

"I expect Isabelle can't mount a horse with that skirt she
was wearin'," Clyde said.

Luke paced away from the horse and mule, packed and
ready to go. *Women are just too damn complicated.*

Cloud was a good strong horse and had no problem carrying Isabelle and Luke. The problem was entirely with
Luke. Riding with Isabelle's arms around his waist was the
most delightful torture. The poor girl probably had no idea
what she was doing, squeezing her arms around his chest so
tight he could feel her bosom pressing against him. The fact
that layers of clothing separated them did not keep Luke
from imagining exactly what those soft mounds would feel
like pressed against his skin.

While he suffered through this torture, Isabelle kept up a cheery monologue. It seemed to Luke the woman commented on every blade of grass they passed until at last she was interrupted by Pennigan's noisy greeting.

"Oh!" Isabelle said as Luke helped her down. "What an interesting-looking dog."

Not suitable for the standards of propriety?

Luke was ready to set Isabelle back in the saddle and take her to the trading post, but she bent to scratch behind Pen's ear. She had a good instinct for dogs, he'd give her that.

"What's his name?"

"Pennigan."

"Pennigan. Oh, we're going to be friends, aren't we?"

The dog seemed delighted to have attention from another human being. And why not? Everyone else seemed to like the idea of Isabelle taking over Luke's ranch.

His eyes drifted away from the dog and back to the woman who had befriended him. Charlotte's quick solution for the ride from town was to lend Isabelle a pair of Clyde's britches. They were just a bit too long for Isabelle when she stood upright. Now, as she squatted next to the dog, they pulled tight over her bottom. Luke's eyes were drawn to that fine round surface until he felt his own trousers growing tight at the crotch. *Damn.*

Before Luke could stop him, Pen showed his pleasure by slurping Isabelle's chin. Luke took a step forward to intervene, but stopped when Isabelle giggled and turned so that the dog could lick her nose and cheeks as well. At least the dog would have some female affection tonight.

While Luke took care of the animals, Isabelle made coffee to go with the supper Charlotte had packed for them. At least she was trying to make coffee. The first problem was that Luke didn't have a stove. The large stone fireplace was equipped for cooking with several iron arms for hanging pots. Everything she'd learned from Charlotte about using the stove and oven would be useless.

She'd managed with some difficulty to light the fire and started water heating while she searched Luke's meager supplies. She stopped and looked around the room. It was small and Spartan with rough pine flooring and no carpets. A table and four chairs sat in the center of the room. There was a coatrack near the door and a bookshelf beside the window. The top shelf held an old almanac, a Bible, and a worn copy of Cooper's *The Pioneers*. The lower shelves were covered with a range of tools, harnesses in need of mending, and other items Isabelle couldn't identify. There was a small cupboard next to the fireplace. The open shelves above held tin plates, cups, a container of lard, and a supply of tallow candles. A drawer held knives, utensils, matches, and string. Pots and pans were stored below, along with some coffee, sugar, corn meal, and flour.

"Lookin' for somethin'?" The rumble of Luke's deep voice caused Isabelle to jump.

"Yes," she managed once her heart started beating again. "I couldn't find the eggs."

"Eggs?"

Isabelle tapped her foot. She was certain Luke was not dim-witted, yet his propensity for single-word sentences sometimes made him sound mighty foolish. Not to mention the fact that it was impossible to decipher his meaning.

"For the coffee?"

When Luke scowled, as he was doing at this moment, his dark eyebrows met, and lines creased his forehead in a most unbecoming manner. His smiles were far preferable.

"An egg in the coffee to avoid bitterness." She had reviewed that part of the guide just this morning.

"No."

"Of course it does. You simply—"

"I mean, no eggs." Luke marched across the room and

threw some coffee into the hot water, making no attempt to measure. "No chickens."

"I don't see what—" Isabelle cut herself off. No chickens, therefore no eggs. The man's logic was flawless, even if his vocabulary was limited.

"No milk or butter either."

"But you have cows." Isabelle's voice sounded whiny even to her own ears, and she regretted it when she saw the flash of anger in Luke's eyes. "No matter," she said. "We'll make do."

"Coffee's boilin'," Luke said as he pulled a chair out from the table and sat.

Isabelle jumped to work, moving the pot to the side so that it wouldn't boil hard. That would also cause bitterness, according to *A Lady's Guide*. She set the table with the two tin plates she found on the shelf and laid out the supper from the sack Charlotte had packed.

"You have a lovely home." Isabelle wasn't used to silence. Her mother had always managed to keep a civil conversation going at the table. It was an important skill for a proper hostess.

"It suits two bachelors."

"You keep it very neat and clean."

Luke shrugged and grabbed another biscuit. Charlotte had included a jar of her strawberry preserves, and he spooned a great glob on top of the bread before stuffing half of it into his mouth.

"The view from your window is more beautiful than anything you'll find at the finest homes in Boston."

"Ain't been to Boston, but expect you're right."

She earned one of his brightest smiles for her effort, and decided to eat rather than press her luck with further conversation.

"For breakfast I'd like some beefsteak and gravy. And I have the makin's for some biscuits if you don't mind an early start."

"Biscuits?" Isabelle used her practiced smile to hide her

panic. She'd helped Charlotte make biscuits twice. It had seemed easy enough; perhaps she could manage. "I don't see an oven."

"We have one—there." Luke pointed to a door on one side of the fireplace. "The old stonemason who built our fireplace insisted upon it. Use it mostly for warming, takes too long to get hot for makin' bread and such. You might just use the Dutch oven for the biscuits."

"Of course." As soon as supper was over she'd search *A Lady's Guide* to see if it mentioned Dutch oven. Then she'd find instructions for preparing beefsteak.

Luke shut and latched the door on the cold October night. He hung his coat on the peg and stood for a moment watching the candlelight dancing on Isabelle's dark red mane as she rested her head on the book that was propped open on the table. He smiled. She was certainly dedicated to reading that thing.

He pulled it out from under her, and she stirred, but did not wake. "The preparation of meats," he read from the open page. He flipped through the book, finding instructions for making everything from beans to puddings. In the chapter on making a home he read:

A proper wife makes certain that her husband need not concern himself with matters which to him will be trivial, though the smooth running of the household may depend on them. To this end, the wife must take complete charge of the servants. She must be careful to instruct them in their duties and to manage their time. Idle hands, it must be remembered, are indeed the devil's workshop. For the good of the household, and indeed for the good of the servants themselves, they must be kept busy so as to lead happy and productive lives.

"Very useful information," Luke muttered. "If you happen to have servants, which ain't never gonna happen to me. Come on, darlin'. Time for bed."

"What?" Isabelle bolted upright, knocking the chair over as she stepped away from Luke. "No!"

She inched farther away from him, her arms locked across her chest.

Luke raised a hand. "I'm not gonna touch you." He pointed to the door to Matt's room. "You're goin' to your bed." He pointed to his door. "I'll be in mine."

"Of course." She dropped her hands to her sides. "I . . . was merely startled." She reached for her book and clutched it like a shield. "I'm sorry, I didn't mean to imply . . ."

Luke considered telling her she was right to worry. No man should be trusted alone with her. *No point frightening her.*

"Good night," she said as she backed toward the door to her room.

Luke nodded and walked outside. The cold air that slapped his face as he stepped onto the porch was just what he needed.

Five

The next morning as he was feeding Cloud, it occurred to Luke that it was nice to have someone inside cooking a hot breakfast for him while he attended his chores. He emerged from the barn, stomach growling and ready to eat. When he caught sight of the smoke coming out the door of his house, he dashed first to the cistern, then up to the house. Isabelle was standing on the steps, fanning in front of her face, when Luke arrived with a bucket full of water.

"Where's the fire?" he shouted.

"It's not a fire!"

Luke dashed inside, looking for flames. Smoke was spewing into the room from the fireplace. *What the hell?*

"It just started smoking," Isabelle said.

He grabbed a long-handled spoon and fork and managed to extract the meat and toss it onto the table. She stood behind him. In the clearing air he could see the tears streaming down her cheeks, and his inclination to shout at her diminished. Instead he reached back into the fire and pulled the tin plate away from the burning wood.

He dropped it on the table. "I suppose you have an explanation?" He couldn't keep the anger out of his voice.

She took a deep breath and choked on the smoky air. He waited.

"I wanted to keep the meat warm while the biscuits cooked and—oh!" She grabbed an iron hook and lifted the lid from the Dutch oven.

"Hellfire and damnation!" she muttered as she pulled the heavy pot full of blackened biscuits away from the coals. "I don't understand." She looked up at the clock Luke kept over the mantel. "These should have taken another five minutes to cook."

"Dependin' on how hot your coals are."

"Well, yes. I suppose so." She glanced at him, then down as though examining the floorboards.

"A wonder in the kitchen, Charlotte said."

Isabelle kept her eyes cast down. "She may have exaggerated a bit."

"It seems she meant to say it was a wonder anyone survived you in their kitchen." Luke brushed his hair back from his eyes. "What the hell was that tin plate doing in the fire?"

"I put your steak on the plate. But it was growing cold. I thought surely it would keep warm if I put the plate at the edge of the fire."

"And the grease dripped into the fire, causin' all this smoke."

"Please don't throw me out, Mr. Warring." Isabelle took hold of his shirtsleeve. "I'll earn my keep, I promise."

Luke searched her clear green eyes for some sign that she had a lick of sense. All he could tell for certain was that she was desperate and frightened. He pulled his sleeve out of her grip.

For some reason he'd put himself in charge of keeping her safe, though he'd hoped to get a few decent meals in the bargain. "Should have known better," he mumbled.

"I beg you, sir—" She started to grab him again, but this time he stepped back.

"No beggin'!" It was hard enough keeping hold of his

senses without her hanging on him. "No need for that. I promised you can stay until your father comes. I mean to keep my end of the bargain. You're gonna have some work to do to keep yours."

"Yes, sir. You won't regret—" Isabelle stopped short. She swallowed.

He could see he'd frightened her again. He just didn't know how to behave around a woman. And he didn't aim to learn, either.

"You can start by cleanin' this mess."

Isabelle managed not to burn the biscuits at dinner. Although they were rather heavy, Luke seemed to enjoy them with some of Charlotte's strawberry preserves. Taking no chances, Luke had cooked the beefsteak himself on a grill over the white-hot coals. Isabelle studied his movements. She watched closely as he poured the meat juices into a pan before turning the beef. No drippings hit the fire, and there was very little smoke.

Once she understood his method, her eyes wandered to where the fabric of his trousers stretched over the muscles on his legs. When she moved around behind him she found herself staring at the rounded shape of his bottom. It was a far more interesting view than the sizzling meat presented.

Luke turned to hand her the pan, and she jumped, startled.

"Sorry," she said, balancing the pan carefully so the drippings wouldn't spill.

"You can use that to make gravy."

"I can?"

"Don't tell me you've never made gravy?"

"I . . . no, I haven't."

"Bring me the flour."

Although Isabelle knew she deserved the disdain in Luke's voice, she felt the hurt still. She vowed to learn quickly, to somehow repay Luke for his kindness.

The dinner was excellent, which was lucky because it turned out to be their only full meal of the day.

While Luke checked on the cattle, Isabelle set about making supper. To be certain they would have something substantial to eat, she chose to roast some potatoes. Nothing could be easier, according to *A Lady's Guide*. Apparently not simple enough for Isabelle.

Luke had stoically eaten the potatoes she set before him. Either he was exceptionally kind or extremely hungry. Both, Isabelle decided. It had seemed logical to her that the potatoes would cook more quickly if she put them directly on the hot coals. Unfortunately this resulted in potatoes that were burned black on one side and raw on the other.

Isabelle cleaned the dishes quickly and went to work on the large basket of mending while Luke kindly disposed of the wash water. Fortunately she'd spent years perfecting the art of needlepoint. During her stay with the Havermans, she'd easily adapted her needle-working skills to mending. She sat close to the candle and weaved the needle back and forth, mending a stocking that had so many holes in it, Isabelle wondered why he didn't simply throw it out. Seeing what a frugal life the rancher lived made her all the more grateful for his generosity to her.

"What's this?"

"Ouch!" She pricked her finger with the needle.

"Didn't mean to startle you."

"It was entirely my fault." She smiled up at him. "My thoughts were wandering." She pointed to the object he held in his hand. "That's my flute."

Setting her sewing down, she took the small case from his hand, pulled the wooden flute out, and showed it to him. He touched the keys and seemed impressed with the way they bounced back when he lifted his fingers.

"My mother sent to Europe for this when I was a little girl. There are tiny springs—do you see them?"

She pulled a chair next to his, and they both bent close,

holding the instrument up to the candle. Luke tapped a silver key and watched it bounce back. He looked at her, a lopsided grin giving him a boyish look that was enhanced by the single lock of hair hanging down over his forehead. When his eyes captured hers, the heat there banished all thought of little boys. The look warmed her chest and belly like a sip of brandy on a winter's night. She sat back in the chair, needing to put some space between them.

"Can you play it?" he asked.

She smiled, relaxing a little. "It is my only talent."

He handed it to her. "Play somethin'."

"Mozart?" she asked, standing and moving a few steps away.

"Any song you like," he said.

She started to explain that Mozart was not a song, but thought better of it. Instead she played a lively version of "The Blue Tail Fly" with special flourishes that she'd invented to entertain her young cousins.

"That's nice," Luke said. "But I never heard it called 'Mozart.' "

"That wasn't the Mozart. He's a composer." Isabelle smiled. "Would you like to hear something that he wrote?"

"Yes, ma'am."

She moved her fingers over the keys of her flute, allowing the orchestral opening of the Adagio from Mozart's Concerto for Flute and Harp to play through her mind. "This is meant to be played with an orchestra and a harp. Well, I've only ever played it in my mother's parlor with a piano—but I think it will work as a solo."

Luke pulled his chair around and straddled it, facing Isabelle with his arms resting on the seat back. He waited patiently, watching her fingering the keys with her graceful hands. She lifted the wooden instrument to her lips, took a deep breath, and closed her eyes. The first few notes rang bright and clear. It was softer and smoother than the little tune she played before. Sweeter than birdsong. She seemed to be almost floating as she swayed with the music, like a willow in the wind.

When she stopped her face was glowing pink, like a woman who had been well loved. Luke cleared his throat to banish that thought. "That was fine," he said.

"It's better with the harp." She wiped her instrument carefully before putting it back into the leather case.

"It was real pretty to me, harp or no." He took the few steps over to her.

"Thank you," she said. "You're very kind."

"I'm not one for sugarin' my words to make someone feel better." He touched her shoulder.

Isabelle looked into his eyes. "I'm glad you enjoyed it."

He nodded. "I reckon it ain't an easy thing—makin' music so fine and sweet."

Her smile opened wide. It was probably the candle's reflection, but her eyes seemed brighter just at that moment. "I wouldn't call it easy, but I love it too much to think of it as difficult."

"I think I know what you mean."

"Not anything half so hard as cooking."

He chuckled, and she favored him with a genuine grin. He leaned closer, inhaling her fragrance, the usual flowers nearly covered over with smoke from a day working over the fire. Her tongue peeked out as she wet her lips. It seemed she was inviting him to those lips, and he was helpless to stop.

When his mouth touched hers, a small shock jolted them apart for the space of a heartbeat, but something stronger drew them back together. Her sweet touch was warmer and softer than he'd imagined it. The heat surged through him. A man with half a lick of sense would walk away now. Instead, Luke pulled her into his arms.

She did not resist. In fact, she gripped his waist and leaned into him until her breasts pressed against his chest. Encouraged, he teased her lips open and touched his tongue to her teeth. She opened for him, and his tongue met hers for only a moment before his sanity returned.

He stepped back, taking a moment to recover his breath. Words of apology came to him, but he couldn't quite bring his tongue to speak them. *Sorry?* He simply was not.

Six

Isabelle dropped the broom she was using to clean the porch and ran out to greet the wagon that was pulling into the yard.

"Charlotte!" she screeched as the wagon rolled to a stop.

"Brought your trunks," Charlotte said as she jumped down and gave Isabelle a quick embrace. "How've you and Luke been getting along?"

"Just fine." Isabelle clamped her teeth together to keep from adding anything about the kiss they'd shared. The wondrous, magical, unforgettable, dangerous, not-to-be-repeated kiss. She turned away, pretending to examine the contents of the wagon bed so as to avoid Charlotte's scrutiny. No doubt the other woman had noticed the sudden rush of heat to Isabelle's cheeks.

"Isabelle?" Charlotte scowled. "He hasn't treated you—"

"He's been wonderful, Charlotte." Isabelle put on her best party smile. The one that hid every real feeling she had. "He's ever so patient with me."

"Had some trouble with the cookin', have you?"

"Besides nearly burning the house down and failing to make one edible meal, my cooking has been quite a success," Isabelle said as she reached for a trunk.

"I'm sure it isn't as bad as all that." Charlotte grabbed

one end, and the two of them lifted it together. "Burned the house down?"

"It was only smoke. I let grease drip into the fire."

"I reckon I forgot to warn you about that problem."

Isabelle fought an urge to beg Charlotte to take her back to the trading post. Staying out here alone with this man was going to be trouble. Not because she couldn't cook. And not because she couldn't trust him. It was her own desires she couldn't trust. That was something she wasn't willing to confess to her friend.

"I brought you somethin' that might help." Charlotte pulled a basket out from under the wagon seat. "Buttermilk and eggs."

Isabelle hugged the basket to her as though it were filled with diamonds. "This is wonderful. But I haven't any money—"

"Don't worry." Charlotte winked. "I've already added it to Luke's bill. He'll be eatin' 'em after all."

Isabelle shook her head. "You're a very clever woman, you know that?"

"I've been told as much on many an occasion. My husband sometimes tells me I'm too smart."

"Any news from him?"

Charlotte shook her head. Isabelle could imagine how difficult the waiting between letters was for her friend. Isabelle had lived for each letter from her father for the past ten years. A letter meant he was alive and well. And the fact he'd taken time to write meant he'd thought of her, cared about her. Still loved her. Someone loved her.

"I wish I could stay and visit," Charlotte said. "I have to get back."

"I understand." Isabelle set her smile firmly in place again. "Thank you so much for coming."

She watched Charlotte drive away until the wagon disappeared into a cloud of dust.

* * *

Isabelle glanced at the clock sitting on the mantel. Five o'clock. Luke would soon come in for his supper. After the disaster last night with the potatoes, she was afraid to check tonight's fare, but there was no avoiding it.

She set aside the shirt she'd been mending, walked across the room, and grabbed a kitchen towel. She sent up a silent prayer before bending to peek inside the small Dutch oven. The sound of Luke scraping mud from his boots caused Isabelle's stomach to turn a quick somersault, whether it was nerves over the supper, or anticipation of another kiss, she wasn't certain.

The corn bread had risen in the center just as the guide said it would, and it was a golden color, browned at the edges. At least the buttermilk and eggs wouldn't go to waste. She breathed the rich aroma of the sweet cornmeal as she grabbed the iron pot and set it on the table.

When she lifted the lid on the large pot that hung over the center of the fire, her nose twitched with the smell of charred sugar. "No," she mumbled just as the door opened behind her.

"That corn bread looks mighty good," Luke said.

She glanced over her shoulder at him. He'd taken the trouble to wash and slick his hair back as he always did before the evening meal. She looked back at the pot of beans. The sweet smell of molasses greeted her nostrils as steam rose from the bubbling mixture. Perhaps only the beans at the bottom were burned. Her shoulders relaxed. At last she'd managed to cook something edible.

She spooned some of the beans onto two plates and carried them to the table. Luke waited for her to sit before seating himself. She wasn't certain whether he was practicing more refined manners for her sake, or simply wary of any food she had prepared. If it was the latter, she could hardly blame him. Glancing at the tin plate in front of her, she decided the beans did not look very appetizing. She'd been careful not to scrape the bottom of the pot, yet bits of charred black beans could be found scattered over her plate. The corn bread would make up for any shortcomings, she told herself.

Isabelle pressed a knife into the beautiful golden crust and found the mound jiggled in a most disconcerting manner. She made another cut, pulled the slice out, and set it on Luke's plate.

"No!" Isabelle leaped to her feet so quickly she knocked the chair over. The center of her beautiful corn bread looked like pudding. A thin pudding at that.

"It ain't so bad," Luke said, spooning some beans into his mouth. He chewed and swallowed before taking a spoonful of the half-liquid corn bread.

"I'm no good at this, Luke!" Isabelle pushed the beans around on her plate. The beans that weren't burned were still hard and uncooked. "*A Lady's Guide* lists baked beans as an easy hearty meal for a hard-working man. I can't make the simplest dishes. I don't even know how to do laundry. I'm just like my mother!" She brushed a tear from her cheek and threw Luke a challenging look.

Her mother had managed quite well after her father had left them, taking on a succession of wealthy lovers. Surely Isabelle had inherited that natural talent. "There's only one thing I'm good for. If I'm going to earn a living here, I've got to develop a saleable skill."

"Now, you settle down, darlin'." Luke walked around the table and pulled her against his chest.

Isabelle burrowed her head into his shoulder and sobbed. "I'm useless!"

"Now, now." He patted her shoulder with one hand, but held her firm with the other. She stretched her arms around him and hung on. "Most women spend their whole lives learnin' their way around the kitchen. You can't replace that trainin' with a book."

She swiped away the tears from her cheeks with the back of her hand. "Then I'll not have any way to make a living.

What if," she sobbed, ". . . what if my father never comes for me and I'm stuck here forever? What will I do with myself?"

"Come spring, you'll go back to that uncle of yours in Boston. He'll take—"

"No!" Isabelle pushed away from him. "I am not going back to Uncle Elliot. I'd rather . . ." She looked up into Luke's beautiful gray eyes. They revealed tenderness far deeper and warmer than his words. She knew what she needed to ask him. Knew he was the only man she could ask. "There is a way, if you will help me."

"I'll do what I can for you. You know that."

Isabelle nodded. She knew she could depend on Luke. She also knew that she was asking something far beyond friendship. "You told me men will pay for what they need. And they'll pay dearly if the commodity is scarce."

"True enough."

"There's nothing more rare around these parts than . . . women." She pulled in a deep breath. "Teach me."

"What?"

"I don't want my first time to be with a stranger." Isabelle could not imagine any of the ruffians that she'd met being gentle with her. She was certain Luke would not hurt her. It might even be nice. Her mother, she was certain, enjoyed her time with the men who visited. "Teach me, please."

"I . . . can't." Luke stood and walked to the window. He looked outside. "You don't know what you're askin'."

"Yes." She walked over to him and took his rough hand in both of hers. "Yes. I do."

Luke stared at her. "This is foolish."

"I need to find my father, and I don't have any other way to pay."

"I'll loan you—"

"I can't ask you to do that."

"And yet you'd ask me to do this to you—to make you a . . . a fancy woman?"

"Fine!" She set her hands on her hips and glared. "You won't help me? I'll just walk to the trading post tomorrow. I have no doubt I'll find a willing man—maybe several."

"You want me to show you what a whore feels like?" he bellowed.

Perhaps she was wrong about Luke. The fire in his eyes at this moment didn't seem at all gentle.

"Take off your clothes," Luke growled.

"What?"

"You didn't hear?" A victorious grin spread across Luke's face and vanished when Isabelle reached for the first button.

"No." He held up a hand. "Stop."

Isabelle released another button and another. His eyes widened as her dress fell down over her shoulders, and she tugged her arms out of the sleeves. She wriggled her hips, and the simple work dress fell to the floor, but Luke's eyes stayed on her chest. She stepped out of the pool of blue fabric at her feet and looked up in time to see Luke's Adam's apple bob.

Isabelle felt a surge of power as she watched this big man frozen, seemingly helpless before her. She stuck one leg out, slowly removed the stocking, and tossed it aside before doing the same with the other leg.

Luke tried to wet his lips, but his mouth was dry. *She wants me to teach her?* Hell, she was giving him a lesson right now. Good sense told him to walk away, but every male instinct in his body kept him in place as surely as if his boots had been nailed to the floorboards. He watched her tossing her undergarments carelessly, exposing more and more of her skin until at last she pulled her chemise over her head and revealed a pair of full breasts, small pink nipples protruding, inviting.

"Now what do I do?" she whispered.

He inhaled and let out a long, slow breath at the sight of

her naked curves. The truth was he'd never seen a woman entirely nude. His body's response even with half the room between them was nearly overwhelming. He held back, not wanting to frighten her. *Hell with that!* Frightening her was exactly what he should be doing to stop this crazy scheme of hers.

Two long strides forward and he captured her in his arms. She gasped, but didn't fight him. He pulled her up against him, letting her feel the fullness of his arousal through his trousers. Her eyes widened, and he saw his plan was working. He lifted her off her feet and bent to bite her shoulder. She yelped.

He dropped her and stepped back, trying to get himself under control. "You ain't ready for this, Isabelle."

"I . . . I want to learn." Her trembling voice betrayed her nerves.

He shook his head and took another step back. She approached him this time, placing her hand over the bulge that pressed against the buttons on his pants.

"I know what this is," she said, her voice steadier this time. "You want me."

Want? I need you, like I've never needed anything. "A man can't control that," Luke whispered. "He can control his actions."

She slipped her hand inside the waist of his pants, touching him lightly with her graceful fingers, then stroking him until he could barely keep his legs under him. Another minute of this and she would prove his assurance that he could control his actions was an empty boast.

"Show me now, or I'll walk to the trading post tomorrow." She continued stroking him.

He grabbed her wrist, intending to pull her hand away from him so he could escape.

"Maybe Simon will be there," she said.

He pulled her hand away, then lifted her into his arms,

cradling her. His eyes swept over her rounded breasts, her flat belly, and down to the mound of curls at the apex of her shapely legs. He bent to nuzzle a breast.

"A smart whore charges extra for this," he growled before taking the breast into his mouth.

"Oh!" was all she could manage as a shiver went up her spine. The animal grunts that came from Luke's throat as he suckled her breast frightened her, but also sent fire burning through her.

He set her back on her feet, and she stood watching him as he opened his buttons and pulled his pants and underpants down. His erection came out straight. When he pressed it against her belly she felt it hard and hot. Her fear was quickly replaced by curiosity.

"Touch me," he said. "Like you did before."

She reached out first with one finger, then her hand, grasping him and stroking the textured surface.

"Ahh." He shuddered over his entire body as she continued stroking. "Kiss me there, now!" he demanded.

She dropped to her knees and kissed him as she continued to stroke him with her fingers.

He groaned. "Take me in your mouth."

She looked up at him, surprised. She took the gleam of victory in his eyes as a challenge and opened her mouth, tasting the tip. It felt smooth against her tongue. Warm, salty. She opened wider and allowed more of him inside. With her tongue she stroked and licked as she drew him farther inside.

Isabelle knew that people did not mate with their mouths. A small part of her mind occupied itself with taking his measure and wondering how he could possibly fit. Perhaps he was unusually large and couldn't fit inside a woman. That would explain why he wanted to come inside her mouth. He groaned again, a deep rumble that she could feel in her own throat, and she felt a bit of joy in knowing she'd provided him with some pleasure.

"Enough!" He lifted her, and she felt the smooth cold wood as he laid her flat upon the table, with her buttocks at the edge and her legs dangling.

He opened her legs and moved between them, pressing the tip of his male part against her. He was going to try to fit. She gasped as he pushed inside her.

"Open up, darlin'!" he commanded, and he moved his hands to her buttocks, helping her open farther.

She wrapped her legs around him, trying to get a purchase as he pressed harder, settling himself deeper inside her. She was tense from her shoulders to her knees, and she felt a tear drip into her ear. This had not been a good idea, but there was no stopping now. She forced herself to relax, to open as he thrust inside her.

"Oh!" she cried in pain.

"That was the worst of it, sweetheart."

She opened her eyes. He was looking at her with tenderness again. She bit her lip and forced herself to breathe. "It wasn't so bad. I'm fine."

Impossibly, he pressed deeper still, then grabbed her shoulders and held her in place as he rocked inside her. Each thrust sent peculiar sensations through her. The pain remained, but there was also a pleasant throbbing as he pushed into places that had never felt a touch before. A glimmer of pleasure ran all the way down to her toes. She reached up to hold him just as he pulled out of her and spilled his seed over her belly.

She sucked in a breath, feeling as though she'd just run a race, and she noticed that Luke, too, seemed breathless as he leaned over her. She drew in air, trying to find words to express her feelings.

"Having you inside me was . . ."

He kept his eyes away from hers as he stepped back and pulled his trousers up around him.

"Make sure you get the money first. You'll be in a poor position to collect once the man has satisfied himself. And don't let him stay too long after. You'll have other customers waitin'."

He walked out of the room, forgetting his coat and hat. Isabelle stood, shivering. There was a pleasant ache inside her and an emptiness that longed to be filled again. Except that his quick departure told her more certainly than any words could that he wouldn't touch her again.

She slipped back into her clothes and peeked out the window. A glow from an open door indicated Luke had retreated to the barn. She thought of taking his coat out to him, but was sure he didn't want to see her. Instead she started picking up the chairs and cleaning the mess of spilled beans around the table. She ignored the tears. Whores, she was certain, did not cry.

Seven

The next morning Isabelle dragged herself out of bed after a near sleepless night. Every time she had shut her eyes, trying to forget the previous day, the aches and pains of her newly discovered female organs reminded her. She'd been impulsive last evening. The one lesson her mother had actually tried to teach her.

"Men," her mother had said. "Are foolish when it comes to women. A clever woman can use this to her advantage. Never act on impulse. Always plan carefully and you shall have whatever you want from a man."

Isabelle had not paid attention to the advice. She had been certain she would never want to use a man the way her mother had. Unlike her mother, she would earn an honest wage for a good day's work. Instead she had turned to the nearest man and used him.

Even worse, there was a part of her that had enjoyed it. She was indeed her mother's daughter.

Isabelle dressed and stepped into the kitchen where Luke was already at work building the fire. She found the sack of ground coffee and spooned some into a pot.

"I'll make some flapjacks, if you like," Luke offered.

Isabelle nodded. "That would be nice."

He went to work, digging some lard out of the tin on the shelf. Isabelle watched him out of the corner of her eye. She wanted to learn, but was a little afraid that asking him to teach her would remind him of the lesson she'd requested last evening. They would have to speak about it eventually, but she was in no hurry. Instead she made herself busy making the coffee and hauling in water for washing.

They worked together in silence, then sat to eat. There was only the small table between them, but it might as well have been a wall. The sound of the mantel clock echoed around the room like a drum.

Luke shifted uncomfortably in his seat. He stared at the pancakes on his plate, unable to look at her. It wasn't enough he'd violated her yesterday—he had done it on this table. How the hell was he ever going to be able to eat a meal here?

"I want to thank you, Luke."

He shrugged, figuring she meant to thank him for breakfast. No thanks necessary, he was too hungry to risk her cooking this morning.

"For teaching me what I asked you last night."

He looked up at her. She was putting on a brave smile, but there was hurt in her eyes.

"I'm sorry, Isabelle . . ."

"Please don't apologize." She reached across the table and squeezed his hand. "I mean it. You did only what I asked of you, and I do truly appreciate it. I'll always be glad that you were the one who taught me . . ."

Luke pulled his hand away and pushed back from the table, increasing the distance between them.

"I know I was rough with you, but I thought it was necessary." He cleared his throat. "I only wanted to put the foolish notion out of your—"

"Oh, no." Isabelle shook her head. "No. You were . . ." She squared her shoulders and raised her chin. "It was quite nice." Tears pooled in her eyes. "I'm so very glad that you were my first."

"You still intend to sell yourself?"

"I don't know. I . . . I may have no choice," she said. "But you've made it easier for me, and I do appreciate that. Truly."

He scowled. *Fine. She wants to be a whore—good luck to her!*

"I won't trouble you again, unless . . ." She brushed at her hair as though it weren't pinned perfectly to her head. "If you want me . . . or perhaps you find me . . . perhaps I'm distasteful to you?"

Distasteful? He only wished she were; then maybe he could keep his hands and the rest of his body away from her. He studied her for a moment. *Damned woman!* She had that look of perfect innocence, but he knew better. She knew exactly how to torture him.

"I try to stay away from whores." The words sounded more vicious than he'd intended. No matter. The important thing was for him to keep his distance from her. Lucky he already had an escape planned. "I'm going to be gone most of today," Luke said. "I promised my neighbor some help." He forced himself to lift his fork. Work needed doing, and he couldn't do it on an empty stomach.

"Neighbor? I don't remember seeing another house on our entire journey here."

"Zeke Petersen has a ranch about two miles west." He shoveled another bite into his mouth.

"Does he have a family?"

"He ain't likely to be a customer, if that's what you mean," Luke growled.

"He's married, then?"

"No." Luke slapped his fork down on the table and stood. "He's a friend of mine."

"Oh." Isabelle frowned. "I don't understand. What has that to do with it?"

"He won't touch you if I ask him to stay away."

"Oh." She smiled.

Luke studied her lips. They were spread slightly, showing a row of neat white teeth. Something about that smile made him feel uneasy.

"Don't worry." She used a knife to cut a small piece of pancake before spearing it with her fork. "I have no intention of offering myself to anyone but you so long as I remain here under your roof."

"That's right you won't. I ain't runnin' a whorehouse."

Isabelle stirred the stew, feeling certain of her success. Luke was off at the neighbor's ranch again. It was the third time this week he'd left her alone. Isabelle hated the solitude, but she'd had the most marvelously productive day. Not only had she put together a fragrant bubbling stew, but she had also fired up the oven for the first time. While the oven heated, she'd mixed and kneaded bread as Charlotte had taught her. It had taken hours for the oven to heat and the dough to rise. Finally, she'd removed the ashes from the oven and placed three loaves inside on the hot stones.

While the bread baked, she'd mended two of Luke's stockings and replaced the buttons on his best woolen shirt. Isabelle's stomach growled as she set the lid back on the pot. The coals were hot enough to keep the stew warm without burning it. At least she hoped it wouldn't burn. She moved the pot another inch away from the fire.

She pulled the loaves from the oven and set them on the table. According to Charlotte, the bread should cool a bit before she cut into it. They were a perfect golden brown and made a lovely hollow drum sound when she tapped on the bottom of each loaf. These were signs they were cooked through. She covered them with a clean cloth and left them to cool.

Isabelle returned to her mending for only a moment before curiosity drew her back to the table. Using the big knife, she cut into the center of one loaf. Her shoulders relaxed when she found no raw dough in the center. Her first good meal. She couldn't wait for Luke to taste this supper. She'd show him that she wasn't completely useless. Maybe then he'd speak to her again.

It was too much to hope that he'd touch her again. Kiss her. Share more intimate secrets.

At that moment she heard footfalls on the porch. She smiled. *Perhaps I summoned him with my thoughts.* She sawed off a slice of warm bread and rushed to the door.

"Look what I have for—" Isabelle dropped the bread and stepped back into the house, slamming the door on a thick hand.

"Damn bitch!" Simon Vemonde's shout sent shivers up her spine.

She leaned all her weight against the door, but this did not provide much of a barrier for Simon, who pushed his way into the house. She ran for the table, hoping to grab the knife she'd used to slice the bread, but Simon tackled her before she was halfway there.

He straddled her, beaming a triumphant grin. "You are so lovely, my dear."

Not bothering with the buttons, he ripped her dress open, pulled a knife from his boots, and cut through her undergarments, baring her chest. Isabelle felt a cold hand squeezing her breast, but she'd closed her eyes, not wanting to look at him. Her stomach roiled. She thought it likely she would vomit on him. In fact, she hoped she would. She shoved hard with her arms and her hips, trying to force him away.

"Hold still now," he shouted and pressed her arms over her head, pinning them to the floor with one huge paw. He bent to give her a slimy kiss, and she felt bile rising in her throat.

When he pulled away she spit in his eye. He laughed.

"Damn you to hell!" she yelled. He slapped her so hard her head jerked to one side. She blinked, feeling heat throbbing where his hand had landed on her cheek. He bent close to her again, and she spit up at him.

This time his fist pounded her jaw. "You don't learn, do you?" Another blow sent her head spinning through shadows. "Now. All I want is a share of what you've been givin' ole Luke." Simon's smirk forced its way through the fog in her head. "Don't worry. He's miles away. I made sure we would be alone for this."

"He'll smell your stench on me when he gets home."

"Shut up, woman!"

Isabelle squirmed under him. She felt trapped, helpless. If she could get him to release her hands, she might have a chance to grab one of the pistols that hung from his belt. No matter how she struggled, he held her fast. Fear combined with the terrible odor of the man pressing down on her hips caused the bile to climb up her throat again. She choked it back, but it kept coming, spewing out onto her face and neck.

"You disgustin' bitch!" Simon bellowed as he moved away. He found a towel and cleaned himself, then tossed it to her. "Clean up!"

She used the towel as best she could to clean the floor and herself, holding her dress closed with one hand as she worked.

"Come on, come on."

"I just need some water." She walked to the door and slipped outside before breaking into a run.

"Stop!" Simon shouted. "Stop, dammit!"

An explosion sounded behind her, and she froze.

"Come back here, now!"

She turned slowly and found herself looking up into the barrel of the largest pistol she'd ever seen. Her knees nearly gave way, but she refused to collapse. A small voice inside urged her to turn and run, though she was in easy range of that pistol. *Better dead than in that man's hands again.*

A calmer voice prevailed. She was determined to survive this. With deliberate steps, she moved back toward the house. Simon fired a shot at the ground a few feet in front of her, and she jumped.

"Faster!"

She choked back a sob and forced herself to take a step and then another, stopping a few feet in front of him. He closed the distance and slammed the back of his hand against her chin. The world blinked dark. When the light returned, Isabelle felt the cold earth against her back.

"There now, you hold still this time. It will only take a minute." He straddled her, pointing the gun directly between her eyes. "I just as soon kill you as fuck you, do you understand?"

She stared at him.

"Answer me!"

 movement sending waves of pain ...d at her, baring his green teeth as ...The cold barrel of the pistol now ...r as he bent to kiss her. She tried ...s smothered hers. She was afraid ...t her lip. Blood from the wound ...e lifted his head. He laughed and ...olster.

"There now." He pinned her to the ground with a hand to her throat. "You can be good when you've a mind to."

He moved to the side and pulled the hem of her skirts up over her belly. Isabelle tried to cry out, but he leaned down hard on her throat until she could scarcely breathe.

"Why not stop fightin' and enjoy this?" He tore her pantaloons away. "I think you'll find me much more excitin' than Luke. He's an old woman in men's clothin'."

Isabelle felt a pounding where her head touched the ground. She thought at first it was her heart racing. Then an earthquake. When she saw a movement out of the corner of her eye she knew it was Luke.

His boot connected with Simon's ribs. Before Simon could

draw on him, Luke shoved the big man away from her. Within seconds the two men were rolling in a whirlwind of dust, feet, and flying fists. Isabelle grabbed Cloud's reins to keep him clear away from where the men were fighting. They were on their feet again, and Luke threw a powerful blow to Simon's head, knocking him to the ground. The big man lay still, blood streaming from his nose. Luke turned to face Isabelle, who stood with one hand holding Cloud's reins, the other clutching her dress closed. Luke took a step toward her. Behind him, Simon pushed to his feet.

"Luke!" she shouted.

Pennigan leaped on Simon, burying his teeth in the big man's thigh just as he fired his pistol. The shot went wild. Simon kicked the dog away. As the yelping dog flew through the air, Luke spun around.

A fog closed in on Isabelle, swallowing her. She lost her grip on Cloud's reins and sank to her knees. "God please," Isabelle whispered as gunfire seemed to echo around the valley. "Please spare Luke."

She curled into a ball on the ground, shivering as the world went dark.

Something warm and wet touched Isabelle's nose. A whimper pierced her skull.

"Isabelle," Luke whispered. "Isabelle," he said with more urgency.

She half opened her eyes and saw Pennigan's muzzle inches from her face. She looked up into Luke's worried gray eyes. It was too damn hard to keep her eyes opened, and she allowed them to close. Strong arms lifted her.

"Hang on, Isabelle." She felt the rumble of Luke's voice through his chest.

"Thank God," she mumbled. *Thank God Luke is unhurt.*

"Isabelle," Luke said again.

He set her on the hard wooden floor. She could feel the

fire to one side of her—a distant warmth that couldn't touch her. She knew for certain she would always be cold.

Luke opened her dress. "No!" She pulled it shut, curling away from him.

"I don't want to hurt you, darlin'." Luke's quiet, steady voice seemed reassuring. "I just need to check you."

She remained curled into a tight ball.

"Isabelle, darlin'." Luke rested a hand on her shoulder. "I need to know, are you shot?"

"No."

"Are you sure?" Luke leaned over her so that his face was inches from hers. "The way you went down, I was afraid . . ."

"Oh, Luke. I thought he'd killed you."

"No, Isabelle. He didn't hurt me."

She rolled onto her back and looked up at Luke. "Is he gone?"

Luke nodded. "He's dead."

Luke's eyes went from her head down over her body. "You're sure a stray bullet didn't hit you?"

"I'm not injured." Isabelle sat up. The pounding in her head reminded her that wasn't quite true.

"You rest here," Luke said.

He wrapped her in blankets and washed her face with warm wet cloths. His touch was so gentle, Isabelle wanted to beg his forgiveness for pulling away from him before. But she didn't have the strength. All she really desired was sleep. To curl under the blankets and never emerge again.

By the time they sat at dinner that night, the stew was burned at the bottom of the pot. It didn't matter. Pennigan was the only one eating. He'd lapped up a huge bowlful and was taking a well-earned rest in front of the fire. The humans were not inclined to eat, but they both sat at the table pretending.

Isabelle pushed a piece of meat from one side of her tin plate to the other. Luke chewed on a slice of bread as he watched her. She looked up at him. Just looking at her bruised and tear-stained face brought Luke new waves of anger. *How could I have left her alone? Defenseless?*

"What will they do to you?" Isabelle asked.

"Me?" Luke scowled at her. "What do you mean?"

"You . . . you killed a man. I know you had to, but . . ."

"Ain't no one gonna blame me for defendin' my woman."

She worried her lip for a moment and went back to pushing her food around her plate. "I'm not . . . not legally yours."

"No matter. Folks in these parts don't care so much about a weddin'. You livin' with me makes you my wife if I say so."

"Oh." She set her fork down. "Luke. Everyone knows you didn't mean to make me your wife when you brought me here. Simon figured he was entitled to . . . the same services I was providing you, and who's to say he wasn't right about that? I mean, what right did I have to deny him?"

"No!" Luke slammed his fork down on the table. "That makes about as much sense as milkin' a bull. It don't matter that you give yourself to me. Don't matter if you take money for favors. Even whores choose who they spread their legs for. Simon was forcin' himself on you. He got what he deserved."

Isabelle closed her eyes. Luke would die to protect her, but he would never stop thinking of her as a whore.

Eight

The rest of October slipped by in a fog that settled deep into the cold, damp valley. The chill continued into November with weeks of slate gray skies that held no promise of sunshine. Isabelle tromped up the mountain behind the house, the frozen grass crunching beneath her feet. Pennigan bounded in front of her, behind her, and around her. Luke had given the dog strict orders to stay close to her, and Pennigan seemed to take his duties seriously. She pulled the scarf from around her neck, wrapped it over her head to cover her numb ears, and drew her coat tight around her. She'd trade a trunk full of gowns for one truly warm coat today.

"Look, boy!" Isabelle pointed down to the frozen banks of the river. "It won't be long before it's frozen across," she said. Pennigan nudged her knee, and she bent to scratch behind his ear. "No more swimming for you until spring."

The thought of spring brought heaviness to Isabelle's heart. Though she longed to be warm again, melting snow meant the passes would open again, and she would be able to travel west to find her father. She belonged with her father. Not here in this remote valley with a man who far preferred to be alone. And yet she was certain leaving Luke would break her heart.

She wondered what life would have been like married to Luke. It hadn't been necessary for him to claim her as his wife. No one had questioned their story about Simon's attack. He'd been buried without ceremony and forgotten. Except in Isabelle's nightmares.

She was glad for Luke's sake that he hadn't been forced to pretend marriage to her, but part of her was sorry. Though she would not dare speak such thoughts to Luke, she felt more at home here in the wilderness with this quiet man than she had ever felt in her mother's house in Boston.

The sun peeked out from behind a cloud and reflected off the narrow stream of flowing water in the center of the river for a moment before its light was blocked again. Isabelle looked up at the dark sky. They'd had several small snows, but nothing heavy yet. Perhaps today would bring her first real western snowstorm.

She walked farther up the hill, stopping to examine the grave. A neatly etched granite stone bore a simple inscription:

Jonathan S. Warring,
loving husband and father.
b. 1810—d. 1859

Strange. Luke never talked about his mother. Isabelle wondered where she'd been buried. A cloud of dust coming over the rutted trail near the house caught Isabelle's attention. She checked the pistol at her side. After several lessons, she felt confident that she could use it, if necessary. In any case she had no choice but to wear it. Luke wouldn't let her out of his sight unless she had the pistol strapped to her waist. If wearing the gun made her less of a burden to him, then she'd wear it.

The dog yapped twice, and she squinted back at the dust cloud. "I believe you're right, Pen. That is Luke's wagon."

She broke into a run right behind the dog and perhaps just as happy to greet the master of the house.

Pennigan being much swifter got the first greeting. Isabelle stood back, wanting to throw herself into Luke's arms, willing to trade places with the dog so that she could at least have a pat on the head. At last, Luke lifted his eyes to her.

"Any problems while I was gone?"

She shook her head. "Everything was quiet. I made soup and some fresh bread. It was all ready, so I took a short walk."

"I like to walk up there, too."

"It's so peaceful," Isabelle said, "watching the river wind its way through the valley."

Luke led Cloud to the barn to settle him in for the night. Isabelle followed.

"River's nearly frozen over," she said.

Luke removed Cloud's saddle while Isabelle described the details of her day. Outside of an occasional grunt, or nod, Luke didn't respond, but Isabelle knew he was listening. She watched him removing Cloud's bridle, checking him carefully for any sore spots. Luke stroked the animal, and the old gray gelding responded to the gentle touch.

She decided Charlotte had been right when she said it wasn't fancy clothes that made a gentleman. Some men had it in their nature to consider those around them. Luke was the gentlest man Isabelle had ever known.

After Luke made certain Cloud had feed and water, Isabelle and Luke walked side by side up to the house. "How was everything at the trading post? Did you talk to Charlotte?"

"She asked after you. And she had a letter for you. Come through with some soldiers about a week ago." He pulled it from his pocket.

Her hand trembled as she took the folded and sealed letter. "It's from Papa," she said, recognizing his hand.

He watched her brow wrinkle as she read. When she finished, she refolded the letter and stuffed it into the pocket of her coat.

"What does he say?" Luke's gut twisted with that awful, helpless feeling Isabelle's tears always brought him. Hell, if he'd known the letter would make her cry, he'd have burned the damn thing.

She blinked back a tear, then sniffed. "To hell with it. I'm tired of trying not to cry."

Luke knew he should say something, but what? He pulled her into his arms. "What is it, darlin'?"

"He's changed plans again. He's in San Francisco."

"San Francisco? But he's comin' to get you, isn't he?"

She shook her head. "Oh, Luke. I'm so sorry. I know you were counting on my father coming for me."

"Now, don't you worry about that. At least you know where he is. Come spring we can find a way to get you there."

Isabelle sniffed. "He doesn't want me to come!"

She handed the letter to Luke, and he read it through.

"He calls me a foolish girl for coming out West on my own." Now she was getting angry. "He was the one who left me. What right does he have to worry about me now?"

Luke used his thumb to brush a tear from her cheek. "He's your pa."

"I thought my father loved me," she said. "It was Mama he was leaving, not me. He told me that." She closed her eyes. "He doesn't want me, Luke. No one wants me."

"I'm sorry, darlin'," Luke whispered in her ear. "I hate to see you cryin', but maybe this man ain't worth your tears."

She looked up at him, her gaze so filled with hurt it seemed to pierce his chest.

"He's my father. I . . . I need to see him again."

Luke nodded. "Of course you do. You should be with your kin." He looked back at the letter. "You know, darlin', he never says he doesn't want to see you."

She took the letter and read it over again.

"In fact, seems to me what he's sayin' is, he's afraid for you. Afraid you'll get all the way to San Francisco and he won't be able to take care of you."

"Do you think he's . . . sick?"

"Maybe he's just feelin' old. Look. He says he'd worry about you in that rough town after he passes on. That's why he wants you back in Boston with your uncle. Not because he doesn't want you."

Isabelle took in a deep breath. "It doesn't matter. Whether he wants me to come or not, I have to go to him."

Luke considered offering her the alternative of staying with him. A part of him wanted that more than he liked to admit. But the list of reasons it wouldn't work was long and started with the fact that Isabelle deserved more than he could ever give her. "I'll help you find a way to get to San Francisco."

She threw her arms around him. "Oh, Luke. You are too good to me. I . . ."

She tilted her head up, inviting a kiss. He forced himself to turn away from her tempting lips.

"You said somethin' about supper?"

Nine

Isabelle stood on the porch staring up at the bright white orb that seemed to fill the black sky. She heard Luke's confident footfalls approaching, and her foolish heart skipped a beat.

"You'll catch your death," he said as he stepped across the porch to stand behind her.

She felt the weight of a heavy woolen blanket draped over her shoulders. "The light woke me," she said. "It was so bright I was certain I'd overslept." She glanced up at him. The stark light illuminated the stubble on his jaw as he stared out across the valley, white with the fresh snow that had fallen as they slept. He looked so damned handsome she wanted to kiss him.

Even more she wanted to feel him inside her again. He'd held her and comforted her, but not shown the least interest in more intimacy. Each day with him left her with a horrible longing, an emptiness that was becoming more difficult to bear.

She wanted to blame him for using her. For giving her desires she'd never guessed were possible, then refusing to satisfy her needs. Logic told her the blame was entirely hers, but that didn't keep her from being angry.

Poor pitiful Isabelle. The man takes you into his home, protects you with his life, and you are not satisfied.

As usual, she hid her misery behind pleasant conversation. "Seems almost like midday, but it's the moon reflecting off the new snow." She was proud of the way she managed to sound almost normal. "It's not like rain that wakes you when it falls. Snow comes in silence. It's a surprise." *Like love.*

Luke nodded. "It woke me, too. The light." He pulled an arm around her, and she allowed it, relishing the warmth of him against her. "Come inside now, Isabelle."

She closed her eyes for an instant, imagined staying in the shelter of Luke's arms, and knew it was not to be. "I'm fine out here on my own." She was a responsibility to him. He didn't care for her, but he wouldn't want her damaged. She blinked back a tear.

"Suit yourself." But he didn't leave.

They stood in silence gazing out into the night for a few moments. Isabelle felt the chill creeping up from her bare feet and knew she should go back inside. Still she remained.

"I owe you somethin'," he whispered.

"You owe me nothing." She sucked in a breath to keep from shouting. "You've given me bed and board, and I'll . . . I'll do what I can to repay you for that." *Then I'll take my broken heart and be on my way.*

"I'm not talkin' about that. You've done your share of work to earn your keep. Now that the meals aren't all charred."

She beamed a smile, brighter than the moonlight, and Luke clean forgot what he'd intended to say. He leaned closer until his nose touched hers. And then he sought her lips. The chill of her face shocked him for an instant before the heat flamed between them. Her lips were softer than he remembered, sweeter. He teased them open and drew her closer, wrapping his arms around her shoulders. He pulled her so tight he could feel her breasts, firm yet pliant, against his ribs. Her tongue danced against his, inviting him deeper.

He pulled his head back an inch. "That's what I owe you—I've been wantin' to kiss you, but I knew I couldn't stop at kissin'. . . ." He took a step back.

A tear streaked down her cheek as she looked up at him. "I don't want you to stop. I want you, Luke."

A gentleman might have given her a chance to change her mind. Luke was not about to risk that. He lifted her into his arms, carried her to the bed that still held her warmth, and set her gently down. Pulling his pants off, he tossed them over a chair before sliding under the covers next to her. When her icy cold feet touched his leg, he dived under the blankets to find them. She giggled as he took each foot in turn between his hands, rubbing them until some heat returned to them.

"You don't have to—" she started.

"You shush now." He kissed her ankle as he continued rubbing her feet. "I want to make this nice for you."

He bent over her foot and blew warm air on her toes before he kissed each one. He repeated the ritual with the other foot before commencing to work on her ankles in the darkness. Not wanting to lose a chance to see her, he lifted his shoulders to toss the blanket back. The view of those shapely legs was one of many things he wanted to remember after she left him. Her skin was so pale the moonlight glowed against it. He ran a hand over one lovely calf while he kissed and licked his way up the other.

"Oh!" she cried as he pressed a kiss to her sensitive inner thigh and probed against the muscle with his tongue. Somehow that action, inches below, had generated a throbbing in her womb. The sensation was magical, and yet it left her feeling empty—feeling she must have him inside her again.

"Luke?" She wanted to beg him to come closer, but her mind couldn't form the words. "Luke," she sighed his name again.

"Like that, do you?"

"Oh, yes," she whispered. "It's wondrous!"

"Wondrous?" He chuckled, a quiet, throaty rumble that she could feel echoing deep inside her.

He moved over her, and she could see he was hard and ready, so she opened her legs, sorry that this delight would soon be over. Even a few minutes of his tender caresses were well worth the pain of him driving into her.

He pulled her nightgown up to her hips, but instead of plunging inside her, he cupped her bottom and squeezed. With his other hand he reached under her gown, sliding up until he held one breast. She felt the cold against her bare skin—but the warmth of his touch was more powerful. He flicked a thumb against her nipple, and all her senses seemed to jump alert.

"Breathe," she muttered.

"Hmm?"

"I've never felt anything—"

Her words cut off when he took the breast into his mouth, suckling and teasing her with his tongue until she feared she would faint from the sheer delight of it. And then he brought his knee up between her legs, and she gasped, surprised he would put anything other than his male parts up against her most intimate place.

"Oh!" Isabelle moaned as he pressed against her, sending delighted shivers through her.

So many sensations at once. Her mind couldn't find a word to describe the pleasure. He kneaded with his knee while he suckled her breast, sending waves tingling across her skin and a pulse deep inside. No, not a mere pulse, a throbbing that drove her to the edge of oblivion.

"Luke!"

As she called his name he lifted his head to watch her wriggling with the pleasure he was giving her. Her hair was strewn across the white pillows, and her face glowed pink and red. He pressed a kiss to each cheek before finding her lips. His own need was growing, but he was determined to see her completely satisfied before he took her again. His tongue was fierce, pushing deep inside her mouth.

His erection pressed against her belly, causing a deep ache that demanded action. He groaned, suppressing his need once again.

He nuzzled the hollow behind one ear while his hand explored below, reaching gently down into the curls that guarded her womanly places. His fingers probed and rubbed until he found the point that would bring her the deepest pleasure. He stroked gently, then harder and faster until she let him know that he'd found the rhythm she needed to climb over the brink. His tongue pressed against her throat so that he felt more than heard her joyful cries.

"Oh . . . oh, my! That's perfect, how did you know? Oooh!"

"You told me, darlin'."

She ran a hand gently over his chest, and he shivered with anticipation.

"I didn't say anything, how—"

"I can feel your pleasure, Isabelle."

She felt his need through his husky whisper, the way he responded to her touch. "I want to give *you* pleasure."

"You will, darlin'." He brushed a kiss to her shoulder, her throat, her lips. "May I come inside you now?"

"Yes. Yes, please. I need you there. Oh, Luke, I need you."

"Then we'll enjoy this together."

He was careful this time. Mindful that he was larger and stronger. He pushed slowly inside her.

"Yes," she breathed. "That's what I need."

He pressed deeper still—feeling her soft, moist heat tight around him. The cold air of the room beyond pressed against his backside, his legs, his feet. All the heat from both of them seemed concentrated on the single point where they joined together. He rolled onto his side and pulled her close, feeling her breasts through their shirts.

"Wait," she said. She leaned away and pulled her gown over her head. "That's better. Now you."

She helped him lift his shirt over his head and pulled her bare breasts against his chest. The supple mounds sent pleasure shuddering down through him and straight into his cock.

"Isabelle," he groaned into her ear. Their lips found each other, and she surprised him by thrusting her tongue into his mouth—deep and deeper still until he could feel her throbbing around him below. She wrapped her legs around his bottom and locked them together in a tight bond. He began rocking, slowly, inside her. Pressing deeper and harder. Thrusting to the rhythm she set with her tongue.

All thought flew from his mind. He felt only her, knew only her and the fury of their joining. Harder and faster until her cry echoed through his head and he cried out in joy with her.

Afterward they remained entwined, and she rested against his shoulder, her warm breath contrasting with the cold around them. They managed to pull the blankets up and cuddled still locked together in their warm nest, their hearts slowing together until they seemed to beat as one. He could still feel the pulse of her pleasure as he slipped out of her. In a moment, her breathing was quiet and steady. He started to pull away, thinking she was asleep.

"Stay close for another minute?" she asked.

He brushed a kiss to her forehead and another to the top of her head as she curled up against him.

"Luke?" Isabelle said while she made lazy circles on his chest with one finger. Luke started to doze. "You've made me so happy tonight."

"I'm glad."

"I was afraid you didn't want me." She kissed his lips and settled back down against him. "I love you."

Luke's heart jumped to his throat as the meaning of those last words hit him with their full force. He sat up.

"Isabelle, you don't know what you're sayin', darlin'."

"Did I say something wrong?" Isabelle sat with her arms crossed over her breasts. "I only meant . . . You do want me, don't you, Luke?"

"There's a difference between wantin' and lovin'." Luke stepped out of the bed and took his pants from the chair. "This is new to you. You're confused."

He walked out and closed the door behind him. *Dammit, Isabelle. You cannot love me.*

Ten

By the first of December, little snow remained on the ground. The cistern froze, and Luke had to carry all their water up from the river. The days grew shorter. They each worked hard to get all their work done so that they could spend the long nights together.

Isabelle had convinced Luke that she'd been confused, but now she understood. What she felt for him, she'd told him, was simple wanting. She was certain he believed her. Unfortunately, it was more difficult to lie to her heart.

She worked the needle through the heavy woolen fabric of Luke's shirt, weaving the stitches back and forth until she was satisfied her mend would hold. She held the sleeve out in front of her to examine it.

"More mendin' done?" Luke pushed his chair back from the table.

"You need this shirt with all the cold we've been having."

"You determined to keep me warm, are you?"

Isabelle felt heat rush to her face at the thought.

"What are you thinkin'?" he asked, but his grin betrayed him.

"You know very well what I'm thinking."

"Thinkin' about ways to keep warm that don't require shirts."

Nor any other clothing. "I am done with my evening chores, sir. If I can be of service."

"You're certain it isn't a bother?"

"No trouble"—Isabelle sat on his lap and started opening the buttons on his shirt—"I assure you."

"In that case . . ." He lifted her chin so that she was looking into his eyes. "Perhaps you would be more comfortable in your bed?" He covered her mouth with his before she could answer his question. Or perhaps her kiss was answer enough.

They didn't make it as far as the bed, didn't even manage to take their clothes off before she wrestled him to the floor and rode him fast and hard. Although she knew she had no right to think of him as her man, she allowed herself to pretend. To demand pleasure from him and give him what she could in exchange. They found their release together and held each other, panting. She pressed her palm against his rough cheek, a kiss to his throat.

"You're . . . full of surprises," Luke said between breaths.

Pennigan came and pressed his muzzle between them, demanding attention. Luke gave him an affectionate pat, then shooed him away.

"Perhaps we should find the bed after all," she suggested.

"You want more?"

"Yes." She kissed him, teasing him with her tongue. "More, please, sir."

He rolled them both over until he was straddling her. "You might give a man a chance to catch his breath."

She had no chance to reply as he captured her lips and kissed her until she groaned with the odd mix of pleasure and need that Luke's kisses always gave her.

"Bed," Luke said.

"You'll get no argument from me."

He took the candle from the table and followed her into the bedroom.

"I don't think we need a light," she said.

"Yes. We do."

He helped her with the buttons on her dress and leaned back against the wall to watch. It was almost a dance. He could imagine music, perhaps Mozart, playing as she slowly removed her clothing. The thought of her performing this dance for any other man tore at him like a knife to the chest. He shoved it away. Not tonight. He wouldn't let thoughts of her leaving spoil this moment.

When she stood naked before him, he took her in his arms and kissed her, long and deep. He lifted her and set her on the center of the bed. The old straw mattress did not offer much more comfort than the floor. She should sleep only on deep feather mattresses covered with silk. One day she would—far away from him. But tonight she was here. He couldn't give her the luxuries that were her birthright. He blew out the candle and settled next to her to give her what pleasure he could, caressing every part of her lovely body while he built his strength to join with her again.

When she cried his name, he took his release with her, then gathered her in his arms, holding her close, as though he had the right to call her his. He knew he was a selfish bastard. He should go to his own bed rather than allow himself the luxury of sleeping with her supple body against his, but he couldn't let her go yet. He cupped one breast in his hand, memorizing the feel of it, soft and heavy against his palm, while he nuzzled her shoulder, her neck.

"Luke?"

"Hmm?" He nibbled an ear.

"Will you answer something for me?"

"If I can."

She turned toward him, though it was too dark for him

to see her face. "You talk about your father all the time, but you never mention your mother."

He waited. She caressed his face, one finger trailing the line of his jaw.

"Can you tell me about her?"

Luke took her hand in his. Kissed her fingers, then her palm. "She was pretty. Hair the color of sunshine."

"She died?"

"It was a long time ago. We were livin' in Kentucky. I was nearly eight years old. Matthew was four."

"That must have been difficult."

It had been hardest on their father. He had missed her so much. Luke tried to help take care of Matthew, but he could never make up for Mama being gone.

"What happened to her?"

"You don't want to hear—"

"I do. If you don't mind telling the story."

Luke drew a breath. He'd never told anyone. Had kept the secret of his failure all these years. Perhaps it was time. "I was like any young boy. Mama and Papa were the strongest people in the world, and I was sure they could do anything. Mama especially never seemed to tire. Even when Matthew was born, Pa tried to make her rest, but she laughed at him."

He turned and stared up at the ceiling. "She had two more babies after Matt, but they were sickly. They didn't live long. I . . . remember Mama and Papa were sad. And then there was another baby on the way, and Papa told me I had to help take care of Mama. Papa was huntin' and trappin' then. Huntin' for our meat. Sellin' fur. He was gone a good bit of the time. He hated leavin' Mama with the baby comin', but he had to make a livin'."

"But surely there was someone. A midwife? A neighbor?"

"No one within miles of our cabin. And he thought he'd

be back before the baby came." Luke closed his eyes, trying not to remember the way Mama had cried. He'd felt less than useless. "I tried to help her."

"Oh, dear God, Luke. You were alone with her when she died?"

"Papa always said he was proud of me. I did the best I could for Mama and my baby sister."

"Damn him!" Isabelle sat up. "Damn him, Luke. You were eight years old. How could he do that to you?"

Luke pulled her to his chest. "Shh, shh. No sense cryin' over somethin' that happened twenty years ago."

She pulled away. "No!" She wrapped her arms around herself. "I won't forgive him that easily. I don't know how you can."

"How do you forgive your father," Luke said in a low rumble, "for leavin' you and your mama?"

"Forgive him?" Isabelle whispered. "My mother as good as threw him out. She . . . she slept with any man who would buy her the things Papa couldn't afford. No man could be expected to live with that."

"Isabelle." He touched her hair, her shoulder. He tried to pull her into his arms, but she would not allow it.

"No." She took a deep breath. "I'm glad you know the whole truth about me. You see why I'm certain I've chosen exactly the right profession."

"I think there's more of your father in you than your mother."

"If that were true, I wouldn't be your whore, would I?"

"You aren't my whore."

"Then what am I? You're the one who said there's no love between us. You give me food and shelter and take your pleasure from me. Doesn't that make me a whore?"

For two days he didn't touch her. Isabelle cooked and cleaned and fought tears all day, but when she fell into bed she wasn't exhausted enough to sleep. Mrs. Browning's poetry did not touch her as it once had. Words could not. All she wanted was Luke.

She knew he'd never love her as she did him. He'd made it clear that he wanted no wife, least of all her. Still, she had expected a few months of his tenderness. Memories she would carry west with her when she left. Now all she had were cold days and colder nights alone in a house where only the dog seemed to notice her. And even Pennigan preferred Luke's affections.

Eleven

The sound of quiet footfalls in the kitchen brought Isabelle alert. She burrowed deeper into the covers, hiding from the cold of the room outside the bed. Winter mornings meant rising in darkness—but surely it wasn't morning yet. She listened for a moment and didn't hear Luke starting a fire—always his first task of the day. She sighed and pulled the blankets over her head. She must have imagined the footsteps.

The door to her room creaked, and someone stumbled inside. Isabelle smiled. Luke was up—but not rising for the day. He'd decided to forgive her. To come rest beside her. It would make getting up even more difficult, but she'd be glad of his warmth. And if he was feeling restless—she'd be glad to have something more than heat from him. Her heart leaped with hope.

She heard a loud belch and the sound of first one then another boot hitting the floor. Seemed strange Luke would wear his boots to walk from his room to hers—perhaps he'd gone out back to relieve himself. She braced herself for the cold as he lifted the blankets and sat at the edge of the bed.

"What the hell?" a strange male voice boomed.

Isabelle screamed and jumped out of the bed, pulling the

quilt and blankets with her. She held them in front of her to cover herself.

In the darkness another man entered the room. Isabelle's heart was in her throat as she pressed up against the wall, wishing she could simply melt into it. Cursing herself for failing to grab the pistol from the bedside table. *Why the hell hadn't Pennigan barked to warn them of an intruder?*

The sound of fists pounding flesh preceded a crash as the men fell to the floor. Too late, Pennigan started barking. Isabelle couldn't see a darned thing. Gathering her wits, she sidled over to the table, feeling for the gun and the candle.

She prayed the second man was Luke. She had no doubt that he could handle the stranger, unless the man was armed. "Dear Lord, protect him," she whispered.

The thrashing stopped just as Isabelle managed to light the candle. Luke held the stranger flat on the floor, his forearm over the man's throat. "Matthew Warring—what the hell do you mean sneakin' in here in the middle of the night?"

Luke sat up, but he didn't get off his brother. Isabelle peered over Luke's shoulder at a man who seemed to be as long as Luke, but considerably leaner. It was hard to tell what his face looked like since it was bloodied and swollen at the moment. Isabelle set the candle down, intending to fetch some water to clean the cuts on Matt's face.

"Sneakin'?" Matt's voice boomed at precisely the same timber as Luke's. "I thought this was my room. I didn't know you'd taken to keepin' your mistress here."

Isabelle froze, heat rising to her face. Though she'd become exactly what Matthew suggested, the word hurt.

Luke dropped back down, pinning Matt's shoulders to the floor. "Don't you ever call Isabelle by such a name again, or I just may forget my obligations as your older brother."

"I keep tellin' you, Luke. You don't have to look out for me like I'm some young colt needs breakin'. I can take care of myself."

"Sure you can." Luke didn't sound convinced. He stood and held a hand down to his brother.

Matthew refused the assistance and pushed himself to his feet. He wobbled there until Luke guided him into a chair in the kitchen. Isabelle followed with the candle and used it to light another that sat on the center of the table. She placed her candle up on a shelf where it could cast more light into the room, then poured cold water into a basin while she gathered a few cloths.

"So—you decided to come home." Luke spit the words, anger mixed with frustration.

"I'm home." Matt belched.

"Drunk."

"It's bitter out there. I had a bit of whiskey to keep warm."

Isabelle set the basin on the table and dipped a cloth in it. She dabbed at a cut on the corner of Matt's lip. He winced and pulled back.

"I can take care of myself," he snapped and snatched the cloth out of Isabelle's hand.

"Some respect, Matthew. The lady is tryin' to help you."

Matt quirked a half smile. "Lady?"

Luke leaped to his feet, and Isabelle pressed her palm against his chest. "Leave him be, Luke. He isn't far wrong."

She regretted her words as soon as she spoke them, for Luke reacted with a look of pain as though he'd been punched. He collapsed back into his chair. "You go on to bed in my room, Isabelle. I want to talk with my brother."

She nodded and dropped the remaining cloths on the table before padding out of the room.

"So, who's the whore? And are you willin' to share?" Matt asked just as Isabelle closed the door behind her.

"I've asked you to keep a decent tongue, and I mean it. Isabelle is a lady."

"My dear brother." Matt held the wet cloth against his eye, though Luke thought it was likely too late to prevent swelling. "I believe you're smitten. How did this happen? Could it be that your heart is not made of stone after all?"

Luke shoved his hair out of his face. He only wished his heart were as strong as Matt implied. He wouldn't be suffering so right now. If his heart were truly made of stone, it would not have been so easy for Isabelle to melt it.

As things were, he didn't know how he'd manage without her in his life. Fact was, as much as he wanted her in his bed every night, as much as his arms seemed empty when she wasn't in them, he knew he could get along without her body.

What he couldn't imagine giving up was her smile. The sunshine she brought to his life. Her words—that constant commentary on everything that she saw or heard. The lilt of her voice when she paused to admire the sunset, the stars on a clear night, or the moon reflecting off the snow. It was the loss of her company, not her touch, that had made the last few days a living hell.

He hated to admit it to himself—he loved her. Smitten? That didn't express the half of it. He loved her with his whole, soft, vulnerable heart. But he had to let her go for her sake. And though his heart might break, at least he'd never have to endure the guilt and pain his father had suffered when his mother died.

"You don't have any idea what you're talkin' about, Matthew."

Matt laughed. "I may be drunk, but I know you better than you think, dear brother." He punched Luke's shoulder.

"The hell you do!"

Matt belched and chuckled again. "Afraid, are you?" Matt shook his head.

Luke glared at his brother. Leave it to Matt to come to exactly the wrong conclusion. Luke must let Isabelle go for her sake, not his. He had reminded himself a thousand times in the last several days. Isabelle deserved better than to die here in the wilderness. "Hell," he muttered. That was his fear, not hers. Luke wasn't worried about Isabelle as much as he was afraid of repeating his father's experience. "Why would I be afraid of happiness?"

Luke noticed his brother staring at him as if he'd sprouted an extra nose. An inkling of an idea began to form in Luke's head. Maybe it was the lateness of the hour. Maybe it was simply that love had made him foolish. He opened his mouth without thinking through all the consequences. "Brother, it is high time you took a turn watchin' this ranch. I have some business that needs tendin'."

"Me?" Matt muttered.

"Zeke Petersen is just a shout away if you need help."

"There is no way in hell that I'm stickin' around here to run this ranch for you. You had better get yourself another man. . . ."

The protests continued, but Luke wasn't listening. He had to talk to Isabelle.

"Isabelle, are you awake?"

She sat in the bed, leaning against the wall. "Of course I'm awake. How could I sleep after all that commotion? How are you?" She let out a long breath. "You've been so worried about your brother, but it wasn't the best of reunions, was it?"

"No." Luke sat on the edge of the bed. "Do you mind me bein' here. I mean . . . the standards of propriety and all."

She set her hand over his and squeezed. The flickering candlelight increased the natural glow of her bright green eyes. How he loved to look into those eyes.

"I'll be glad to share a bed with you again," she said. "Standards of propriety be damned!"

He smiled and reached out to caress her smooth cheek. She leaned against his palm. He'd forgotten just how soft she was.

"Does your brother need anything? Something to eat?"

"He'll be fine after a good long sleep. Don't worry about him. His homecomin's are generally . . . interestin'." He brought her hands up to his lips and kissed each one. "Havin' Matt here, well, it made me think about us. Our future."

"Future?" Her eyebrows furrowed into a pensive bunch.

He squeezed her hands. "I know it's askin' a lot of you. I've been thinkin'. about this for several days. Every time I considered it, I felt so selfish. But Matt just said somethin' that convinced me. We should be married."

"Is this your way of protecting me? My reputation?"

"Hell no." He smiled. "I mean. It isn't that. I want you . . . need you."

"Luke." She shook her head. "This is not what you bargained for when the Havermans foisted me upon you."

"Remind me to thank them, next time I see them." He held her gaze. "I reckon, I forgot to say—I love you?"

"You what?" She stared at him. "Luke . . . do you know what you're saying?"

He nodded. "Will you be my wife, so I can show you every day just how much I love you?"

"Oh, Luke." She put a hand to her head. "I can hardly believe it . . . I . . . Oh, my father . . ."

"I'll take you to find him. Matt will have to run the ranch for a season while we travel west and find your pa."

"You're serious? You would leave your ranch in Matt's hands?"

Luke nodded. "I will if you'll have me. I can't offer you wealth, or servants, or even the comforts—"

She threw her arms around him and pressed her cheek against his broad chest. "Oh, Luke. Don't you understand? I have all the wealth of the world right here. To have the man I love by my side. To share my bed, my life. To be father to my children. If you want." She pulled back and looked up at him. "Do you want children?"

He stopped to consider the question. "Yes, darlin'," he whispered.

She smiled and caressed his face. "Luke. I love you so much. I can't begin to tell you what I'm feeling right now. I should be able to write volumes, yet I don't seem to have a word for you."

He pulled back a few inches, lifted her chin with his thumb, and bent to look into her eyes. "Isabelle."

He pressed his lips to hers and spoke the finest love sonnet ever written, in actions far more eloquent than any words.

AUTHOR'S NOTE

Before Fannie Farmer's famous cookbook was published in 1896, cookbooks did not offer recipes as we know them today, with precise measurements, temperatures, and cooking times. Instead there were books for wives, which included recipes along with general advice on keeping a husband happy and the household running smoothly.

These books dispensed practical cooking and dietary suggestions as well as moral advice, though the emphasis was often on the latter with the cooking instructions lacking many important details. The authors seemed to take very seriously the notion that the hand that rocks the cradle rules the world.

A Lady's Guide to Home and Kitchen, quoted in this story, is an invention of this author based on many similar books that would have been available in the middle of the nineteenth century.

THE
RELUCTANT
HERO

Lorraine Heath

One

He rode in from the west, a tin star on his chest, a six-gun at his hip, and the promise of justice smoldering in his dark eyes.

—From *Tex Knight Tames the Town,*
by Andrea Jackson

Gallant, Texas
May, 1884

"I'm in desperate need of a hero."

With his thumb, Matthew Knight slowly tipped up the brim of his black Stetson and stared at the lady standing before him. Her unexpected pronouncement had awakened him from a pleasant afternoon nap. As a rule he didn't tolerate rudeness well, but he thought for her, he might make an exception.

He recognized her only because he'd seen her arrive on the noon stage. He'd been sitting right there, on the worn wooden bench outside his office, watching the comin's and goin's, thinking it was a fine day to be alive, praying nothing would happen to change his opinion on the matter.

The warmer weather was still a month or two away. He

hadn't even been bothered by the spiraling clouds of dust stirred along Main Street by all the wagons, horses, and people going about their business. Then the stagecoach had barreled in, causing the dust to thicken. The coach had rolled to a stop in front of the only hotel in town. Its owner, Lester Anderson, sadly lacking in imagination, had named the place Hotel, which to Matt's way of thinking was as bad as calling your horse "Horse" or your dog "Dog." With a poorly painted sign, Lester proudly boasted that his hotel had twenty-eight rooms—which seemed to be twenty-seven rooms too many. Matt had never noticed the vacancy sign come down, and he tended to notice everything. It was his job to notice.

The woman had caught his eye the second she'd stepped out of the stagecoach, like some princess arriving at her castle, expecting her minions to see to her bidding, her dark green outfit clearly belonging to a woman who'd never done without.

She had city gal written all over her, from her fancy, frilly hat to her polished black button-up shoes. Spoiled city gal, at that.

He'd watched as the driver and the guard who rode shotgun had struggled to get her trunk down from the roof of the stagecoach, then carried it into the hotel, while she'd been issuing directions he couldn't hear, moving her hands wildly toward them and back again as though she thought they were going to drop her precious petticoats and she wanted to be ready to catch the trunk if need be.

As soon as she'd disappeared into the hotel and the entertainment was over, Matt had tugged his hat down lower, settled back, and drifted off to sleep.

And now she was standing before him, disturbing his peace, as though she thought he'd be only too glad to jump up and do her bidding as well, do whatever she demanded of him. Be the hero that she claimed to need so desperately.

He didn't jump, but he did extend his manners, unfolding his body until he reached his full height. Some people found his height imposing, but she didn't seem to. Maybe because she was tall for a woman; the top of her head would tuck up neatly beneath his chin. The green of her hat with its bows, ribbons, and lace matched the green of the dress that matched the green of her eyes. Eyes the color of summer clover and hair the shade of golden wheat. He wondered what it would take to get her to unpin that hair for him, so he could fill his hands with it. She was slender, with soft, lily-white hands. No, not soft. Smooth. Except for that little bump on the side of the middle finger of her right hand, as though she'd spent a lifetime pressing something up against it until it had formed a callus to protect itself.

He swept his hat from his head in a gallant gesture he seldom used, because women were a rarity in these parts. "Ma'am, if you're looking for a hero, you're looking in the wrong place."

She angled her chin as though that small action was needed to ignite her courage. Her steadfast gaze dipped to his chest, and he refrained from taking a deep breath to make it appear broader, stronger. What did he care if she found him lacking?

"You're wearing the tin star, so you must be the sheriff," she said.

Now that he was fully awake, he found her voice to be the sort that a man carried with him into his dreams— where he *could* be a hero, even if only until the sun came up.

"You're observant," he responded dryly.

"Sheriff Matthew Knight?"

"Yes, ma'am," he acknowledged warily. It was one thing for her to be searching for the sheriff, another entirely if she was searching for him specifically. Others had searched for him, but been unable to find him, and as far as he knew none had been a woman.

"Then I'm definitely looking in the right place for a hero, Sheriff." She smiled triumphantly as though she'd accomplished an impossible goal. "Perhaps you've heard of me. Andrea Jackson?"

Something about the name teased at his memory. He didn't think he'd find her name on a wanted poster tacked on the wall behind his desk. Outlaws weren't usually in the habit of introducing themselves to the local law. She was too old to be his kid, too young to be his mother, too slender to be growing his kid in her belly. Although, considering how long he'd gone without the close company of a woman, any kid of his would be walking by now. Not that he truly thought he had any children wandering around. He took what precautions he could to prevent that from happening.

If he'd ever crossed paths with this lady, he would have remembered. Not that she had an unforgettable face, but her spirit intrigued him. Not many women stood before him as boldly as she did. The doc said it was Matt's perpetual scowl that kept them away. He tended to think it was his reputation for being a man without feelings, emotions, or dreams. It was easier to face dying if a man wasn't fond of anything he stood to lose.

He slowly shook his head. "Can't say as I have."

"I'm a writer of dime novels, sir. *Lone Star Lily and the Treacherous Cattle Drive?*"

Her voice ended on a rising ring of hope as though she expected her words to mean something significant to him. He simply shook his head. He wasn't known as a kind man, but he figured she'd prefer a shake over, "Never heard of it."

"*Lone Star Lily and the Notorious Outlaw?*"

"Sorry, ma'am."

Her face fell, and it occurred to him that maybe her features weren't as forgettable as he'd first surmised. She wasn't a great beauty, not by any means, but her expressive eyes were enough to hold a man's attention, her nose small enough not to get in the way when he kissed her, her lips plump enough to provide a comfortable cushion for a man's questing mouth.

"Do you read, Sheriff?" she asked pointedly.

And he wondered if she'd gauged the direction of his thoughts and was seeking to put him on another path.

"Yes, ma'am."

"Dime novels? Or are you one of these unenlightened people who consider them frivolous trash?"

Her green eyes held a spark of anger, hurt, resentment, and he thought if he answered wrong, judging by the determined set of her jaw, he might actually be on the losing end of a fight for the first time in his life. Now, wouldn't that be interesting?

"I read them on occasion," he admitted. Every night before he went to bed, but he didn't want to encourage her to linger by offering up a topic of conversation that might interest her. Not if she was searching for a hero.

"Which one is your favorite?"

"Ma'am, I just read the stories to pass the time."

"But you enjoy them?"

He nodded. "They're usually entertaining."

Her smile returned, a smile that could darn near blind a man, a smile that spoke of intimate pleasures. Oh, she was definitely not forgettable.

"I want you to be the hero of my next story," she announced.

His gut clenched; his mouth and throat were suddenly parched as though he'd reached down, grabbed a handful of dust from the street, and swallowed it. Breathing deeply, he shook his head. "Sorry, ma'am, but I'm not interested in having a story written about me."

"You're a little late in making that clear, Sheriff." She reached into her reticule and pulled out a scrap of newsprint. "An article appeared already in the *Fort Worth Daily Standard* when you delivered the Ace in the Hole Gang to the Tarrant County courthouse."

"Did that piece happen to mention that I delivered them in pine boxes?"

"Of course. It also explained that it was your daring actions that resulted in the trio needing those very same coffins."

"There was nothing daring about any of it. And I didn't take them to the courthouse so people could sing my praises. I took them so I could collect the reward money, and that's it. Money for corpses. Nothing heroic in that."

"Perhaps not in that particular aspect of your adventure—"

He lowered his head until his nose was even with hers, until he could see tiny black specks in the green of her eyes. "It wasn't an adventure. I killed three men."

"Who left death and destruction in their wake. Sam Jenkins had a five-hundred-dollar bounty on his head, his cohorts a hundred each. No one can argue that they didn't deserve to die. The newspaper wrote about your exploits and how you faced the gang alone—"

Matt grimaced. He didn't want to hear any of this. He didn't want his role in the events of that day to be scrutinized any more closely than they'd already been. "If my *exploits* have already been written about, then I don't see the reason for you to write anything further."

"On the contrary, Sheriff, I believe you'll make a wonderful hero for my next series of dime novels."

"Series?" His voice sounded as though the dust had taken up permanent residence in his throat.

"Yes. It seems that readers love to read about the same characters over and over. They become emotionally invested in them. Lone Star Lily did well for me, but not nearly as well as the stories written by others that featured heroes like Wild Bill Hickok, Buffalo Bill, Jesse James—"

"I don't consider Jesse James a hero."

"Well, neither do I, actually, but stories that involve him sell like wildfire. So I decided that I should begin a new series. Texas Knight." She gave him a gamine smile. "A little play on your name: Matthew Knight. When I'm finished you'll be as famous as all the others."

She looked at him as though she thought she was doing him some sort of tremendous favor, rather than presenting him with an opportunity to destroy his life.

"That's a right kind offer, ma'am, but I don't want to be famous."

"Look, Sheriff Knight—"

"No, ma'am, you look. I don't mean to be rude, but I've got no interest whatsoever in being the hero of any dime novel."

"Why not? Your name, your likeness will be on the cover. And I swear to you that I will do your reputation justice."

"Not if you're painting me to be a hero."

She released a short burst of air. "This is unbelievable. I can't fathom . . ." She looked out in the street as though she'd find an answer there.

He found himself gazing at her profile, the side of her long, slender throat. He imagined trailing his mouth over that sensitive skin. He'd really gone too long without a woman when he was showing any interest at all in one who could prove to be his downfall.

She whirled back around, and he felt his cheeks burning, as though she might have known what he was thinking.

"All right, Sheriff. I won't use your name or identify you in any way. But I would still like to use you as my inspiration. If I could spend some time with you—"

"No," he barked. "You're writing fiction. Make it all up. You don't need me."

"Unfortunately, Sheriff, I do need you, desperately."

Her eyes held a sadness, and he felt as though he'd just kicked a puppy.

"I don't see how I can be of any service," he muttered.

"Can we sit? I'm getting a crick in my neck looking up at you."

"Lady—"

"Andrea. Or Andi." She sat down as though he'd invited her to stay.

Obstinate, stubborn woman. He ought to just go into his office, leave her out here alone. But he found himself sitting, drawn by the appeal in her eyes. She was much closer to him sitting on the bench than she'd been standing on the boardwalk. He caught a whiff of her fragrance, a flowery scent that he couldn't place. He hadn't spent much of his life sniffing flowers and memorizing their scents, but he recognized sweetness when he smelled it.

She'd clasped her hands in her lap, and that knobby little knot on her finger was more visible. Now he knew how it had come to be. Pressing pencil to paper to write stories.

"Sheriff, do you know what a muse is?" she asked.

"No."

She sighed. "It comes from Greek mythology. Supposedly, there are nine sisters, known as muses, who preside over an artist's ability to paint or a writer's to write. A muse is intangible, but a writer is always aware of it lurking in the corners of the mind, helping us to create our stories." She shook her head. "I'm not explaining this well, and I'm not sure if anyone other than a writer can truly understand. But basically my muse has . . . deserted me. I try to write, and no words come forth, no story evolves. I see nothing except a yawning abyss of emptiness. For a writer it's terrifying, to have nothing inside me except a void where I once had stories."

Sighing, he settled his hat back on his head. "Then don't write."

She laughed, a sad sort of laugh. "I *have* to write, Sheriff. It's who I am."

She smiled at him, a dangerous thing. A man could start to think about doing whatever was necessary to keep that smile visible.

"And being paid for the writing doesn't hurt either," she continued. "You deserved the reward money for those outlaws, and you shouldn't feel guilty that you hauled them to the courthouse so you could get paid."

So they were back to the outlaws now, were they?

Something must have shown on his face, because she shook her head. "I'm just explaining my situation in a manner that would make sense to someone who isn't intimately familiar with the muse. If you can't understand the creative side, you can at least understand the practical side. I need the money . . . desperately. I thought if I came here and spent a few days observing you, experiencing the various duties that are involved in doing your job, then inspiration might strike; my muse would return. The words would once again flow. I know my request may sound frivolous, but trust me, Sheriff, I truly need your help. Be my hero. Please."

Damnation. He averted his gaze because he found himself staring too deeply into her eyes, mesmerized, actually considering the pleasant ramifications of having her near, until he almost forgot what the end result would be: the destruction of a life he'd worked so hard to build.

"I'm not a hero," he said quietly. "I don't want to be seen as one or portrayed as one."

"As I said, Sheriff, I can use another name for your character."

He dared to look back at her. "You're looking for a hero. I'm not him. You're gonna have to look elsewhere."

He heard hurried footsteps on the boardwalk. Turning his head, he saw a woman rushing toward him, two small boys in tow. He came to his feet.

Andrea Jackson did as well. "Is that trouble coming, do you think?" she asked, and he heard the excitement laced in her voice at the prospect of witnessing him doing his job.

He ignored her.

The woman who was approaching him smiled. Lanetta

Logan. Her husband had been a teller in the bank before the Ace in the Hole Gang arrived. Now he was merely a marker in the cemetery.

Matt removed his hat as Lanetta stopped in front of him, still clutching the hands of her sons. Matt had been the one who'd had the unenviable task of telling her that her husband was dead and she was now a widow.

"The stagecoach will be leaving soon," she said. "The boys and I are getting on it. I'm going to my parents' house for a while." She released her sons, who immediately wrapped their arms around her legs. One was three, the other five. Matt had never noticed before how much they resembled their father, even at their young ages. It was the eyes, he thought. The shape of the chin.

Lanetta handed him a piece of paper. "Here is where we'll be staying if you need me for anything. I don't know how long we'll be away, but I was hoping you'd keep an eye on the house, maybe tend the livestock. There's just the cow and a few chickens. I've boarded the horses."

"I'll be happy to do that for you. If you decide you don't want to come back, send me a letter. I'll load all your things onto a wagon and bring them to you."

Tears sprang to her eyes. "You've been so good to me. I can never repay you."

He thought he might double over from the pain of her words slamming into him. "You don't owe me anything, darlin'. You just take care of yourself and the boys."

"That'll be easier to do, since you gave me the reward money that you collected on those outlaws. You didn't have to do that, Matt. You earned that money."

He shook his head, his stomach knotting up. "We've already discussed this."

"I know. I just wish you'd kept some of it."

"I don't need it." Then because he didn't want to discuss the topic any longer, he hunkered down in front of her sons. "So your ma's taking you on a trip."

They bobbed their heads.

"You ever been on a stagecoach before?"

They shook their heads.

"It's an adventure. I want you to be real good for your ma now, ya hear?"

They bobbed their heads again.

He reached into his shirt pocket and withdrew a quarter. He pressed it into the pudgy hand of the older boy, closing the youngster's fingers around it. "Have your ma take you to the general store before you leave, and you use this two bits to get some sarsaparilla sticks to eat on the journey."

The boy smiled.

"Gotta share them with your brother," Matt said.

"I will." The boy looked down at his boots, then lifted his gaze back to Matt. "Pa ain't coming with us."

Matt's heart tightened. "I know, son."

"Wish he could come, but Ma says he had to go to heaven."

He thought the boys were too young to understand that their father was gone forever. It was something that he'd never forget.

"Yeah, he did," Matt said quietly. "He was a good man, your father."

The boy opened his hand, looked at the quarter, and closed his fist around it. He peered at Matt. "Can I get me some licorice instead?"

Matt ruffled the boy's hair. "Get yourself anything you and your brother want."

He was suddenly afraid the boy was going to say he wanted his father back and would use the two bits for that, but in the way of children, the boy had moved on to other things. "Sammy runned away."

Matt lifted his gaze to Lanetta.

"The dog," she said. "We haven't seen him since . . ."

He could see her struggling with the words. "Since that awful day?" he finished for her.

She nodded.

"If he shows up, I'll see he's taken care of."

"When something like this happens, I guess everybody feels like running away," she said.

That was a fact. Sometimes the hardest part was staying.

He unfolded his body and met her gaze. "You're not running away. There's just nothing here for you now."

Reaching out, she squeezed his hand and gave him a tremulous smile. "Thank you, Matt. Thank you for everything."

"You take care now, Lanetta."

She grabbed her boys' hands, spun on her heel, and rushed toward the stagecoach.

"Why, Sheriff, you're a liar."

Matt grimaced. He'd forgotten the dang dime novel writer was standing behind him.

"You didn't go to get that reward money for yourself. You went to get it for her. You *are* a hero."

He spun around, disgusted with the pleased expression on her face, as though she thought she had him all figured out.

"If I was a hero, her husband would still be alive."

With that he retreated into his office, slamming the door in his wake.

Two

The difference between right and wrong, good and evil, was branded on his soul.
   —From *Tex Knight in Pursuit of Justice,*
   by Andrea Jackson

Pacing within her hotel room, Andrea Jackson could barely contain her excitement.

She'd found him at long last. Her hero.

Reluctant though he may be, she had no doubt that he was the one. The one she'd been searching for. He stood tall and straight, and she could envision him sitting just as tall and straight in the saddle. His black pants hugged thighs that no doubt spent a good deal of time guiding a horse. He wore a black jacket over his white shirt, leaving his gun barely visible, but his hand had been at his side, curled slightly as though with the slightest provocation, it could grab the gun and have it accurately aimed, possibly even fired, before she had time to blink.

When he'd removed his hat, his midnight black hair had fallen across his brow, landing just above his incredibly deep brown eyes. Smoldering eyes. Without compunction or embarrassment, he seemed to assess every aspect of her being, as though cataloging her features to memory. She thought any desperado caught by his intimidating stare would surrender on the spot, without hesitation, without a gun being drawn or a bullet being fired.

The Ace in the Hole Gang being a notable exception.

She'd certainly thought twice about staying in front of him, and it had taken every ounce of courage she possessed not to back up and off the boardwalk, not to head for the street and the hotel when he'd tipped back his hat and pinned her with his hard glare.

But she'd reminded herself that he was the good guy. Not that the features of his face revealed even a hint of goodness.

His thick mustache had framed a mouth that didn't seem prone to smiling, but she had little doubt that it did its fair share of kissing. He had an animal magnetism that drew her in even as it held her at bay. Dark, feral, dangerous.

Her heart was only just now stopping its rapid thudding. He'd unsettled her more than she wanted to admit. She hadn't been this flustered since the founders of the bank where her father had served as president had knocked on her door to announce that following his death, they'd discovered he'd been swindling funds. They'd threatened to take her house, everything she owned, put her and her aging mother on the street, and smear her family's good name unless Andrea was willing to repay what he had taken. She was willing. Only too willing. She didn't want his epitaph to read, "Here lies a swindler." Besides, she'd known why he'd done it. He'd spent a fortune trying to find a cure for her mother's frail health—to no avail. Andrea had signed an agreement promising to pay back the bank with steady payments. She'd only have to write two hundred and fifty dime novels.

She thought that looming task was probably what had caused her muse to flee. But she could feel the tickling of its return.

She walked over to the table that the hotel owner, with the help of the stagecoach driver, had moved up to her room. When she'd arrived, the room had only a bed, dresser, washstand, and chair. She'd desperately needed a desk. So Lester Anderson had accommodated her request as much as he was able, taking the table from his office. Probably because, as far as she could tell, she was his only guest and source of business, and he would do whatever it took to keep her happy, to keep the coins coming in. She sometimes wondered if money, the root of all evil, was the root of all goodness as well.

Once the desk was placed in front of the window, she'd opened her trunk, and the men had lifted out her most recent and most precious purchase, heaved it across the room, and set it on the table for her.

Now, she slowly trailed her fingers over the Remington No. 2 typewriter. She'd bought it when her muse had deserted her, hoping it would help her find the stories. She'd heard that other dime novelists were producing a manuscript a week using this newfangled contraption. She'd quickly discovered, however, that the keys had to be pressed in order for them to deliver ink to the paper.

And in order for the keys to be pressed, her fingers had to know what story her mind was conjuring up. Unfortunately, her mind had become a perpetual blank slate. She'd once written purely for the joy of telling a story. Now she desperately needed the two hundred dollars that the next novel would bring her.

Her mother's nurse, Beth, had suggested Andrea turn to real-life heroes for inspiration, but only a few had yet to be claimed, and quite honestly, they didn't interest her. Then the article on Matthew Knight had appeared in the Fort Worth newspaper, and Andrea had begun to feel the first stirrings of excitement.

Now, it was full blown, and she felt her empty well of creativity beginning to fill, at long last, with possibilities.

She dragged the chair over and sat. She wound a piece of paper into the typewriter. She wove her fingers together and bent them backward, as was her usual ritual before writing—because of all the cramping in her hands she'd had in the past—took a deep breath . . .

And looked out the window, inviting the elusive words into her soul.

"Mind if I join you?"

Matt jerked his head up and stared at the woman who'd spoken. He'd been enjoying his beef at McGoldrick's Family Home Restaurant, alone, in silence. A shame he didn't have the authority to chase a citizen out of town for upsetting a man's digestion.

Suddenly remembering his manners, he came to his feet and announced, "I'm almost finished."

With a demure smile, she said, "Then you won't have to endure my company for long."

Before he could respond that he had no plans to endure it at all, she sat in the chair opposite him, not even waiting for him to pull it out for her or to issue an invite. He thought about walking out. That would make his position clear. But he still had a good portion of meat and potatoes remaining, and he was hungry. He took his seat and went to slicing off another bite of beef, ignoring her as much as he was able, considering he'd yet to find any aspect of her worthy of ignoring.

"You cleaned up real nice," she said.

He stilled, the beef halfway to his mouth. He hoped the sudden heat in his face wasn't visible. On his way over to McGoldrick's, he'd stopped off at the barbershop where a man could get a bath and a shave for two bits. And he hated to admit that he'd done it on the off chance that she *might* come here for supper, since it was the only business in town that served meals, other than the boardinghouse. He'd thought he might have the opportunity to discreetly observe her, but he'd never entertained the notion that she'd join him at his table.

He swore under his breath. He *had* entertained the notion. About a hundred times. He hadn't been able to stop thinking about her since he'd met her, and it aggravated him. He wanted to ignore her completely, but he didn't have the strength of will to carry through on his wants.

He lifted his gaze and felt as though he'd taken a solid punch to the gut, because her eyes clearly reflected interest as strong as his. Her cheeks turned a faint shade of red. Clearing her throat, she looked away, casually signaling to the serving girl, McGoldrick's eldest daughter, Lucy.

"I'll have what Mr. Knight is having," the woman said, her voice as soft as a spring rain shower. "Only I prefer that mine be cooked."

"Mine's cooked," he growled.

"Barely."

He felt the heat in his face intensify. He wasn't accustomed to people criticizing his habits. He could just imagine what she might write in her book. *He ate his meat raw, like the barbarian he was.*

"You could sit elsewhere," he said, before eating the slice of beef that had grown cold.

"I could," she said. "But then how would I get to know you?"

"Look, lady—"

"Andrea," she interrupted. "Or Andi, if you prefer."

"I *prefer* to be left in peace."

"Is that the reason you became a sheriff? So you could ensure the peace that you seem to prefer?"

Refusing to be baited into revealing anything, he sliced off another piece of meat and chewed on it. His reason for becoming a sheriff was his and his alone, none of her concern.

"Excuse me? Miz Jackson?"

Matt and the woman turned their attention to the man

standing beside the table, clutching a tattered dime novel to his chest. Matt recognized the skinny cowpoke who worked out at the Triple D ranch, several miles south of town.

"Yes," she said.

"I'm Joe Sears, ma'am. Are you the writer that come to tell the sheriff's story?" he asked eagerly.

"What?" Matt asked, swinging his gaze from Joe to Andrea—Andi—Satan's bride. "Where did he get that fool notion?"

Blushing, she gave him a smile that he thought might have appeased many a man, and he was having to work dang hard to make sure that it didn't curtail his anger.

"I might have mentioned my purpose in coming to Gallant to the hotel proprietor when I took a room."

Matt shook his head. Lester Anderson gossiped worse than any woman Matt knew. Town didn't even need a newspaper with Lester living here to announce any and every little thing that happened.

She lifted a delicate shoulder in apology. "I didn't realize he was the town gossip."

"Oh, he ain't," Joe said. "He just likes to talk about things that are going on."

"That are none of his business," Matt said. "That's what a gossip is."

"A gossip says mean things," Joe said, pouting as though Matt had hurt his feelings. "Lester ain't mean."

Before Matt could respond to that, Joe pulled out a chair and sat down, angling himself so he was facing the lady. Matt wondered if he ought to start selling tickets to seats at his table.

"I gotta tell you, Miz Jackson, that I love Lone Star Lily," Joe said with so much earnestness that Matt was taken aback, and it appeared that Miss Jackson was as well.

"Thank you, Mr. Sears," she said.

"She's got so much courage, it humbles me," Joe said.

Matt could see her cheeks turning pink. She looked at a loss for words. Not that he could blame her, although he imagined not finding words wasn't a good thing for a writer. On second thought, she was apparently accustomed to losing the words. It was the reason she was here.

"I was wondering"—Joe cleared his throat—"I was wondering if you'd be kind enough to tell me where she lives."

Unable to believe the question, Matt stared at the fella, then turned his attention to Miss Jackson to see how she was going to handle the ridiculous question.

She gave Joe a kind, tender smile, the smile of someone who was trying to break the harshness of bad news. Matt wished she'd been there the day that he'd had to tell Lanetta about her husband. A smile as comforting as hers would have come in handy.

Miss Jackson laid her hand over Joe's. "Mr. Sears—"

"You can call me Joe."

Her smile somehow grew more tender. "Joe, Lone Star Lily lives only in my imagination."

Joe's face took on an expression of disbelief. "But Buffalo Bill is real. And Jesse James." He pointed his thumb at Matt. "And the sheriff here. You're gonna write his story. The stories are about real people—"

"Not all of them, Joe," she said softly. "Some are based on the daring exploits of actual people, but most are characters that we simple create ourselves. We give them names and personalities and try very hard to make them seem real. But they aren't."

Joe looked at Matt, a sadness in his eyes that Matt had only ever seen at funerals.

"They're writing lies, Sheriff. Ain't that against the law?"

"It's not against the law to entertain people, Joe. And that's what Miss Jackson does. She writes stories to make you forget that your body's aching from hard work, or you're miserable, or you're sleeping alone. If she writes the story so you believe it's true, well, now that's a testament to her gift for storytelling."

"I thought Lone Star Lily was real," Joe said. "Like Buffalo Bill." He released a bitter laugh. "Don't I feel stupid."

"You shouldn't feel stupid, Joe," Miss Jackson said, drawing his attention back to her. "People are always asking me where she lives."

"You wouldn't be funning with me now, would you?"

"No."

"Would you mind putting your mark in my book?" Joe asked, pushing his book and a pencil toward Miss Jackson.

She smiled. "Certainly."

Matt watched as she turned back what remained of the cover and, gripping the pencil, wrote her name. She held the pencil so tightly it was no wonder she had a bump on that middle finger.

When she was finished, Joe took the book from her. "Thank you, ma'am." He stood and looked over at Matt. "Sorry to have disturbed you."

Matt watched him walk away. "That was a strange encounter." He shifted his gaze back to Miss Jackson. "And no one else ever asked you where Lone Star Lily lived."

She grimaced. "Was I not convincing? I didn't want to hurt his feelings."

"He believed you."

"Thank goodness."

Lucy arrived with Miss Jackson's platter of food. Matt couldn't call her Andrea or Andi, not even in his own mind. Either would invite an informality that might lead to other things . . . like piquing his curiosity about how a woman thought she should travel from Fort Worth to Gallant to meet a man she'd read about. Brazen. Bold. He wondered what other things she might be bold about.

Kissing, maybe. Maybe those plump red lips had no

qualms about traveling either, only the journey they would take would involve a man's flesh. Maybe they'd light upon his mouth—

"Sheriff?"

He jerked his gaze up from her lips to her eyes, wondering how long he'd been staring, watching her eat, watching her tongue slip out and capture any lingering juices. She didn't seem particularly offended. Rather she seemed amused.

"Your food is getting cold," she said, a twinkle in her eye as though she may have realized that she rattled him.

"It's long past the getting part," he muttered.

To his utter astonishment, she stood, picked up her plate, and moved to the chair beside him, the one Joe had vacated.

"I realize mine is probably not quite to your tastes, since it's actually cooked, but it is still warm," she said, while cutting her piece of beef in half. She set a portion on his plate.

"I can't take your food," he said.

"Don't be silly. I could never eat this much."

Silly? Matthew Knight had been called a lot of things in his life, many of the names not repeatable in the presence of a lady. But silly?

That was a word with the potential for disaster.

"I hope you've got no plans to describe me as silly in your book," he said, glaring at her.

She gave him a bright smile. "So you've decided to assist me in writing your story?"

"No, but it sounds like you don't give a care what I want. You're gonna write what you're gonna write."

"Now, Sheriff, that's not entirely true. I would like to portray you as accurately as possible, but if you won't spend time with me so I can determine your true character . . ."

He narrowed his gaze. "How many desperadoes would ride through this town if you wrote that the sheriff was *silly?*"

"You're assuming that desperadoes read—"

206 / Lorraine Heath

"I'm serious," he said, cutting her off.

"I can see that. I won't identify you; I won't identify the town. And I promise the word 'silly' will appear nowhere in the book."

"Since you've agreed not to do any of this identifying, you ought to do just fine making things up."

"I explained to you why I can't. And even though I write fiction, I want it to be as realistic and accurate as possible. All I need is one day. Just following in your footsteps. If you won't give me that, then I'll interview the townsfolk. I'm sure Joe could share a lot of interesting stories about your adventures with me."

"Lord have mercy," he muttered, shuddering at the thought of her basing a story about his life on the ramblings of a cowboy who was a couple of bullets shy of having a loaded six-gun.

"As a matter of fact, it might be better if I went to people who weren't quite as close to the truth. It would give me a more objective—"

"Wait." He rubbed his brow. "You don't have to get your information from a man who might not be living in the real world. I'll give you a day."

"Thank—"

He held up a finger, silencing her with it and his glare. "One day. That's it. And I need your promise that you won't ask the people of this town any questions about me."

"Have secrets, Sheriff?"

None that the people of this town knew about, but if there was one thing these good people excelled in, it was exaggerating the truth. They'd have him killing a dozen men with a single bullet.

"Those are my terms. If you want time with me, you limit asking your questions to me, and you only get one day to do it."

"That's going to give me a rather biased view."

"What difference does it make? You write fiction, not fact."

"All right. We have a deal," she said resolutely.

"Good." He stood. "Be at my office when the sun comes up. That's when my day begins. If you're late, you lose the chance to follow me around."

Her eyes grew big and round, her lips parting slightly. Like a woman on the verge of having pleasure roll through her.

"You mean when it comes up overhead, like at noon?"

"I mean when the sun first starts to push back the night."

"Dawn?" she asked, clearly horrified.

"Yes, ma'am. Before the rooster crows or you're too late, and you've lost your opportunity."

He walked out of the restaurant, feeling triumphant. He wouldn't see her tomorrow unless it was seeing her climb into a stagecoach at noon.

Three

He was a man to be reckoned with, and she was just the one to do the reckoning.
— From *Tex Knight Meets His Match,*
by Andrea Jackson

Before going to bed the night before, Andrea had considered searching out every rooster and wringing its neck. Then there would be no crowing roosters, and she wouldn't have the sheriff's unreasonable deadline to meet. But since eliminating the sun was a bigger problem, she'd left the roosters alone. She wasn't accustomed to starting her day at the crack of dawn, since she usually favored working by lamplight late into the night. It was when she did what she considered her best writing.

Last night had been no exception. With a kerosene lamp to provide the light in her room, she'd alternately hit the keys on her typewriter and stared out the window at a town encased by shadows. Her hero was beginning to take shape. And he strongly resembled the sheriff. Even if the man didn't want a book written about him, she could still write it. Change his name, the color of his eyes, the strong shape of his jaw. Remove the mustache. Although she couldn't quite envision him without it. She thought removing it from his face might be like removing the leaves from the trees. In winter they always looked to her as though something else was needed. She thought he might appear the same.

No, she would describe her hero so he *was* Matthew Knight in her mind. Her description of him would ensure that she would remember him after she left. Although she thought it unlikely that she'd ever forget him . . . or the manner in which he'd looked at her lips as though he were contemplating devouring them with more enthusiasm than he had his meal. She was certain the feral intensity of his gaze had made her blush. She'd never had a man look at her with his thoughts so blatantly revealed.

Memories of the sheriff's gaze had been quite exhilarating. She'd been unable to sleep, because every time she closed her eyes, she saw the hunger. And so she'd written until, while looking out her window, she'd seen someone passing through the town, extinguishing the flames in the few street-lights. Only then had she realized that the sun would no doubt soon be peering over the horizon.

She'd forced herself away from the typewriter, and perhaps that was the most exhilarating feeling of all. It had been too long since she'd anticipated writing a story, too long since she'd greeted moments away from her work with impatience.

While she washed up, fixed her hair, and put on a fresh dress, she was surprised that she wasn't yawning and looking at her bed with undisguised longing. As much as she didn't want to be away from her typewriter, she wanted to be with the sheriff. Spending the day with him, observing him. What if he were involved in another gunfight? She'd be right there, able to witness it. He might arrest any number of people. Today she would gather fodder for her novel.

Tonight she would write with even more enthusiasm and direction.

Making certain that she had plenty of paper for writing

down her experiences throughout the day, she walked out of her room, locked the door, and took the stairs down to the lobby. Only an occasional lamp guided her way. Shadows lurked at the edges of all the rooms. A perfect setting for committing a crime. No doubt the reason that the sheriff began his day just as the sun was coming up.

She stepped onto the boardwalk. Based on the barely perceptible light in the distance, she was close to losing her opportunity. The blasted, uncooperative man would no doubt keep his promise and send her away if he saw the sun before she reached his door. Hurrying along the boardwalk, she was determined that wouldn't happen.

She didn't notice anyone stirring as she rushed across the wide dusty street to the brick building at the distant edge of town. The last building at the end of the boardwalk, it ensured that few townsfolk would have to be bothered by the outlaws who would be held within its walls.

She reached the sheriff's office. His windows were as dark as every other window in town. Shouldn't he already be at work? So why was there no light? Was he already out, seeing to business? Had he not waited on her?

Dang the man! He'd promised to let her spend the day with him. The sun was only just now starting to lighten the sky. She wasn't late. Disappointment and anger reeled through her. She kicked the door. She took three steps toward the hotel, before going back to kick the door again.

How dare he fill her with hope!

She kicked the door yet again and again and—

It swung open, and she found herself staring not so much at the gun directed her way, as she was at the bare chest of the man holding the weapon.

"Woman, what in tarnation are you doing?" he asked, his voice scratchy as though it hadn't yet been used today, his gaze boring into her.

"You told me to be here when the sun came up." She pointed east. "It's coming up. I thought your day began now."

Yawning, rubbing his chest with his free hand, he nodded. "It does. It is. Reckon you can wait out here—"

"I'm not waiting, Sheriff. It's an ungodly hour, and I dressed practically in the dark so I could observe your day. I'm observing." Without waiting for him to respond, she marched past him, into his office, resisting the urge to reach out and touch his chest as she went by, then stood there in the shadows wondering what to do next. Perhaps she should have waited outside, but she was here now, and retreat was not in her vocabulary.

"Don't you think it's a mite inappropriate for you to be here this time of day?" he asked in that same raspy voice.

She spun around. "You suggested it, Sheriff. It's your office—"

"And where I live."

Ah. That explained the absence of light, shirt, and . . . boots, now that the sun was easing into the room, giving her a clearer look at him. "Just leave the door open."

He moved a little farther inside. "Thought you wanted a true accounting of my day."

"I do."

"I don't leave my door open."

A resounding echo filled the building as he slammed the door shut.

Even in dawn's shadows, Matt could see those gorgeous green eyes of hers grow wide with alarm. Made him feel like a villain. And why not? He was suited to the role.

He strode over to his desk, struck a match, lit the lamp, and glanced back at her. He sure as hell hadn't expected her to show. Kicking on his door at dawn for God's sake. The woman was as tenacious as a starving dog that had latched on to a bone.

Moving around to the corner of his desk, he opened a drawer, then laid his gun inside. The way she was looking at him, he didn't want her near a weapon.

"Did you lie when you said your day began with the sun?" she asked haughtily, as if she had a right to be aggravated with him.

In a way, he guessed she did.

"No." But he usually didn't have such a horrendous night of tossing and turning, haunted by her fragrance and the mystery of what that enticing mouth of hers tasted like, what her skin would feel like beneath his fingers. "I'm just a little slow getting started this morning. Make yourself comfortable while I see to my morning *duties*."

He went to the stove in the corner, lit the wood he'd shoved into it last night, and set the coffeepot in place. He needed coffee bad. While it was heating, he walked to the small back room where he lived and lit the lamp that sat on a table beside his bed. Other than his horse, his spring bed was his most prized possession. He'd ordered it from the Montgomery Ward catalog for two dollars and seventy-five cents. Unfortunately, the damned freight charges to have the thing delivered had darn near sent him to the poor house.

He went over to the washstand and poured water from the ceramic pitcher into the ceramic bowl. He turned around, came up short at the sight of the woman in his doorway, then marched past her to the stove.

"Why don't you take a seat by my desk?" he suggested.

"Nothing interesting happening at your desk."

He wrapped a small towel around the handle on his coffeepot and took it back to his room. "Nothing interesting happening here as far as I can see either."

"What are you doing?" she asked.

"Heating up my shaving water." He poured a little of the hot water in and carried the pot back to the stove. He opened the lid and dumped in some coffee grounds. "Coffee'll be ready soon."

He returned to his room, stirred up his shaving lather, lifted the brush, looked in the mirror, and nearly yelped at

214 / Lorraine Heath

the sight of her unexpected reflection as she stood in*side* his room, peering over his shoulder. Slowly, he turned. "What are you doing?"

"Observing your day."

"I didn't watch you get ready."

"And I wouldn't be watching you if you hadn't started your morning by lollygagging."

"Don't push me, lady."

"Don't push you? You told me that I'd suffer consequences if I wasn't here early enough. So here I am. Now you can suffer the consequences for not being ready."

He heaved a sigh, reluctant to go back on his word. He had told her to be here or else. Well, she was here, so the *or else* fell to him now.

"It's unseemly for you to watch me," he said, conviction ringing in his voice.

"I've watched my father shave."

"Then you don't need to watch me."

He turned back around and began lathering his face. Dang fool woman stood right where she was. Paper and pencil suddenly visible in her hands. They must have been hidden within the folds of her skirt. Rolling his eyes, he picked up his straight razor, wondering if slitting his own throat might be the way to go this morning.

"How long have you been sheriff?" she asked.

He glared at her reflection in the mirror, before tipping up his chin and scraping the razor along his neck. "Long enough."

"Long enough for what?"

"To be good at what I do."

"Which is what, exactly?"

"Guess you'll know by the end of the day. How long are you planning on staying in town?"

"Long enough."

He ground his teeth together to keep himself from smiling. She looked so danged pleased with herself, throwing his words back at him. If she just didn't look at him as though he was a hero, her being here might not be so bothersome.

She'd gone back to scribbling. What could she be writing about? She wasn't asking questions. Whatever had possessed him last night to invite her to spend the day with him? He'd done it because he hadn't thought she'd show. She was a tenacious little thing.

"What are you writing?" he asked, as he finished scraping away his beard, reached for the towel, and wiped away the last of the soap.

"I'm just making notes about your sparse surroundings. Do you think all sheriffs live as you do?"

"Nah. Some have houses, wives, families."

She lifted her gaze. "So you don't have a wife?"

He shook his head. "Or a house. Or a family. And that suits me just fine." He took his shirt off the peg on the wall and shrugged into it. "You had breakfast?"

"That's a silly question. Where would I have breakfast this time of day when I'm staying in the hotel?"

"Give me a minute of privacy, and I'll fix you something."

Her gaze dropped to his shirttail, and he thought in the dim light that she was blushing again. Lord, she was sugar and vinegar, and both aspects intrigued him.

She spun on her heel and walked away. He tucked his shirt into his trousers, cursing his thoughtless tongue that had offered to fix her breakfast. He didn't want to give her any excuse to stay.

Hell of it was, he had to admit that he didn't want her to leave either.

Four

He was in the habit of getting up before the sun to thwart any man intent on doing harm.
—From *Tex Knight Saves the Day,*
by Andrea Jackson

Andrea had never started her day off with a warmed can of beans and black coffee so strong that even now she feared what it might be doing to her stomach. He'd apologized for not having sugar or milk to lessen its harshness. Or eggs. Or biscuit makings. Or flapjacks. Or syrup. Or jam. Or a second plate.

He'd been gentlemanly enough to give her the solitary plate, chipped on one side, after scooping some beans onto it. He spooned his breakfast straight from the can.

He was leaning back in his chair, his booted feet crossed on the corner of the desk, his spoon scraping the sides of the can. He placed what had to be the last of the contents into his mouth and closed his eyes as though he were in heaven.

"Now, that's the way to start the day," he murmured, opening his eyes and tossing the can into a nearby empty box. He reached for his cup and took a long, slow swallow of the bitter brew, not grimacing once.

She wondered what his stomach was made of. Iron maybe?

He released a contented sigh, placed the cup on his stomach, and wrapped his hands around it. After a few moments, he sighed, took another sip, then went back to doing nothing.

Andrea stood. "Where can I wash the plate?"

He peered over at her as though he'd forgotten she was there. "Just put it on the stove. I'll wipe it down later."

"Wipe it down," she muttered.

"Feel free to pour yourself more coffee," he offered.

When they were throwing snowballs in hell.

"Thank you, but I don't drink much in the morning." She set her plate on the stove and proceeded to walk around the outskirts of the room. The more interesting items—the wanted posters—were tacked to the wall behind his desk. She walked to the cabinet that housed the rifles—locked up and secure.

"Why do you need so many rifles?" she asked.

"If I ever had a need to deputize any of the menfolk, I'd want to be able to provide rifles to those who needed 'em."

She peered over at him and arched a brow. "Menfolk? Why not deputize some ladies?"

He scowled. "That doesn't even deserve an answer."

"I've heard they have a woman serving on the police force in Denver."

His scowl deepened. "They're just asking for trouble."

She scoffed. "You can't be serious. Women have worked just as hard as men in settling the West."

"Do you know how to use a gun?"

"No, but I'm sure I could learn if I set my mind to it."

He shook his head and went back to staring at the empty cell on the other side of the room.

"Do you know how to use a typewriter?" she asked.

He snapped his head around. "A what?"

"A typewriter. It's a machine that allows you to press a button and a letter appears on a piece of paper."

He just gave her that intimidating stare.

She sighed. "It's supposed to make it easier on those who do a good deal of writing."

"Stop them from getting that bump on their finger?"

Self-consciously she glanced down at her hands. She'd always been embarrassed that her fingers weren't quite straight and that she did indeed have a raised place on the finger where she'd been pressing a pencil since she was five years old and had first been taught the magic of creating letters.

"I brought it with me," she said to change the subject.

"Don't see how you could leave the bump behind."

She scowled. "The typewriter. It's in my room at the hotel if you have an interest in seeing it."

His eyes narrowed. "They have a name for ladies who invite men to their hotel room."

"I wasn't inviting you to my room. I was inviting you to see a typewriter."

He took another slow sip of coffee. "Is that the reason you looked so skittish yesterday when they were hauling your trunk into the hotel?"

"I wasn't skittish, but yes, I did have concerns. The machine was an investment, and I'm not in a position to replace it if it's mishandled."

"Don't see why you need a machine. I can accomplish the same thing by pressing pencil to paper."

"But is your handwriting legible? Is every letter perfect?"

"I can read it. That's all that matters."

She crossed the room back to his desk. "Well, unfortunately, in my profession, others have to be able to read what I write. Although my point was that I'm sure you could learn to use a typewriter and I could learn to use a gun."

"Well, teaching you isn't part of my job."

"Why are you so ornery?" she asked, sitting back down in her chair.

"You're disturbing my peace."

There it was again. That word "peace." He was cantankerous. And had gone back to staring at the cell.

She sighed. "When do you actually start to work, Sheriff?"

"I'm at work now."

"You're in your office, but I don't see you working."

"I'm waiting."

"For what?"

"For trouble to come calling."

She glanced around. "Surely, you must do something more than sit there all day . . . waiting."

He slowly shook his head. "No, ma'am."

"How will you know when trouble arrives?"

"I'll know." He took another leisurely sip of that disgusting coffee. He turned his head to the side so he could see her. "Reckon there's really no reason for you to stay."

"On the contrary. I see no reason to leave."

She noticed that a muscle in his jaw twitched.

"My day would make for mighty boring reading, Miss Jackson."

She scooted up to the edge of her chair so she could rest her elbows on the desk. "It might, Sheriff, if I didn't have such a vivid imagination. Besides, my job is to embellish the mundane."

He narrowed his eyes, and that muscle twitched again. "I don't see that there's really anything for you to write about."

Oh, but there was. Simply because he didn't want her here was reason enough to be here. It was her stubborn nature that had allowed her to get published to begin with. Several of her works had been rejected by the publisher before she'd found a story that an editor had thought was worth telling.

She had a feeling that Matthew Knight had a story worth telling. Why else would he so desperately guard it?

"Where are you from, Sheriff?"

"Around."

"Is that a town in Texas? I'm not familiar with it. Whereabouts is it located?"

She wasn't certain, but she thought a corner of his mouth

quirked up. Rather than answer her, he took another sip of his coffee.

Her stomach growled like a dog that had spied the sheriff's undercooked tossed-out meat. She pressed her hand below her ribs, embarrassed by the noise.

"I have another can of beans," he offered.

"Thank you, but I'm not really hungry." If anything, she was feeling nauseous. She wondered if the only restaurant in town was open yet. She should probably go and have some decent breakfast, but she was certain that as soon as she left, the excitement would begin.

Settling back in her chair, she studied the posters on the wall. Men wanted for breaking the law. Rewards offered. Only a few had a likeness of the man printed on them. Most were descriptions only.

"Do you suppose outlaws take pride in the amount of their reward?"

"I doubt they take pride in anything."

"Why would a man steal?" she asked. "Why would he kill?"

The muscle in his jaw jerked, and she remembered that he had killed. Was he haunted by his actions? How could he not be?

"Do you know the time?" she asked, refraining from asking him how it had felt, how he had dealt with it. If he wouldn't tell her where he was from, he certainly wouldn't share with her the doubts that might plague him.

He stretched back and pulled a pocket watch out of his trousers watch pocket. "Twelve minutes after seven."

That was all? She'd thought it had to be at least ten. She got up, went to the window, and looked out on the town. She could see people moving about, sweeping the boardwalk, unloading wagons. "Shouldn't you be out walking around?" she asked.

"Better to stay put in one place so people can find me if they need me."

She spun around. "Don't you get bored?"

He tipped his head back so he could see her. "I tried to tell you. Nothin' exciting about my life."

She released another sigh and returned to her chair. She wasn't going to leave. "It would be a mite less boring if you'd at least answer my questions with some enthusiasm."

"You wanted to follow my footsteps. I granted permission. I never said I'd answer questions."

"It's a little difficult to follow your footsteps when your boots seem to be permanently at rest."

She was certain this time. His mustache moved; a corner of his mouth did shift up.

"This is my life, lady," he said flatly.

"Fine. I can do this the hard way." She picked up her paper and pencil. He said that he'd been around long enough, and she thought she might be able to gauge his age, but based on the deep lines fanning out from the visible corner of his eye, she didn't think he was referring to years with his cryptic statement. The lines were many and deep. No doubt a result of squinting at the sun or carrying heavy burdens. Ruggedly handsome, he wasn't at all hard on the eyes. Before he'd shaved this morning, she'd noted how thick his morning beard was. Probably one of the reasons he grew the mustache. He probably looked like a desperado by the end of the day. She wondered if that mustache would tickle if he kissed her. She supposed she could ask for research purposes. In her stories she always had a damsel in distress, and her hero always received a kiss at the end.

But she'd never had a hero with a mustache.

Her stomach rumbled again.

"Why don't you mosey over to McGoldrick's?" he suggested. "I'll go over and get you if there's any excitement."

She presented what she hoped was her sweetest smile. "Why would I even contemplate exchanging the pleasure of your company for food?"

The door opened, and he grimaced. His booted feet hit

the floor with a resounding thud as he sat up. "Not now, Doc," he fairly growled.

"What do you mean not now?" asked the man standing in the doorway. He was dressed in a white shirt with a black jacket. Over his arm dangled a wicker basket. "I have no plans to eat a cold breakfast."

Breakfast?

She could smell enticing aromas wafting out of the basket as the man walked farther into the room.

"I didn't know we'd have such lovely company for our morning ritual," he said, setting the basket on the table.

"Morning ritual?" she asked, coming to her feet.

He removed his hat. His blond hair was shaggy, his light blue eyes twinkling. She thought he was close to the age of the sheriff, whatever age that might be.

"Why, yes, ma'am. The owner of the boardinghouse where I live cooks a hearty breakfast for the sheriff and me each morning. Since my cantankerous friend isn't one to make introductions, allow me. I'm John Martin, and I'm assuming that you're the writer everyone is whispering about this morning."

She didn't know whether to be glad that food had arrived or to throw something at Matthew Knight for feeding her horrid beans when he'd known food was coming. Warring against her instincts, she fought back her anger and decided to be pleasant. This man could no doubt provide her with information.

"I find it difficult to believe the sheriff has a friend," she said sweetly.

"Not cooperating, is he?" He glanced at her cup on the desk. "Don't tell me he gave you his awful coffee to drink."

"Nothing wrong with my coffee," Knight said.

John Martin shuddered. "As long as you were born without the ability to taste. Matt, why don't you start setting the food out, while I fix us something proper to drink?"

He walked over to the stove, and Andrea leaned over the

desk until her nose was almost touching the sheriff's. While he'd offered beans, he'd known something better was coming.

"Don't think I haven't figured out your game. You promised me today, and I'm not about to walk out without a fight."

"'Sadly, his aim failed to equal his courage.' One of your more memorable lines," John told Andrea. "Although I was saddened that the poor man was done in by the outlaws."

Matt sat behind his desk, watching with disgust as John poured on the charm and Andrea—Andi—lapped it up.

"I can't believe that you'd remember the exact words," she said. "I'm not sure the sheriff has even read one of my stories."

"I'm not even sure he can read," John said with a chuckle.

"I can read," Matt muttered.

She looked at him now, a pinch of strawberry jam nestled at the corner of her mouth. His gut clenched with the thought of what it might be like to taste the jam and her mouth at the same time, just dip his tongue into that corner and . . .

"Have you ever read any of my novels?" she asked.

He wanted to lie, wanted her sparkling gaze directed at him instead of John, but his friend was a more likely hero. After all, he saved lives; he didn't take them. "Not that I can recall."

He dunked the biscuit into the bowl of gravy that Mrs. Winters had sent over with John. She prepared them a breakfast every morning, and John always brought it over. Matt felt a bit spiteful for having hoped that sitting here doing nothing, offering his poor excuse for a breakfast, would have sent Andrea on her way.

And when had he started to think of her as Andrea? Maybe as she'd watched him shave, the intimacy of it making him long for a woman who was there every morning as he prepared for the day. But a woman in his life would no doubt mean him being peppered with more questions than a writer might ask him.

Not that Andrea had asked him a lot of questions, but she'd sure taken a lot of danged notes.

". . . sheriff going on three years now," John said.

Matt snapped to attention, realizing he'd been focused on Andrea rather than the conversation going on around him.

"That's not long considering the reputation he's acquired," she said. "Do you know where he lived before—"

"It's not important," Matt snapped. He glared at John. "Think you could content yourself with telling her your history instead of mine?"

"I was telling her my history. She asked how long I'd known you. Although I'll admit that my history isn't nearly as interesting." He leaned toward Andrea. "Quite honestly, I don't know his history. People come to Gallant to start over. Most leave their past at the edge of town."

"Did you?" she asked quietly.

John shifted his gaze over to Matt, who took satisfaction in the look of discomfort on the man's face. "Not so interesting when the questions are about your past, is it?"

John cleared his throat. "No, reckon it's not." He clapped his hands together. "So, are you going to give Andrea a tour of a day in the life of a lawman?"

Matt set his empty plate into the wicker basket, leaned back in his chair, and folded his hands behind his head. "This is it. What I do all day."

"I didn't fall for it before," she said. "I'm not going to fall for it now."

And dang it, if she didn't look somewhat hurt.

"Dadgum it," he growled. He stood, his chair making an awful scraping sound as it scooted back.

She jerked, her eyes growing wide.

"Let's go," he said, heading for the door.

"Where are we going?" she asked.

"To do my job." He snatched his hat off the peg on the wall and looked back in time to see John grinning with satisfaction. The man probably thought he'd accomplished something. Lord only knew what.

"Reckon you'll clean up the mess you made while you were here," Matt said to John.

"As much as I'm able. I'm assuming you won't be available for our weekly chess game this evening."

"We'll be back before sundown."

"Still, I'll assume you'll be otherwise occupied, answering Andrea's questions."

"I'm not answering anything. I only promised she could follow in my footsteps, so following is all she's going to do." He glared at her, and she backed up a step before squaring her shoulders and taking a defiant step forward. "And you're not going to ask anyone any questions about me." He arched a brow. "Ain't that right?"

"I'll only observe, Sheriff. You won't even know I'm there."

Was she joshing? The only way he wouldn't know she was there was if he was dead and long buried.

Five

Without hurry, he strode down the street as though
he owned the very dust that his boot heels kicked up.
—From *Tex Knight and the Devil's Rope,*
by Andrea Jackson

Andrea couldn't believe that he was actually allowing her to accompany him. Considering the various ways he'd attempted to discourage her this morning, she wasn't quite sure if she should trust him now.

She wanted to ask where they were going and what they were going to do when they got there, but based on his unwillingness to share even the most mundane of facts with her, she decided peppering him with questions would only increase the tension radiating from him and possibly result in their returning to his office before she'd had an opportunity to observe anything of interest.

So she walked beside him . . . and periodically came to a stop so he could catch up. How could a man with such long legs walk so dang slow? It was obvious that he was a stranger to impatience, and she supposed that was a good thing in a lawman.

"In here," he said when they reached the general store.

"What are we going to do here?" she asked.

His mustache twitched. "You're the most question-asking person I've ever met."

"If you'd willingly carry on a conversation, I wouldn't have to prod you with questions."

"I need some supplies."

She sighed. Supplies. Specific was obviously not in the man's vocabulary.

He held the door open, and she preceded him inside. It was typical of a general store, offering almost everything a person could think of.

"Morning, Matt," the man behind the counter said.

"Tom. This here's Miss Jackson—"

"The writer?" Tom asked, perking up. He came out from around the corner, wiping his hands on the white apron that circled his substantial girth. "I heard you were in town, and gonna write a story featuring the sheriff here. I'll tell you there ain't a finer man in all of—"

"Tom?" the sheriff barked.

Tom peered over at him. "Yes, sir?"

"She doesn't need to hear all that. We're just here for a lock."

"Back of the store, bottom shelf." Tom turned back to her. "Ma'am, it is an honor and a privilege to have you in my store. I have one of your books over here, just waiting to be bought. Would you like to see it?"

"I'm sure she's seen her books," the sheriff said.

She scowled at him. "It's always exciting to actually see one in a store." She turned back to Tom. "I'd love for you to show it to me."

"Right this way."

She glanced back at the sheriff. "Holler at me when you've got all your *supplies.*"

She fell into step beside Tom. "Do you sell a good many dime novels?"

"Yes, ma'am, especially when the cattle drives come

through." He stopped at a shelf on the far side of the counter and puffed out his chest. "Right there, ma'am."

She had a sneaking suspicion that he'd moved her book to the top of the stack as soon as he'd heard she was in town on the off chance that she might just happen to come through.

"Do you know yet what you're going to write about Matt? What kind of story it'll be?"

She shook her head. "Right now the idea is just a seed." Glancing back over her shoulder, she couldn't see the sheriff. She'd promised him only that she wouldn't ask the townsfolk questions about him. She turned back to Tom. "I'm trying to gather some information about the day the bank robbers came through."

Tom shook his head like a buffalo on the range. "It was a sad day in this town. They killed Josh Logan before anyone knew what was going on. They came out of the bank shooting, guess they figured to scare people off, so they could hightail it out of town. But Matt didn't hesitate. He just rushed toward 'em, rifle ablazing. Don't know how he managed to be so accurate considering he was sick as a dog that day."

"Sick?"

"Yes, ma'am. Saw him out behind the bank some time later, shaking like he had a terrible fever, puking up his insides, something violent. I fetched the doc right away. He couldn't do nothing for the dead men, thought he needed to see—"

"We had a bargain."

Rage slithered through the voice that had spoken, nearly stopping Andrea's heart. Considering that Tom had gone as white as a sheet and was pressing his fist against his chest, she had a feeling that he felt the same way.

She twirled around, then stepped back. The sheriff's anger was palpable, and it was terrifying to be on the receiving end of that heated glare.

"I gave you my word that I wouldn't ask any questions about you, and I didn't. I asked about the bank robbery," she said, amazed that her voice came out as calmly as it did.

"You're splitting hairs."

"I need information that you're not willing to give."

"You're morbid. Feeding on the misfortune of others. There's no story here. I'm no hero. I told you that. Three men rode into town intent on taking money from the bank. Four men died. End of story. No happy ending." He jerked his thumb over his shoulder. "Tom, tally up my expenses so I can get about my business."

"Matt, I don't think she meant any harm," Tom said.

"Doesn't matter if she meant harm or not. I've got a job to do, and I need those supplies to do it, so if you'll please add what I owe you to my account, I'd be much obliged."

"Yes, sir."

Tom bustled over to get behind the counter. Matt's gaze still had Andrea pinned to the spot.

She swallowed hard. "I'm sorry. I might have been a bit deceptive."

"A bit?"

"I'm not going to write anything that will embarrass you."

"Lady, you don't know me well enough to know what will embarrass me."

"Exactly!" she shouted. "Exactly the reason why I want to get to know you. But you keep giving me these cryptic answers, thinking that you're going to discourage me, and all you're going to do is make me dig in deeper."

She took a step toward him, raised up on her toes until she could gaze directly into his eyes. She saw his startlement, and it emboldened her.

"Sheriff, *you* don't know *me* well enough to know how to effectively get rid of me. But if you're a man who thrives on failure, keep doing what you're doing. I guarantee you'll fail."

Marching past him, she glanced over at Tom, whose jaw looked to have come unhinged. "Thank you, Tom."

"Yes, ma'am."

Then she went on out the door with her head held high and her tears held back. In the past few months she'd become a master at holding back those tears.

When Matt walked out of the general store, Andrea was still standing on the boardwalk, her arms crossed over her chest, hurt, anger and stubbornness clearly mirrored in her eyes. If anything was going to send her running, it would have been the exchange between them that had taken place inside the store. Strange thing was, seeing her anger had defused his. If anything, it intrigued him.

He thought events in his life had made him tough. Something in her life had made her even tougher.

He held up the sack. "I'm going over to Josh Logan's house. Most folks around here don't have locks on their doors, and I figured since Mrs. Logan was going to be gone a spell, I ought to make sure that her house is secure from intruders. So I bought some locks and nails. I figure I'll find a hammer there. I'm going to walk down this boardwalk until it ends. Then I'm going to take a right and head up the road until I get to her house. Probably about a good ten-minute trek. Then I'll secure the house and walk back to my office where I have some papers that I need to look at."

As far as peace offerings went, it wasn't much, but it was all he had.

Her mouth twitched, and a sparkle returned to her green, green eyes, as though she recognized that apologies were foreign to him. He had a powerful urge to draw her into his arms and latch his mouth onto hers until the sun set and the moon rose.

"Thank you, Sheriff," she said.

"I won't put you off any longer. I'll answer your questions, if you give me your word that you won't ask anyone about me or that day."

She tilted her head slightly, studying him as though she thought she could decipher exactly why he was so set on her not bothering the folks. She finally relented. "I give you my word."

"And no splitting hairs, trying to ask a question because I wasn't specific enough with the rules I was laying down."

She nodded. "No splitting hairs. And I owe you an apology—"

"Yeah, you do."

She angled her chin. "Are you going to let me finish?"

"Do I have a choice?"

The corner of her luscious mouth tipped up higher. "I owe you an apology for attempting to get around my promise."

"All right," he said brusquely, so she wouldn't get the impression that she'd gained more advantage than he wanted, "now that we've delivered all our apologies, can we get moving?"

"Certainly, Sheriff. Down to the end of the boardwalk, then to the right. I'm more than happy to oblige."

They headed down the boardwalk, greeting people they passed, as if everything was normal, as if his stomach wasn't knotting up as he wondered what might happen if she ever wrote her story.

He didn't know many women who were as straightforward as she was, women who didn't back down. He didn't particularly like that he found himself admiring her. Respect, trust, caring . . . they were pitfalls that could lead a man into confessing his sins.

Six

He was as quick to deliver justice to a bad man as he was to deliver comfort to a child or dog.
—From *Tex Knight Takes in a Stray,*
by Andrea Jackson

The Logans' house was quaint, two stories, recently painted robin's egg blue with a wide white porch that wrapped around the sides. Honeysuckle grew in abundance next to the porch. The scent wafted on the breeze, made Andrea feel incredibly welcome.

She touched one of two large wooden rockers on the porch, watched it move to and fro with her movements. Beside each one was a smaller rocker, and she imagined a husband and wife watching the sun go down while their sons sat beside them.

Matt had gone through the house, made sure that everything was as it should be, and was now hammering away at the doorjamb. Andrea sat in the rocker and gazed out on the yard. This house wasn't so different from the one in which she'd grown up. A swing hung from an ancient oak tree. She could hear the lingering echo of a child's laughter. She could sense the silent sobs of a grieving widow.

When Matt finished with his task, he sat down on the porch step, his back against the beam supporting the eaves, angled so he could see her, one foot on the step, his other leg stretched straight, his foot on the ground. He patted his thigh. "Come here, Sammy."

She watched as a large short-haired black dog ambled forward, then stopped. It seemed the Logans' prodigal dog had returned.

"Come here, boy," the sheriff said. "Come here. You remember me. I'm not going to hurt you."

"What if he bites?" Andrea asked.

"Now, why would he bite the hand that fed him last night?" he asked.

"You found him last night?" she asked incredulously.

"Yep."

"Where was he?"

"Stretched out across Josh Logan's grave."

Matt's voice was somber, and she thought he might be hurting as much for the dog's loss as he was for Mrs. Logan and her boys.

"Have you ever had a dog?" she asked.

"I was never in one place long enough to take on the responsibility until I moved here three years ago."

Good Lord, she almost fell out of the chair. In that one sentence he'd given her more information than he had from the moment she met him. She wanted to do like the dog, who eased forward until he sat beside Matt and laid his head on Matt's thigh.

"That's a good boy," Matt crooned, petting the dog. "Miss him, don't you, fella?"

The dog released a small whine as though he understood exactly what Matt had said.

Matt peered over at Andrea. "Sammy used to follow Josh to the bank." He shrugged. "I didn't know his name, but I'd see him every morning." She thought he actually blushed, looked uncomfortable. He cleared his throat. "Normally I begin my day by walking through the town, right after the sun comes up, before Doc brings breakfast over."

She glared at him. "Why, you deceitful man! You thought if you didn't do anything that I'd grow bored and leave."

"I was hoping."

She couldn't seem to stop herself from admiring his honesty, nor could she truly blame him for his earlier actions when he was so set against giving her any time at all. She wanted to gain his trust, wanted him to realize that no harm would come from a few embellished stories. She wanted to prolong a conversation that wasn't marred by his dark scowl.

"So finish telling me about the dog," she prodded.

"Well, once Josh went inside the bank, Sammy would trot back over here and keep watch over the family. Then at five o'clock when the bank closed, he was waiting outside the bank to walk back home with Josh. Dangdest thing I ever saw. A dog that could tell time."

She smiled. "He obviously loved his master."

"Yep. Lot of people loved Josh Logan. He was a good man. Even from the short time I knew him, I could tell he was one of the best."

She didn't know what else she could add to his statement, and questioning him seemed inappropriate at the moment, considering the somber mood and the nature of the conversation. They sat in companionable silence, listening to birds, enjoying the slight breeze. She thought this was a pretty spot, a nice place to have a family.

"I always liked this place," he said quietly.

"Perhaps you can purchase it if Mrs. Logan doesn't come back. It would give you a nice place to bring a wife, raise a family."

He shook his head. "A wife and family aren't for me."

"Why not? You're relatively easy on the eyes."

He glowered at her.

"A tad moody, though," she added. "I suppose you might have difficulty holding on to a woman at that. Did you grow up in a house like this?"

He released a harsh chuckle, then shook his head. "No."

This time the silence following his pronouncement wasn't quite as comfortable.

"Are you going to tell me where you grew up?"

He studied her, his eyes narrowed, as though he was contemplating whether or not he should answer her question, when in truth he had no choice unless he was willing to go back on his word. She thought she should remind him that he'd promised to be forthright. Instead, she said, "I did."

She leaned back against the rocker. "At the edge of Fort Worth . . . Well, it was the edge when my father bought the place, but eventually there were a lot more houses and a lot more people. I still live there. With my mother."

"She must be beside herself with worry with you traipsing all the way to Gallant alone . . . in search of a hero."

She felt the tears sting her eyes, but held his gaze. "I didn't tell her that I was coming in search of a hero. I told her that I had to visit with my publisher. Her health isn't good, and I didn't want her worrying."

"What's wrong with her?"

She thought she detected genuine concern in his voice.

"The doctors don't know. My father spent a good deal of money trying to find out." She didn't know why she felt the need to unburden herself, especially to this man, but she did. Maybe it was because in spite of the harshness with which he always addressed her, his eyes held compassion. Perhaps it was his poor attempt at an apology outside the general store that had won her over. Or the fact that he was a man who fed and comforted a dog that held no loyalty to him.

She released a sigh. "My father died recently. Shortly afterward, it was discovered that he'd taken money from the bank to which he had no right."

"You mean, he was an outlaw?"

"I believe in his case that the correct term is embezzler. The founders promised not to say anything if I would pay the money back. My fiancé—"

"You're getting married?"

He sounded horrified, and she wondered if it was because of the times when she'd spotted him staring at her with undisguised longing. She slowly shook her head.

"No." She felt the dang tears sting her eyes. "I lived in a fancy house and had pretty clothes and nice things, but when he realized that I came with a financial burden that would take me most of my life to pay back. . . . I suspect that it wasn't me that he loved, but rather everything I represented: wealth and prestige. We were quite the social family. It will kill my mother if she finds out what my father did."

"It doesn't bother you?"

"Oh, God, of course it does. I'm furious with him. I don't know what he was thinking."

"Maybe he was thinking he'd do anything to save the woman he loved."

She stared at him. "You don't strike me as a man who would put a lot of stock in love."

"I don't." He shrugged. "So that's the reason you need to write a whole bunch of books."

She nodded, looked away, looked back at him. "Yeah."

She got up and moved to the porch steps, sitting down beside him. He had so much strength, seemed so confident of his path. She wanted to simply lean against him and absorb the power that radiated from him.

As though reading her need in her eyes, he leaned forward and trailed his fingers over her cheek. "You shouldn't have to pay for your father's sins."

"What he did was wrong. I won't excuse it. And I'll make it right."

"Not everything is that simple."

"He broke the law. That's unforgivable. Surely you understand that, being a lawman."

"I think sometimes a man loses his way."

"And you think that's what happened with my father?"

"Can't say for sure. I didn't know the man. Should you have left your mother alone?"

"Trying to guilt me into going home?"

He had the good graces to blush.

"I'm figuring you out, Sheriff."

"Don't be so sure. What about your mother? How will she manage?"

"I hired a nurse to take care of her. It gets expensive, and my only means of support is my writing, which brings us back to you."

His hand stilled; she was as grateful as she was disappointed. His touch was a distraction she could ill afford.

"Where is your mother?" she asked.

"Never knew her. And before you ask, I don't recall much about my father or my life when I was younger. Besides, my youth wouldn't make for interesting reading."

She scoffed. "I'm not sure you're exactly an unbiased judge of what's interesting and what's not."

"I'm a fair judge of what's interesting—when it's not related to me. Interesting is the color of your eyes and the way they darken when something excites you."

Andrea felt the heat rush to her face, and before she could tell him he was wasn't going to distract her into changing the subject—

"Interesting is the way you can step off a stagecoach and capture a man's attention. Since I've been in this town, I must have seen two dozen folks arrive on that stage, and you're the first one I couldn't look away from."

She angled her chin. "And now to distract me, you're going to tell me that I'm beautiful."

He shook his head. "Nah, I've seen beautiful women before. The surface might get my attention, but it's not gonna hold it."

She wasn't sure if she should be insulted.

"It's not your surface that holds a man. It's something deep inside you that shines through. Something more than goodness. Kindness, maybe. The way you worried about that dang trunk of yours but tried not to let the men carrying it know that you didn't trust them to get the job done."

"How did you know—"

"The way you kept reaching for it, then pulled your hands back."

"You're observant, Sheriff."

He took her hand and stroked his thumb slowly over the knot on her finger. She could feel his sensuous touch clear down to her curling toes. She'd never felt this way when Elliot touched her, not that he'd been this brazen. He'd always been the perfect gentleman. There were no perfect gentlemen in her stories, and until this moment, she hadn't realized why: they were boring.

"I couldn't see it when you were by the stagecoach, of course, but it was one of the first things I noticed when you were standing in front of me. I couldn't figure out what had caused it."

"Too many hours with a pencil gripped in my hand," she forced out. She wanted to be touching him as well, but she'd never been physically bold. "I've been telling stories since I was old enough to form letters."

"Where do they come from?"

He was looking so deeply into her eyes that she thought he might be able to read all the doubts about herself that she tried to hide, the insecurities that had been built slowly, one by one, as she'd learned about her father's deceptions, taken on the responsibility of caring for her infirmed mother, and been taught by a man she'd cared deeply for that love didn't conquer all things.

She shook her head, becoming as lost in his eyes as he seemed to be in hers. What had the question been? Stories, about stories.

"I don't know where they come from," she admitted. "They've always come so easily, and now they seem so reluctant to appear."

"You know he was a fool."

"Who?" she asked, startled by the abrupt change in topic.

"Your fiancé. To have given you up for the reasons he

did. A man could live with you in poverty for the remainder of his days, and he'd still be rich."

Heartfelt poetry from the sheriff was nearly her undoing. She didn't object when he cradled her face with his large hands, didn't protest when his mouth blanketed hers with a kiss that stole her breath, stole the steadiness of her heartbeat. He snaked an arm around her, drawing her close until her breasts were flattened against the firm planes of his chest. He swept his tongue through her mouth as though he were exploring a long-forgotten trail: tentatively, unsure of the path, his confidence growing as he mapped out the area.

She thought she should break off the kiss, press her palms to his chest and push him away, but it had been so long, too long since she'd felt desired or, more importantly, since she'd felt even the whisper of desire, of the need to be with a man. Demands and responsibilities had put her own needs on hold.

She wound her arms around his neck and returned the kiss with equal fervor. His mustache didn't tickle, but was soft, comforting. She'd never been kissed like this, with so much passion that came as slowly as he walked. As though the journey was to be savored, each step along the way noticed for what it offered.

Slowly, leisurely, he took his fill of her as though he had all day to do so, hungrily, deeply, as though it was his only chance. As though today was all that would be given to him—

Abruptly she pulled back and studied him. He was breathing as harshly as she was. "You're trying to distract me," she accused him.

"I'd say there was no trying about it. I succeeded."

"Well, your reprieve is over. I'm here to observe your day." She stood. "And observe it I will."

After giving the dog a final pat, he got to his feet and gave her the smallest of grins, tilting his head back to the porch. "I guarantee that was a lot more interesting than what we'll be doing at my office."

Seven

He had as gentle a hand as she'd ever known.
  —From *Tex Knight and the Lady in
  Need of Rescue,*
  by Andrea Jackson

Andrea sat at the table in her room, her arms folded over the typewriter, her head resting on her hands as she gazed out the window into the darkness of the night. From her perch, she could clearly see the sheriff's office. A pale, faint light spilled out through the windows, and she wondered what he was doing. Was he reviewing more papers? Was he writing some sort of report? Was he reading? Was he sitting at his desk? Was he doing all the boring things that had occupied him all afternoon and had made her wish that they'd never left the Logans' porch?

Or was his long body stretched out on his bed? Were his boots resting at the foot of it? Was his shirt hanging from the peg on the wall? Did he sleep with his trousers on? Or had he simply put them on this morning so he wouldn't be embarrassed when he opened the door to her?

Had he known it was her this morning? And what would he do if she knocked on his door in the morning?

Would he hold her to the bargain they'd made of giving her only one day?

Or would he welcome her into his office, into his arms?

This man who took in strays, comforted children, helped out a widow, and, whether or not he was aware of it, had befriended Andrea with a compassionate ear.

From the moment Elliot Palmer had told her that her determination to pay off her father's debt was too much of a burden for any man, she'd accepted that love would always be an unattainable dream, that no man would be willing to accept the limitations that marriage to her would bring.

But this afternoon she'd had a taste of desire such as she'd never felt when she was with Elliot. And while she knew her time in Gallant, her time with Matt, would be fleeting, she was a twenty-six-year-old woman, spurned, traveling the lonely road to spinsterhood.

She deserved one night when she wasn't lonely. One night when she wasn't alone. One night when she could pretend that her dream of love was attainable.

She wasn't surprised to find herself getting up from her desk and extinguishing the solitary flame. She'd bathed earlier and washed her hair, as though her heart knew long before her mind that she wouldn't spend tonight alone.

With no hope for anything beyond this day, she walked out of the room, locking the door behind her. The hallway was shadowy and quiet. She did her best not to make a sound. She wasn't worried about waking up any guests, since she was fairly certain that she was still the only one. She was more concerned with waking up the hotel owner, Lester Anderson. How would she explain her wandering out so late at night?

She needn't have worried. Lester was nowhere in sight. A solitary lamp at the registration desk held the shadows back, but based on the snoring she heard, he was asleep in his office. She walked quickly and quietly through the lobby into the night.

* * *

Matt had sat on the bench outside his office, with Sammy lying at his feet, until the sun eased its way beyond the horizon and night crept in. He hadn't taken offense when Sammy headed off to the cemetery. Loyalty was one of the things he'd always longed to have. Loyalty and love. Loyalty, love, and a lady who could accept him, faults and all.

Instead he found himself falling in love with a lady who was looking for a hero. She might think she was only looking for a hero for her story, but he'd figured her out. She was looking for a hero for herself.

And he was about as far removed from being a hero as the devil was from heaven.

He'd sat on his bench until the lights of the town were lit. It was easy to determine which room in the hotel was hers. It was the only room with pale lamplight spilling out of it.

For a while he'd thought he'd been able to see her silhouette sitting there. He'd imagined that she was inviting him over, would welcome him. He didn't remember getting up from the bench or heading toward the hotel. He wanted another kiss. He wanted a night of just holding her, of listening to her, hoarding the final moments of the single day that he'd promised to grant her.

But in the end, he couldn't bring himself to do it, to cross the street to the hotel, to go up to her room and ask her to invite him in. She wasn't the kind of woman who gave herself easily. And he was the kind of man who only deserved the kind of woman she wasn't.

He'd knocked on the door at the closed general store until Tom had finally come out from the back where he was no doubt working on his ledgers, inspecting his inventory. With Tom grumbling the entire time, Matt had gone inside and bought that dime novel that Tom had been boasting about earlier.

Now he was stretched out on his bed, staring at words

that Andi had written, wondering when she'd become Andi to him, wondering what words she might write about him. If there would be any truth in them.

He heard the door to his office open and close.

Very slowly, he reached beneath the pillow and wrapped his fingers around the cold ivory of his Colt. He released his grip when he saw her standing in the doorway to his room.

Swinging his legs off the cot, clutching the book, he came to his feet. "What are you doing here?"

His voice was raspy, strangled.

She licked her lower lip, and he could see the doubts harbored in her eyes. "You promised me today," she said quietly. "It's not yet tomorrow. We've got a couple of more hours."

Reaching out, he set the book on the table beside his bed, then took three steps closer to her. "I don't work at my desk at night."

"I didn't think you did."

"I don't leave this room—"

"I know."

With a low feral growl, he drew her into his arms, slanted his mouth over hers, and kissed her deeply, hungrily, holding nothing back. He was wearing only trousers. He inhaled sharply as she explored his back, the first touch of a woman's hands against his bare skin in so long that the pleasure of it nearly drove him to his knees.

Drawing back from her mouth, he cradled her face and held her gaze. "If you're not wanting any more than kissin', tell me now."

"Are you going to send me away if that's all I want?"

"I couldn't send you away if my life depended on it, but if kissin' is all you want, I'll keep my pants on."

"And if it's not?" she asked, almost shyly.

"Then my pants are coming off and so is your dress and anything that you're wearing underneath it."

He saw the heat of desire flare in her eyes. "I'm not wearing anything at all under my dress."

He felt as though she'd delivered a kick to the center of his chest. "God Almighty."

Then her boldness retreated, and her hesitancy returned. She cupped his jaw, stroked her thumb over his mustache. "Matt, I've never . . . lain with a man before. I'm not afraid of you, but I am—"

"Shh." He placed his thumb against her lips. "I'll make it good for you, darlin'. We've got until the sun comes up."

He lowered his mouth to hers, knowing that if he were indeed the hero she so desperately wanted, he'd send her away.

He wouldn't loosen her buttons, one by one.

He wouldn't part the material and move her dress off her shoulders. He wouldn't watch with rapt fascination as it slid down her body and pooled at her feet.

He wouldn't feel his body tighten with wanting, wouldn't rasp, "You're so beautiful."

He wouldn't take her hand and lead her to the bed, sit her down, and kneel before her to remove her shoes.

When she was completely revealed, he wouldn't ask her to lie back; he wouldn't stand up and unbutton his trousers. He wouldn't take fierce pride in the appreciation he saw in her eyes.

If he were a hero, he wouldn't have done any of those things.

Thank God, he'd never been a hero.

Andrea thought she'd never again in her life see anything or anyone more magnificent than he was. He was beautiful, quite simply beautiful, but Andrea didn't think he'd appreciate the sentiment, and she thought it a shame that she'd never be able to describe the beauty of this moment. It was beyond mere words, beyond telling. It was at once glorious and humbling, to have this man looking at her with such unmasked appreciation in his eyes.

He stretched out beside her and rolled over onto her, raised up slightly on his elbow to keep some of his weight off her, but she wouldn't have minded the pressure. He skimmed his hand along her bare hip, up her side, his gaze following the trail marked by his fingers. He looked so different from this angle. Then she realized with sudden clarity and joy—

"You're smiling," she said softly.

He swung his head around, and the smile made him look so much younger. She thought she could come to love that smile.

"Why wouldn't I, darlin', when you're offering me heaven?"

With his hand, he cradled her breast, a touch that sent desire spiraling through her. He lowered his head and the kiss he delivered to her flesh was as hot as any he'd delivered to her mouth. She scraped her fingers through the thick strands of his hair, dug them into his shoulders, heard him growl, was aware of her own moans.

He was as gentle as the falling of night, as warm as the coming of summer. His hot mouth and skilled fingers teased her, almost unmercifully, until she was begging for release, writhing against him, kissing any part of him that she could reach—his throat, his shoulders, his chest—while he took a leisurely journey over every inch of her flesh.

"So beautiful," he murmured, over and over, a raspy refrain.

Then he was raised above her, his eyes holding hers, and she felt the pressure building as he sought to finish what she'd begun. She saw the strain in his face, felt the quivering in his arms as he fought to hold back, fought to go gently, but her body was beyond the need for gentleness. It was demanding—

"Now," she breathed, "please now."

With a harsh groan, he drove himself home, covering her mouth to absorb her cry, holding them both still as her body grew accustomed to the fullness of his. He kissed away the tear at the corner of her eye, then trailed his lips over her cheek, across her mouth, his breathing harsh and heavy.

Then slowly, slowly, he began to move, rocking against her, cradling her face between his powerful hands, holding her gaze. She could feel his muscles rippling with his movements, feel her own body responding, undulating waves of pleasure flowing through her. Growing, swelling, as his thrusts became quicker, harder, and she was writhing beneath him, seeking the release—

That came upon her with the force of an untamed beast. Her back arched, her cry echoed around them, mingling with his guttural groan and his final thrust that sent him spiraling over the edge with her.

Matt thought that when she was gone, he would still smell her here, in his bed. The expensive freight he'd always resented having to pay to get this bed no longer seemed important. He was grateful he'd had it to offer instead of a cot.

She was nestled against him, her finger trailing up and down his chest while he lazily stroked her hip. He thought he'd be content to stay here forever. He'd extinguished the flame in the lamp, so the only light now was that provided by the moon coming in through the high window of his room. The darkness allowed for an intimacy he'd never before known with a woman.

The women he'd always taken to bed were the kind who expected a favor in exchange for a favor, and once the exchange was made saw no point in lingering.

"You claim that you weren't a hero that day, but Tom told me that you were violently ill and yet you still managed to save the town."

He stiffened. Was that the reason she was here? To gather more information about him? Maybe he should tell her the truth. She'd know then that he was no hero, but he couldn't quite bring himself to reveal everything, to prove to her as her father and fiancé had that there were no heroes. But he could at least nudge her toward the truth. "I wasn't sick."

"But Tom said—"

"I wasn't sick before . . . before the robbery. It was only after . . . after I . . . after it was all over. I'm not brave or courageous. I puked my guts out."

She was quiet for a while, as though she had to ponder the ramifications. Finally, she said, "It says a lot about you that what you did made you ill. You don't take lives lightly."

"Can we talk about something else . . . or better yet, not talk at all?"

He started to roll over onto her, but her hand came up and pressed against his chest.

"How old are you?" she asked quietly.

"I don't know. Is it important to you?"

"Don't you have an idea?"

"I didn't grow up in a house or a town. I grew up on the trail. My older brother"—he cleared his throat—"he taught me to read, to shoot, to fend for myself. If I had to guess, I'd say I'm on the far side of thirty."

"You sound angry."

And she sounded hurt.

"My apologies. I'm not used to talking after."

He was used to leaving, to not hanging around. To never noticing how a woman smelled afterward. This woman at least smelled tempting, her perfume wafting around him, the musky scent they'd created together stirring his passion.

"I know so little about you," she said.

"You know all you need to know," he said, as he nestled himself between her thighs, kissing her with a feral intensity, determined to distract her from the questions.

Andrea was lethargic and sore, but the soreness somehow managed to feel good. Matt was sleeping, his arm draped heavily across her stomach. She thought she should be able to sleep as well, but her mind was conjuring up stories fast and furiously. Heck of a time for her muse to want to come out and play.

Gingerly, she eased out from beneath Matt's arm. Her bare toes felt the blanket that he'd kicked onto the floor earlier. She picked it up, wrapped it around herself, and with only moonlight to guide her, walked into his office.

At his desk, she fumbled around until she located the matches and lit his lamp. She sat in the chair behind his desk. It gave her a different perspective on his room, made her feel closer to him. She thought she would forever see him sitting here, tending to the law.

She needed to write, but his desk was clear except for the lamp. She opened a drawer and found a pencil as well as what appeared to be an old wanted poster. It was yellowed and ragged.

Surely he wouldn't mind if she used it to make a few notes. She laid it facedown and wrote until the words no longer flowed. Yawning, she turned the paper over and immediately regretted that she'd not looked at it more closely before she'd scribbled on the back.

It was a poster announcing the reward for the four members of the Ace in the Hole Gang. Four members? Matt had only killed three. She wondered what had happened to the fourth member. Had he been there that day and escaped? Or had he been captured or killed before?

They had a likeness of each member on the poster. Something about Sam Jenkins tickled at her memory. Something in the eyes. He and his brother, Matthew Jenkins, were worth a five-hundred-dollar reward. Matthew Jenkins.

Her heart slammed against her ribs, because his likeness was much more familiar. She picked up the pencil and began to shade in a mustache. . . .

"What are you doing?"

She jerked her gaze up. Matt stood there wearing only his trousers. She shook her head. "Nothing. I couldn't sleep. I had an idea for a story . . ." She glanced down at the likeness of Matthew Jenkins, then looked back up at Matthew Knight. The resemblance was uncanny.

His gaze dropped to the paper beneath her trembling hands.

"I thought it was an unimportant piece of paper," she whispered. "I was writing a story on the back."

Reaching out, he snatched the paper from her, then balled it up.

"I tried to tell you I wasn't a hero."

She felt the tears burning her eyes.

"You want to know it all, don't you?" he asked, resignation in his voice. "But you're afraid to ask, not sure you want to know the truth."

She couldn't nod or shake her head. She felt as though her heart was being crushed.

"Sam pretty much raised me after our pa died," he said, as though she'd given some indication that she wanted him to speak. "I rode with him, got tired of it, and came here three years ago. I don't know if Sam knew I was here, if he thought I'd be his ace in the hole, or if it was just bad luck.

"I was sitting on the bench, the day he and the gang rode into town. I saw them and recognized my brother. I went into my office, closed the door, and pretended that I didn't know what was going to happen. Josh Logan is dead because he had the courage to do what I didn't. He tried to stop them."

She dipped her gaze to the crushed paper in his clenched fist. "And you're still wanted?"

Not waiting for him to answer, she got up and hurried into the back room. She snatched her dress from the floor, then slipped it on.

"Andi?"

He was standing in the doorway. She couldn't bring herself to look at him as she fastened her buttons.

"Doc told you that people leave their pasts at the outskirts of town. That's what I'm trying to do."

She spun around and glared at him. "You want me to admire you for that?"

"I never asked for your admiration or your hero worship or any of it. Has it occurred to you that you're not searching for a hero for your story, but you're searching for a hero for yourself? I'm willing to bet you once thought your father was a hero . . . and that beau of yours, too."

She was afraid to answer, embarrassed to admit that he might have hit on the truth. That she wanted more than a hero for a story. That she was no different than Joe Scars, wanting to believe in the type of person who didn't exist, someone who only existed in her imagination.

She grabbed her shoes, and without bothering to put them on, she rushed past him, got to the door, and stopped.

"I won't tell anyone," she said quietly, then looked back over her shoulder at him. "I'll be leaving on the noon stage. You finally managed to convince me, Sheriff. You're not a hero."

He looked as though she'd fired a bullet into his heart. She didn't want to think about it, about him, about what he'd done, or who he really was.

As she rushed back to the hotel, she was acutely aware of the horrendous truth of her situation.

She'd fallen in love. Fallen in love not with a hero, but with an outlaw.

Eight

Tex Knight had but one fault. He failed to recognize his own goodness.
—From *Tex Knight Fights His Demons,*
by Andrea Jackson

What was a hero?

Sitting in her library in her home in Fort Worth, Andrea stared at the words she'd typed. She'd thought she'd always known. He was bigger than life and brave. Courageous to a fault. He always saved the day. Was kind to pets and children.

He was a man who looked deep within himself and liked what he saw. He could look himself in the mirror.

The knock on her door barely disturbed her. It opened, and her mother's nurse poked her head through the opening. "I know you're busy writing your story—"

She wished.

"—but there's a doctor here to see you."

"A doctor? Is mother—"

"She's fine. This doctor's not from around here. He says he's from Gallant?"

Andrea came to her feet. "I'll see him."

Her heart was thundering so hard that she was certain

anyone coming into the room would be able to hear it. Wiping her suddenly damp palms on her skirt, she crossed to the door just as John Martin walked in. She gave him a tremulous smile. "Is it Matt?"

His face was somber. "Not in the way that I think you probably mean." He extended a package. "He asked me to bring this to you."

She hesitated to take the offering, but in the end curiosity got the better of her, as well as disappointment that Matt was too cowardly to face her.

Although she didn't know why she should be surprised that he was cowardly. He'd spent his entire life taking the easy way out. Robbing people instead of working hard. Hiding when responsibility stared him in the face.

"Would you like some tea?" she asked as she walked over to a chair and sat, not realizing until she was in place that she was clutching the package as though it were something precious.

Doc took the plush chair nearby and shook his head. "No, thanks, but I would like to stay in case you need me after you open the package."

"Do you know what's in here?"

"A portion of it."

"Do you think I'm going to swoon?"

He smiled. "No."

"Then why would I need a doctor?"

"Not a doctor. A friend."

She released a heavy sigh. "Yes, I could probably use a friend."

She unknotted the string, and when it fell away, she pulled back the brown paper and gaped at the pile of money resting inside.

"Five hundred dollars," Doc said quietly.

She lifted her gaze to him, afraid to ask, afraid she already knew the answer, wondering why the thought didn't bring with it any comfort. "Where did it come from?"

"Matt turned himself in to the authorities. He asked me to bring you the money and that letter."

That letter. She looked at the folded piece of paper resting on top of the money. With trembling fingers she unfolded it.

Dear Andrea,

I'm wishing I had your newfangled contraption for perfect writing right now because my hand is shaking so bad that I don't know if you'll be able to read my words. I've never been so scared in my life, and that's saying a lot.

I'm not like you. I'm not good with words. You wanted a hero, darlin', and I wish I could have been him for you. But I can't be. But the right one for you is out there somewhere, and I hope you find him. Not just for your stories but for yourself.

Matt

With tears burning her eyes, she looked at John Martin. "Did they send him to prison?"

"For ten years."

"Where?"

"He doesn't want you to know. I think that letter was supposed to be good-bye."

With determination she rose to her feet. "The problem with Matthew Knight is that he has no idea what a hero is."

"Are you going to teach him?" Doc asked.

"I'm going to try."

She walked over to her desk, jerked out the story she'd been unable to write, put in another piece of paper, and began typing.

Six months later

Matt Knight noticed her the second she stepped out of the noon stage onto the dusty street. Her blond hair was tucked up beneath a fancy bonnet. The green of the bonnet matched the green of the dress that he knew matched the green of her eyes.

His mouth went dry. His heart was hammering so hard that he thought he might crack a rib. He watched as the stagecoach driver and his guard struggled to get her trunk down from the roof of the stagecoach, watched as they carried it over to the boardwalk and set it down in front of the hotel.

Then to his utter and complete amazement, she left it there and began strolling up the boardwalk, toward his end of town. He swallowed hard, slowly came to his feet, and swept his hat from his head with a shaking hand. He hoped he wasn't going to need that hand to aim his gun anytime soon.

As she drew nearer, he realized that he'd forgotten exactly how pretty she was. Maybe that was a good thing, because it would have only added to his loneliness, and it had been fairly unbearable as it was. He hadn't been able to figure out how a man could be so dadgum lonely when there were other people around, but standing here now with her before him, he was beginning to suspect that his loneliness had come about because *she* hadn't been there. The one woman he'd come to care about more than any other.

He thought he'd be content to simply stand there and look at her for the remainder of his life.

"Hello, Andi," he said quietly.

"Sheriff." She studied him as though she was as hungry to take him all in as he was her. "How was prison?"

He flinched. There was an unexpected spark of anger in her voice.

"Not as bad as it might have been," he said. "Not as long as it should have been. Thanks to you and Doc."

They'd petitioned the governor to grant him a pardon based on his heroics in saving the town. He'd never think of his actions that day as heroic, but he was tired of fighting it.

Considering every citizen of Gallant had signed the petition, Matt figured it was a battle he'd never win anyway.

"And the citizens of Gallant," she said.

"Yep. They even gave me my job back. I hadn't expected that."

"Has it never occurred to you that you're not the man you once were?"

"Every day, but I'm still not—"

She pressed a finger to his lips. "I know. You're not a hero. I'm not here looking for a hero, Matt. I'm looking for the man I've come to love."

He was afraid to reach for her, to take what he so desperately wanted. But she apparently had no such compunctions. She stepped forward, wound her arms around his neck, and reached up to press her mouth to his.

He greedily took what she offered, wrapping his arms around her, holding her tightly against his body, kissing her as though his very life depended on it. And maybe it did.

He drew back and cradled her face between his hands. Here they were in broad daylight, carrying on like no one could see. "I've got a powerful urge to carry you inside, but it would ruin your reputation, and one of us ought to have a good reputation."

"You could come to the hotel tonight, and I could show you my typewriter."

He smiled and touched her cheek. "I'm sorry that the reward offered for my capture wasn't enough to pay off your father's debt."

"Is that why you turned yourself in? To help with my debt?"

He shook his head. "I did a lot of bad things in my youth, Andi. I thought being sheriff here could make up for it. But that morning, the look in your eyes when you realized what I was . . . Until I faced my past, I realized I could never have a future. The thing was, until you, I never cared if I didn't have a future. I'll never be a hero, but I got to thinking that I might not mind being a husband."

Smiling brightly, she wrapped her arms around his neck again and came up on her toes. "Are you asking?"

"Reckon I am."

Her eyes grew somber. "I won't walk away from my father's debt."

"I'm not asking you to. But I will ask you to let me help where I can. As far as I can see your fiancé was a fool. If all I ever have is you, Andi, I'll always be a rich man."

Epilogue

Tex Knight had a heart as big as Texas and dreams to match.
> —From *Tex Knight Rides into the Sunset,*
> by Andrea Jackson

THE END. Andrea Knight finished typing two of her favorite words and sat back in her chair with a sigh, feeling a sense of accomplishment. Her series about Tex Knight had done well for her over the years, and this was her final installment.

She looked at the crumpled wanted poster that sat on the edge of her desk, a constant reminder to her that heroes could be found in the most unlikely of places.

She and Matt had bought the Logans' house shortly after they were married. They'd also bought another typewriter, so she had one in his office where she could be with him for a few hours while he worked and one here at the house so she could write when the muse struck.

Her mother had gone to quietly join her father, and Andrea continued to make payments on her father's debt.

She heard Sammy's barking. She was beginning to think that he really did know how to tell time. He was always waiting outside Matt's office at the end of the day, even though he still spent his nights near his former master.

Andrea got up from her desk, walked through the house, and onto the porch, so she could watch her husband approach. He smiled much more these days.

"Ma!" Their four-year-old son released his hold on his father's hand and rushed straight into her arms.

She lifted him up and hugged him tightly.

"Did you finish?" he asked.

"Yes, I did."

Matt walked up to her, slipped his arm around her, and drew her up against his side. "How did it end?" he asked.

She smiled up at him. "Like any good story. The hero got the girl."

If you enjoyed Georgina Gentry's
rip-roaringly good story,
"The Great Cowboy Race,"
here's a special excerpt from her new
full-length western romance,
TO TEASE A TEXAN.
On sale now from Zebra books!

One

They were cheating the cowboy at the poker table tonight. He must be blind or very drunk not to see Snake Hudson dealing from the bottom. Lark felt almost naked in her skimpy sky blue dress as she paused by the table, tray in hand. Dixie, one of the other saloon girls, stood behind the cowboy, and she was giving slight signals as she watched the cowboy's hand and nodded to her latest lover, Snake.

Lark hesitated. It wasn't really any of her business. After all, the big, black-haired cowboy was a grown man, and she needed this job.

"Hey, you—girlie," Snake snarled, "you ever gonna serve them drinks a'fore we all die of thirst?"

"Right away." Lark began serving drinks around the table as the big cowboy grinned at her a little cross-eyed.

"Left-handed, he drawled, "just like me."

"I'm a Texan, too," she said. His accent told her he was a Texan. Land's sake, he was a grown man and ought to know better than to sit down at a poker table with a crooked bunch like this.

Snake sipped his whiskey and rubbed the whiplike scar

on his forehead. Then he smirked. "Full house. Sorry, cowboy, reckon you lose again." He reached out and began to rake in the pot. "How 'bout another hand, Larado? You might be luckier this time."

Lark continued to serve around the table. The noise and the smoke made her head ache, along with the off-key music.

"Donno, Snake," Larado said, chewing his lip. "You 'bout cleaned me out."

"Just one more hand," Snake urged. "Maybe this hand will win everything back."

The cowboy hesitated, and Lark held her breath. "All I got left is my horse and saddle and my gold watch, and I set a heap of store by it." He pulled the watch out of his leather vest and stared at it as if trying to make a choice.

"Take a chance," Snake urged.

"Yeah, take a chance, cowboy," Dixie urged. She smiled with lips as bright red as her dress, the cigar smoke swirling around her blond hair.

He hesitated again. "Don't know if I ought to." He squinted thoughtfully at the gold pocket watch, his face furrowed in concentration.

Oh, no, I can't let him lose that, too. Without giving it a second thought, Lark dropped a glass of beer in the cowboy's lap. "Oh, I'm so sorry!"

He stumbled to his feet, wiping at his pants. "Reckon I'm through for the night, then." He stuck the gold watch back in his pocket and left weaving in a crooked line toward the swinging doors.

"Damn it," Snake roared, "I oughta get you fired for that, girlie."

"I—it was an accident." Lark put down her tray and followed the staggering cowboy out onto the wooden sidewalk. The night air was fresh and cool but noisy. In this wide-open town, there were a dozen saloons in a two-block area and not much else. Pianos blared a mix of Stephen

Foster songs. Drunken trail hands galloped up and down the dirt street, shooting into the air and shouting.

The cowboy staggered down the sidewalk, whistling: ... *as I walked out on the streets of Larado, as I walked out in Larado one day, I spied a young cowboy all wrapped in white linen, all wrapped in white linen and cold as the clay.* ...

Her blue dress felt thin and skimpy. She wrapped her arms around herself to keep from shivering. "Hey, you!" she yelled at the tall Texan. "You need to stay out of places like the Last Chance."

"Well, now, sweetie." he stopped, turned, and grinned down at her, a charming, crooked grin. "I reckon if you're gonna pour beer on me every time I come in, maybe I'd better."

"I was trying to keep you out of trouble."

He leaned against a porch railing and hiccoughed. "I reckon I can handle my own self, sweetie." He reached out and slapped her familiarly across the bottom.

"Don't do that. And don't call me 'sweetie,' you saddle tramp!"

"Okay, I'm agreeable. You got a name? I reckon we ain't howdied yet. I'm Larado."

"Larado what?"

"Sweetie"—he grinned, pushing his Stetson back—"since you're a Texan, you should know it ain't polite to ask a stranger too many questions. What's your handle?"

"I'm Lark, er, Lark Smith." She held out her hand awkwardly. Since she was a runaway, it wouldn't be too smart to give him her full name.

"Well, Lark, sweetie." His big hand engulfed hers, and he hung on. "I like tall, pretty brunettes. Any more like you at home?"

"I'm a mirror twin," she said before she thought.

"A what?"

"You know, I've got a dimple on the left side; she's got one on the right. I'm left-handed—"

"She's right-handed. Now I get it." He nodded. "Well, how about let's go on up to your room?"

"I only wait tables here, nothing else." She tried to pull out of his grasp and kept her tone cold.

He swayed a little on his feet, and she could smell the whiskey. "I got no money anyway. Maybe you'd take a gold watch?"

"You want to get another beer poured on you?" She jerked out of his hand. "Now, go sleep it off somewhere."

"I reckon maybe I have had a little too much red-eye."

"A little?" she snorted. "Why, I'll bet you couldn't hit the ground with your hat in three tries. You had to be blind not to see the marked cards in that game."

He stumbled and sat down heavily on the edge of the wooden sidewalk. "Now, that Snake fella seemed like a right friendly *hombre.*"

Lark snorted again. "Why, he'd steal the butter off a sick beggar's biscuit. Cowboy, you'd better report back to your outfit and stay out of dives like this one."

He shook his head and rolled a cigarette with unsteady hands, looking up at her. "Came up with a trail herd a few days ago, but now they're sold, and I ain't found another job. Thought I might win enough to ship me and my horse back to Texas."

"Land's sake, partner," she warned, "you won't ever win playing at the Last Chance. I've only worked here a few months, but I spotted the cardsharps right off."

He smoked with unsteady hands and seemed to be thinking it over. "Maybe I should go back in there and demand my money."

She shook her head. "I wouldn't do that if I were you. You don't know how tough the boys in the Last Chance can be."

"I can handle myself, sweetie." He tried to stand up, stumbled, reached out, and caught her arm to steady himself. He was a big one, all right, taller even than her uncle

Trace or her cousin, Ace. He stood swaying and staring down at her, and she was tall for a woman. "You cold?"

"Of course I am!" she snapped and pulled away from him. "This skimpy outfit they make me wear hasn't got enough fabric to cover a broom handle."

"Looks good to me." He grinned at her.

"Get out of here and go sleep it off," she snapped. "Now, I got to go, they're yelling for me inside."

"Lark," he murmured, "can you sing?"

"Not very well. Now *vamoose, pronto.* Maybe tomorrow, you can get on with some outfit."

He shook his head. "Done tried. Nobody around here needs a wanderin' saddle tramp. Reckon I'll go back to Texas."

"Good idea. And a word of advice. Stay away from poker tables when you're blind drunk." She turned and went back into the saloon.

Larado squinted in the darkness and looked after her. He was drunk, all right, but not as drunk as she thought. She was purty, a tall, dark-haired girl in a gaudy blue dress. Like himself, she looked as if she had some Injun blood. His manhood stirred as he remembered the feel of her and the scent of her perfume. What the hell was he thinking? Girls like that one came high, and he hadn't a nickel to his name. He'd have to sleep out on the prairie tonight with his horse, and maybe tomorrow his luck would change. His pants were wet with beer, and he was getting cold in the night wind. He pulled his coat collar up around his ears and stumbled away.

Lark scurried back into the smoky, noisy saloon. Joe, the short owner, stood scowling by the poker table with a cigar between his teeth. "Lark, where the hell you been?"

"Uh, just out."

"Snake here tells me you caused him to lose a sucker he was about to finish off."

"I accidentally spilled a drink in the cowboy's lap." She needed this job.

"Aww, don't believe her," said the blond whore Dixie, perching her rear on the poker table. "That was a pretty good gold watch. Besides, that broke up the whole game."

"Lark," Joe said, "you're a lousy waitress. Any more trouble outta you and you're fired."

"But, Joe—"

"You heard me." He walked away from the table.

Lark looked helplessly at the crowd around the poker table.

Snake frowned and shrugged. "You heard him. Next time I got a sucker on the hook, stay out of it. Now, Dixie, get that talented fanny of yours off the table."

The men all laughed. Dixie laughed, too, and started to saunter away. Lark caught up with her. "You were helping Snake cheat that cowboy."

"So what?" Dixie sneered. "Besides, that Texan's a grown man. He must have been blind not to see Snake dealin' them cards off the bottom. Anyway, what business is it of yours?"

Lark caught her arm. "I ought to slap you, Dixie."

"You do, and I'll pull out some of them beautiful black curls. Did I ever tell you I once got into a fight with your sister?"

Everything else was forgotten. "You know my sister?"

"Yeah."

"I don't think I believe you."

"Don't give a damn whether you do or not. Her name's Lacey, and she's prissy and straight-laced. She wouldn't be caught dead workin' in a saloon."

That was her twin, all right. "Where'd—?"

"I don't wanta talk to you no more," Dixie drawled and started to saunter away, the red satin on her hips swaying as she walked.

"Dixie, tell me where you saw her." Lark ran after her and caught her arm.

"Let go of me, you bitch." Dixie swung at her, and Lark stepped away, but Dixie came at her again. Lark was a Texas girl, and she could give as good as she got. She buried her fingers in the whore's bleached hair and gave it a good yank.

Dixie howled like a stepped-on cat and came at her, scratching and shrieking.

"You southern-fried tramp!" Lark said, and they went down in a mix of short skirts, lace underwear, and tangled long legs.

"Fight! Fight!" The shout went through the crowded saloon and all the men came running to watch. The only thing a bunch of cowboys liked better than a good fistfight was two girls going at it.

Lark wasn't going to let the slut get away with this. She forgot she needed a job; she forgot everything but slapping Dixie silly. They crashed first into the piano, sending the player falling to the floor, then into a pool table, sending cowboys scrambling. Now other girls and male customers gathered around to watch the latest entertainment in the crowded saloon.

Nate, the big bartender, came running. "All right, break it up, you'll have the boss out here." He tried to pull the girls apart, but Lark poked him in the eye as she drew back on Dixie again. Oh, her sister Lacey would be mortified if she could see her tomboy sister in such an unladylike battle—but then, her twin was always so correct and Lark could never do anything right.

"Here comes the boss!" Someone yelled a warning, but Lark was on top, yanking the tart's yellow hair.

Joe strode up, grabbed both girls by the arms, and hauled them to their feet. "What's goin' on out here?"

"She started it," Dixie wailed.

"I was just giving as good as I got!"

"She was, too," the crowd assured him.

Joe took the cigar out of his mouth and frowned. "Lark, damn it, I warned you."

"I know you did, but I'm a Texan, and that poor Texas cowboy was being cheated—"

"So what?" Joe shrugged. "If he ain't a big boy, he don't belong in a tough town like Buck Shot."

"But he was almost broke," Lark protested.

He looked at her and sighed as if speaking to a small child. "That's what we do here at the Last Chance; we take their money. Now, Texas, I warned you, so you're fired. Be out of here by morning." He turned on his heel and stalked back toward his office.

Land's sake, what have I done? Got herself fired over a drunken, penniless cowboy. Chin still high and defiant, Lark headed up to her cramped room to pack. What was she going to do now?

She'd gotten some satisfaction out of giving Dixie's yellow hair a good yank, but that wouldn't pay the bills. She could always wire home to Uncle Trace for money, but she was too proud to do that. Besides, Aunt Cimarron would come after her and take her back to the ranch. They had raised her ever since her parents had been killed and her rich grandfather had decided he couldn't deal with the twins. She'd just be on the run again as she had been for the last couple of years. She wondered where Dixie had run across Lacey. Last she had heard, Lacey was scheduled to marry that perfect paragon of virtue, Homer something-or-other. By now, Lacey probably had a perfect baby while her twin made a mess of her life. Well, Lark would just drift on like she always did. It was easier than facing up to her own imperfections.

She sat down on her bed and listened to the music and laughter from downstairs. Where was she going to go now? Her prominent ranching family would be upset if they knew she was working in a saloon. Of course, ever since she'd dropped out of Miss Priddy's fancy academy in Boston while Lacey graduated with honors, they'd been upset with her. They said they weren't, but Lark knew better. If she ever did anything to make them proud, she'd contact them, but it was tough being the twin who always messed up.

She thought of the Texan. The nerve of him slapping her on the bottom so familiarly! And to think he'd wanted to buy a night in her bed with a gold watch. No man had ever bedded her, and a penniless, drunken cowpoke wasn't going to be the first. Oh my, what did she expect him to think? He wouldn't have believed the truth, that the niece of one of the biggest ranchers in Texas would be slinging drinks in a wild whiskey town along the border between Oklahoma and Indian Territories. The whiskey towns were the roughest in the West, existing to sell liquor and other brands of sin to the Indians and outlaws who hid out in Indian Territory where whiskey was forbidden.

Lark blew out her lamp and went to bed with a defeated sigh. Tomorrow, she'd drift on. She was homesick, but she couldn't go home. Lark was certain her relatives felt sorry for her because she couldn't seem to measure up. It was easier to run. As she drifted off to sleep, she wondered, what had happened to the drunken cowboy? Damn him, he'd gotten her into a mess.

Larado stumbled out to a tree on a prairie where he'd left his horse and bedroll. "Hey, hoss, you doin' okay?" The bay stallion raised his head and nickered as Larado scratched his neck, then returned to grazing on the dried grass. "Maybe you are, but I ain't." Larado shivered in the raw wind, squinted, and looked back toward the long, muddy street of saloons. He could hear the off-key music and the laughter from here. Had the other man been cheating? Should he have called him out?

"Now, pard, that would have been a damn-fool thing to

do, and you know why," he muttered to himself as he spread his blankets and lay down. "You ain't that good a shot without . . . Well, you ain't no gunfighter."

It was a raw night for early April, and he shivered and pulled his blanket closer, thinking about the girl in the blue skimpy dress. She'd have been warm, all right, and he wished he had her in his blankets with him. What was her name? Lark. Like a bird. He remembered the feel of her as he pulled her toward him. He didn't have any money to spend on her, and she must know it, but she'd come out anyway. He hadn't been nearly as drunk as she thought he was; it was only . . . Well, that didn't make no never mind.

Working at the Last Chance, she had to be experienced and really know how to please a man. In his mind, he imagined pulling her close and feeling that curvy body all the way down his. Her legs under the short, skimpy blue dress had looked long enough to go all the way to her neck. "Oh, sweetie," he groaned, trying to get comfortable as his manhood stirred. "If I win couple of hands next time, I'm gonna see how much you cost. The first night I spent a dollar on that Dixie, and she was okay, but I'll wager you're better."

Money. He was flat broke. The ranches around here all seemed to have plenty of cowboys. Larado had been trying to win enough to grubstake supplies to get back to Texas. Just what the hell was he gonna do now?

At daylight the next morning Larado sat before a small campfire, sipping the last of his little stash of coffee and nursing a hangover. He'd drift south now and maybe find a temporary job punching cattle somewhere where it was warm. What he really dreamed of was owning his own spread, but he couldn't see any way he could ever do that.

A sound. He turned his head and squinted. In the early dawn light, he wasn't sure for a moment who the rider was. Then he recognized Snake.

"Kin I get down?" Snake yelled.

"Sure." Larado nodded. He had a bad headache from last night, and he felt as lowdown as a rattlesnake's belly, but a Texan was always hospitable. He stood up. "Want some coffee?"

"You got an extra cup?"

He nodded, pouring the man a cup. Snake sat down on a rock, taking the tin cup in both hands.

"Damn, that hot coffee feels good on a cold morning." Snake took a sip and shuddered. "Don't you Texans make coffee any way but strong?"

Larado laughed. "If it won't float a horseshoe, we throw it out and make another pot." He studied the other man's ugly face with its jagged red scar on the forehead.

Snake touched the scar. "You're wondering how I got this, right?"

Larado felt his face burn. "Naw, I wasn't."

"I don't mind." The other man sipped his coffee. "Looks like a snake, don't it? A long time ago, I got into a whip fight with another fella. Since then, I've learned to use a pistol—safer for me."

Larado laughed, but the other man didn't laugh.

"Listen"—Snake took another sip of coffee—"I felt bad about last night, realizin' you was pretty broke when you left the table."

"That happens when you play poker." Larado rolled a cigarette and shrugged. "I don't begrudge you the money."

"Maybe I could stake you a little," Snake offered. "I got something workin', and I might cut you in on it, being's how my last partner got kilt in a knife fight."

"Oh?" Larado felt a rush of warning. "I don't think—"

"Hear me out," Snake interrupted. "There's a fat bank in this town, almost as fat as the owner. You can't believe how much money goes in there from all these saloons."

"Uh uh." Larado shook his head. "That dog won't hunt."

"Huh?"

"It's what Texans say when it's no go. I ain't never done nothin' crooked much. I ain't hankerin' for no prison cell."

"You got any money to get back to Texas?"

"No. I'm flat busted except for my watch and my horse," Larado admitted as he stuck the smoke in his mouth and reached for a burning twig from the campfire.

"Look"—Snake leaned closer—"this bank would be a pushover. It just opened up and is bustin' with deposits. The sheriff's out of town, and it's too early for the bank to be open."

"Then how would you get in? You gonna blow it?" Larado asked.

Snake spat into the fire. "That'd draw too much attention. I been watchin', and I seen that fat little banker works on his books with his teller early in the mornin' before the bank opens."

Larado shook his head and blew smoke. "I ain't no robber, and I'd like to live a little longer."

"I never heard of no Texan being a coward," Snake said.

"When you say that, mister, you'd better smile. Our motto is 'Remember the Alamo.' Texans go down fightin'."

"I meant no offense." Snake tossed the last of his coffee in the fire where it sizzled and went up in steam. "You could just mosey in there with me and look around, see if you think it's doable."

"Do I look like my mama raised a fool?" Larado shook his head. "I ain't no bank robber, and to be mighty honest, I ain't too good with a gun."

"Hell, I am," Snake said. "I ain't askin' you to shoot somebody, just help me carry all those sacks of money out— they'd be mighty heavy."

"Mighty heavy," Larado repeated wistfully.

"Just come along with me and walk through the bank so I can look it over," Snake urged. "Maybe you can give me some leads on what I ought to do when I do get a partner. You seem like a smart *hombre*."

Larado felt himself redden. "Don't have much book learnin', although my mama did teach me to read. I reckon I'm smart as the next fella, if only . . ."

"I reckon I know a smart *hombre* when I see one." Snake grinned, showing yellow teeth. "That's why I want your advice. It'd be worth a gold eagle to find out what you think."

Larado smoked and stared into the fire. A twenty-dollar gold piece was a lot of money to a busted cowboy. "All I got to do is look over the bank and give you an opinion?"

The tough gunman nodded.

"Okay, here's my opinion," Larado said. "A man can get kilt robbin' banks. Don't do it."

"Hell, I take back my apology. I reckon what they say about Texans is true." Snake stood up slowly. "Folks say they're all gurgle and no guts."

Larado leaped up and grabbed him by the jacket sleeve. "You callin' me yellow?"

"Easy, cowboy, easy." Snake made a soothing gesture. "I wasn't askin' you to rob the bank, just help me look it over."

"I ain't seen the color of your money."

"Fair enough. You're a smart *hombre*, Larado." Snake nodded, reached into his coat, and tossed a coin.

Larado caught it and stared at it. "Ain't you afraid I'll take your money and skedaddle?"

"You strike me as a purty honest man," Snake said. "They say Texans got a sense of honor."

"Reckon that's true." Larado nodded. He didn't like the feel of this whole thing, but he needed the money—Lord, how he needed the money. Chico could use some oats, and he damned sure needed a new sack of Arbuckles, a hunk of bacon, and a little cornmeal to get back to the Lone Star state. "Well, I'll go along and look over this here bank, but I ain't gonna rob it with you."

"Sure, sure. Let's go now while it's still early and there's almost nobody on the street."

Larado put the gold coin in his vest, tossed his cigarette into the campfire, and stood. "I'll saddle up."

Snake followed him over to Chico. "I believe you're the most honest galoot I ever met. Anybody else would jump at the chance to cut themselves in on a fat job like this."

"My mama would roll over in her grave if she thought she'd raised a son that would take another man's money," Larado said. "I don't know what she would say about just lookin' it over."

"Aww, that fat banker has plenty, and you know how bankers is. He probably took half of it from some old folks he foreclosed on or cheated some poor widow out of it."

Larado gave that some thought as he saddled up and mounted. He began to whistle his favorite song: . . . *as I walked out on the street of Larado, as I walked out in Larado one day. . . .*

"I hate that song," Snake grumbled.

Larado stopped whistling. "I was wishin' last night I had a twenty-dollar gold piece. I reckon that's what it would take to buy that gal."

"Dixie?" Snake laughed as he swung into the saddle. "Hell, she's my gal. She's meetin' me at my camp later this morning. I tell you what, I'll give you a few minutes on a blanket with her."

"I didn't mean her. I meant that tall one with the black hair." Silently, he wondered what kind of man would offer the use of his woman to another man as though he were of-fering to share some pecan pie. Maybe he didn't know Larado had had the blonde the first night in town. She was pretty good for a dollar.

"Oh, Lark?" Snake snorted as they rode out. "Don't know much about her 'cept she's a Texan, too. She'll tease you, but that's all. Waits tables, won't work the cribs with the other whores."

"Oh?" Larado's interest heightened. "Damn, there was something about her got my blood runnin' hot."

"You ain't the only one." Snake laughed. "But she don't do nothin' but serve drinks—and not very well. You got your pants soaked with beer, so you know that."

Larado grinned, remembering the girl. "She can pour beer on me any time. She's purty as an ace-high straight."

"After you left, she and Dixie got into a fight, and she yanked some of Dixie's hair out. Don't know what Dixie said to start it."

Larado pictured the scene, the luscious long legs, the tangle of dark hair, maybe a torn and revealing skimpy costume. "Texas gals ain't likely to let anyone give them lip. You can always tell a Texan, but you can't tell 'em much."

Snake yawned and shrugged. "Ain't that the Gawd's truth? A woman is a woman," Snake said. "they'll cheat you and trick you, and they're all the same when the lights is turned out."

"I don't know about that," Larado drawled. "That one wasn't no coyote bait."

Snake scratched his crotch. "Weeks ago, I made a pass at her and got slapped for it. She acts like a lady, but no lady would work in a saloon."

"Reckon you got that right." She was mysterious and interesting. His head hurt, but he remembered the warm scent of perfume that wafted up between her full breasts.

They rode away from the camp and into town. As Snake had said, the streets were almost deserted in the early dawn.

Snake said, "We'll tie up at the hitchin' post out front."

Larado looked toward the bank. "There ain't no hitchin' post."

"What? Oh, hell," Snake grumbled, "I forgot they took 'em down yesterday, doing something to widen the street or some fool thing. Now what we gonna do?"

"Hey," Larado said with a grin, "look who's comin'."

Lark walked along the wooden sidewalk carrying her small valise. She knew the stage stopped in front of the butcher shop near the bank. She'd wait there for it. Where she was going, she couldn't be sure. She ought to yell "calf rope," which was Texan for admitting defeat, and wire her uncle. He would be forgiving, but Lark was not only defiant but proud. How could she go home, hat in hand, where no doubt her twin sister, Lacey, the perfect example of young womanhood, was now planning her perfect wedding to young Homer What's-his-name?

She heard the sound of horses and turned to see that Texan from last night and the bad *hombre,* Snake, who had been cheating him at cards. What was the Texan's name? Oh, yes, Larado. He was either stupid, drunk, or blind not to have seen what was going on at that poker table, yet here he was riding into town with the bad *hombre.*

She was almost abreast of the bank now, trying to decide whether to acknowledge that rascal Snake and the cowboy who had cost her her job.

She heard the two men dismount.

"Miss," Larado called.

She turned, not sure what to expect. The look in the Texan's dark eyes told her what he'd like. Land's sake, just because she worked in a saloon, did every man think she'd fall on her back for a few coins? "Yes?"

The Texan touched the brim of his hat. "Mornin', ma'am."

She almost wanted to scream at him: *You cost me my job, you harebrained idiot, and now you speak to me?* Instead, she gritted her teeth and barely nodded to him.

Larado smiled that engaging, crooked grin. "You don't seem the type for a saloon, miss."

She felt herself color. "That's hardly your business," she snapped. "A girl's got to eat."

"You two stop all that jawin'," Snake griped. "We got things to do."

"Miss Lark"—Larado took off his hat—"the hitchin' rail's down the street for repair. Maybe we could get you to hold our horses while we do a little business?"

"I reckon I can be obliging." She took a deep breath. The Texan was not only handsome with a lock of black hair hanging in his dark eyes—that grin would rock any woman back in her high-button shoes.

They handed over their reins.

Larado pushed his Stetson back. "We're much obliged. Won't be gone a minute."

She set her small valise down, took the reins from the pair, and watched them swagger into the bank. She didn't know what business they had in there. She figured the cowboy was broke after last night and Snake was a ruffian, not the kind who put his money in a bank. She fidgeted a long moment, wondering when the stage would arrive.

Abruptly, the early morning silence was shattered by the sound of gunshots from the bank.

The two horses reared and whinnied at the sudden noise, and she hung on to the reins for dear life. People hurried out of buildings, shouting and running. Lark fought to control the rearing horses. *What in God's name is happening in the bank?*

ABOUT THE AUTHORS

Lorraine Heath is a Waldenbooks and *USA Today* bestselling author, especially known for her emotionally rich and unforgettable historical romances set in Texas. She is a RITA Award winner from Romance Writers of America and has received a Career Achievement award from *Romantic Times*. In addition to romance, she writes young adult fiction under her own name and the pseudonym Rachel Hawthorne. She lives in Plano, Texas. Visit her website at ww.lorraineheath.com.

Georgina Gentry has received great acclaim and a devoted readership for her passionate and well-researched novels set in the American West. She is a two-time winner of *Romantic Times'* Lifetime Achievement Award and has been inducted into the Oklahoma Professional Writers Hall of Fame. She lives in Edmund, Oklahoma. Visit her website at www.nettrends.com/georginagentry.

Teresa Bodwell is a talented new voice in romance. Her first novels, LOVING MERCY and LOVING MIRANDA were both published in 2005. She lives in Missoula, Montana. Visit her website at www.tbodwell.com.

GREAT BOOKS, GREAT SAVINGS!

When You Visit Our Website:
www.kensingtonbooks.com
You Can Save 30% Off The Retail Price
Of Any Book You Purchase!

- **All Your Favorite Kensington Authors**
- **New Releases & Timeless Classics**
- **Overnight Shipping Available**
- **All Major Credit Cards Accepted**

Visit Us Today To Start Saving!
www.kensingtonbooks.com

All Orders Are Subject To Availability.
Shipping and Handling Charges Apply.